MANKIND'S
NEW BEGINNING

MANKIND'S NEW BEGINNING

The Dragon Prophecy and the Tankers' Quest for the Ancient Keys

Charles H. Sherbow

Goneti Press, LLC

For information contact :
Goneti Press, LLC
Mesa, AZ 85205
Permissions@GonetiPress.com

ISBN 979-8-9912616-0-9 (paperback)
ISBN 979-8-9912616-1-6 (e-book)
ISBN 979-8-9912616-2-3 (hardback)

Library of Congress Control Number: 2024919707

First Edition
10 9 8 7 6 5 4 3 2 1

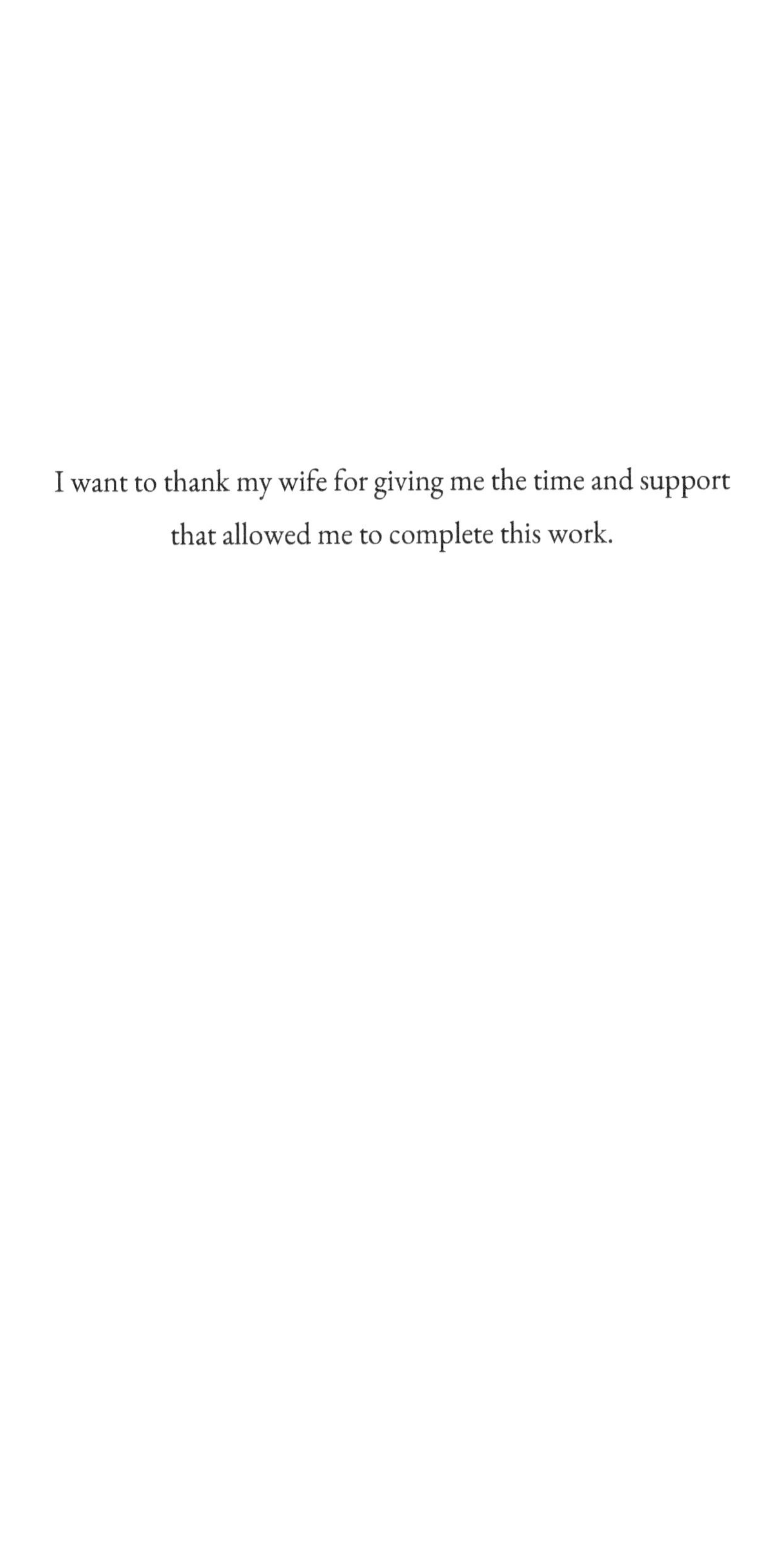

I want to thank my wife for giving me the time and support
that allowed me to complete this work.

CONTENTS

The Request for Service

Steve Johnson's consciousness itched. He sensed something familiar but could not quite place it.

Through the window of his home, nestled at the base of Mummy Mountain in the quiet city of Paradise Valley, Arizona, he viewed the beauty of the northern slope of Camelback Mountain.

Like every other night at this time, Steve sat in his large, overstuffed armchair. He started his meditation session by closing his eyes.

In his mind, the mantra automatically flowed. *Inhale through the nose, hold and exhale through the mouth. Second breath. Inhale through the nose, hold and exhale through the mouth. Now a final third breath. Inhale through the nose, hold and exhale through the mouth.*

Steve drifted quickly into a deep meditative space where he continued inward to contemplate the full mantra. *The gift is how the ancient people of the Dragon Prophecy communicated with one another through their minds. We living people learn this gift a little each time we meditate. When we achieve the gift, we shall seek the Dragon's Teeth hidden out across the planet. With the teeth in our possession, the Dragon becomes whole, and he yields his thoughts of the treasure and our original state of existence. May we find the teeth to make the dragon whole.*

After a time, as his mind sometimes did, a conscious thought overcame the mantra. He thought about one of his granddaughters' issues in school. He willed his thoughts to become a force of positive energy to send her way—to help her—but the focus on the mantra would not come. The awareness of something uncannily familiar yet unidentified overwhelmed his efforts.

Steve brought himself out of meditation.

As he opened his eyes, the sound of Bach's Brandenburg Concerto No. 3 filled the house. The doorbell. Bobbing his head along to the tune, Steve experienced a moment of clarity. As he stood, he felt his eighty-six years in each muscle. He walked slowly and carefully to the front of the house.

Intuition told him who stood outside the front door.

Steve opened the door with a big smile on his face. "Welcome, Imperial Grand Councilor Conway, my home is at your service."

The grey-haired man with the strong chin and striking blue eyes responded predictably with, "I am your servant, and I am here to serve and protect humanity."

Even though Steve had met the imperial grand councilor, or IGC, only once, the two men hugged like old friends.

They had met more than ten years before at a national convention of the Traditional Ancient Mystical Order (TAMO). At that time, Steve served as the head of the local Valley of the Sun Chapter of TAMO. Conway had come to this area to visit Steve's organization.

The fond memory faded, and Steve invited him in and escorted his guest to the great room. He gestured for him to sit on the large comfortable dark leather couch. Steve sat on the matching leather chair facing him.

"Master Johnson, there are some things of great importance to our organization we must discuss." The IGC settled into the couch and leaned forward looking at Steve in the opposite chair.

Steve sat up straight and answered quickly in a serious voice, "For TAMO, I am here only to serve."

The IGC stared intently at Steve. "I have met with three others here in the Valley of the Sun and seven members in other states. You are the last of those chosen for the opportunity to participate in a great medical experiment and subsequent quest." His tone sounded low and subdued. "Here in the Valley in downtown Phoenix, an organization called Twelve-Gen has worked for years on a process of rejuvenation. One of the side effects of this process, I believe, is telepathy. Our teachings from the Dragon Prophecy talk about this as 'the gift.' This skill for people from our organization, and others like ours, is needed."

Steve's pulse quickened. "I have said before I am always willing to serve. This time the service seems to come with great benefit to me and to humanity. Please, tell me more."

The IGC reiterated what Steve already knew. "You learned the basics about the Dragon Prophecy in the first twelve levels of your TAMO studies. By now I'm sure you are aware, the teaching about the Dragon's Teeth is an allegory for the tools to gain the treasure of humanity's ancient knowledge. The exact nature of the treasure is unknown, but we are sure it will be of great value to TAMO and humanity. The Dragon Prophecy explains 'the gift' is needed for the retrieval of the teeth."

The IGC frowned slightly. "The rejuvenation process, known to only a few, comes with some risk." He sounded quite somber. "The last time the experiment was attempted, all twelve participants died. We have a hope that, with a predisposition to meditate along with special training from our Order, the next participants will survive. The issue for the previous participants, our organization believes, comes from the prophetic passages about the gift in the Dragon Prophecy. The gift of telepathy would make anyone unprepared go mad. Your TAMO training should save you from their fate.

"If you are willing to serve, knowing the dangers, tell me now that you accept. Twelve-Gen realizes most seniors still prefer paper verification, so I will have Twelve-Gen send over the paperwork that must be signed and notarized before the first meeting. That meeting, if you accept, will be one week from today at the Twelve-Gen Center at ten a.m."

Steve did not hesitate. "The risk may be high, but the rewards seem to warrant it. Have the company send the papers over to me. I will get them filled out, notarized, and ready to deliver to Twelve-Gen. I will see you next week."

With his nerves firing in anticipation of a new opportunity to serve, Steve accompanied the imperial grand councilor to the front door and watched him as he walked back down the long sidewalk, climbed into his white auto-driver, and left. As the car moved down the driveway without a driver, the sensation of familiarity with the imperial grand councilor also left.

☆☆☆

The package arrived early the next morning by courier. The big stack of papers amounted to a contract: a waiver and release of liability. It indemnified the Twelve-Gen organization in case of death or serious injury. It also provided that all medical expenses for the next ten years would be covered by Twelve-Gen and, for the first year after the rejuvenation was completed for the last participant, each participant would receive room and board and a stipend. Even with all the massive inflation of the first part of the 21st century and the current dollar market, the 24,000 new dollars-per-month tax-free stipend ranked as highly generous.

The task of reviewing the contract reminded Steve of his years in real estate with its massive contracts. They, too, were required to be read and understood. That background made the reading of the Twelve-Gen document straightforward. It did take until mid-afternoon to read and look for loopholes before he was convinced it was a good and fair contract. If all went well, it would be a "win-win" for both the participants and Twelve-Gen.

With everything filled out, he needed a notary. Steve found his identity information, entered the garage, and hopped into his auto-driver. As always, he acknowledged gratitude for the convenience of these great-looking cars that drove themselves. They made it easy for an eighty-six-year-old to maintain freedom and still allow for the safety of others.

He told the car, "World Bank One, closest local branch with a notary."

The car backed itself out of the garage and took him to the bank where he would get the papers notarized.

The discussion at the bank took little time. Within the hour, Steve was back at home eating dinner. He called the provided courier service number and identified himself. They told him the documents would be picked up later in the evening.

The courier came as the beautiful pink and gold Arizona summer sun began to set. Just as the day came to a close, he felt a chapter of his life ending as he handed the papers off to the courier. The action officially marked the first step of something completely new. His belief that rejuvenation would be a reality in his lifetime was now confirmed. Grinning from both nervousness and excitement, he could not wait to learn more about the project.

The Twelve-Gen

Steve had done his due diligence about Twelve-Gen during the week and had found them to be a reputable company specializing in the qualitative description of all genes in the human DNA. Now, apparently, they could manipulate those genes.

Steve put on a nice suit and tie, went out to the garage, and gingerly hopped into the auto-driver.

"Take me to the Twelve-Gen offices in downtown Phoenix."

The garage door opened, and the car left. At that time of morning, the Twelve-Gen office was only twenty minutes away. He arrived at nine forty five, opened the car door and carefully maneuvered his old self out of the car at the office entrance, and told the car, "Park in public parking. I will call you when I am done."

The vehicle raced off to find the closest public parking location.

Steve craned his head as he looked up at the forty-story World Bank One building. He exhaled a quick breath at the sight as he entered the lobby through the revolving doors. His excitement rose while walking the short distance to the elevator. The elevator doors opened, and Steve stepped in.

"Twelve-Gen offices, please."

After a moment of swiftly rising, its system responded with, "Coming up, twentieth floor, Twelve-Gen public entrance." The elevator stopped quickly.

He cleared his ears with a yawn, exited the elevator and immediately faced the receptionist at her massive wooden desk. Behind it hung a big sign with the company logo and its slogan: *"Twelve-Gen—We can make you better!"*

He provided his name to the secretary, who stood up and said in a polite tone, "Follow me, Mr. Johnson. I will take you to the others."

They walked briskly around the corner and down a long corridor to a large corner conference room where she ushered him in. The imperial grand councilor and fourteen other people sat in the audience. One elderly woman, probably in her early sixties, stood in the front of the room next to a seated man in a white lab coat.

The fifteen people who sat in the audience all appeared old, except for the imperial grand councilor. Some appeared older than Steve and some a bit younger. Steve counted six males and eight females.

My involvement makes this closer to an even ratio of genders.

He sat in the last open seat, right up front. The person in the white lab coat was obviously their speaker.

Probably in his mid to late forties, he wore a white medical coat with *"Twelve-Gen—We can make you better!"* emblazoned on the left coat pocket. From it, dangled a bright red badge featuring his photo and name: Director Charles Swenson, PhD, MD. His blond hair and blue eyes matched his obvious Norwegian name.

The speaker stood to reveal an imposing six foot six stature. "Good morning, ladies and gentlemen. My name is Dr. Charles Swenson. My friends call me Charlie. So please, as my future friends, please call me Charlie.

"I want to start by telling you all, at any point in my discussion you can decide to leave. No one will think badly of you. This project is not for everyone." He spoke with a strong but approachable tone.

The woman in the front of the room used sign language to interpret Dr. Swenson's words.

He acknowledged the action with a nod toward her. "I would like to introduce our interpreter, Natasha. She is the seventy-four-year-old daughter of our oldest member, Nadia Belova. As you can see, Natasha looks like she is in her sixties. When you compare her to her mother sitting in front of her, you may not realize Nadia is actually one hundred years old. She looks much younger than most of you. She lost her hearing as a little girl and her daughter has been her friend and companion for most of her life. You can tell longevity runs strongly in their family. When you have a chance today, please introduce yourself. I think Nadia will be one of the most remarkable people in our experiment."

Dr. Swenson talked through the program, what was involved in the rejuvenation process, and the effects of the participants' extended treatment to obtain the desired results. Much of the detail Steve had read in the paperwork he thoroughly reviewed and signed. "If you decide to continue with the project, our staff will take you down the hall to obtain a sample of your blood. We will require two pints of it and an oral mucosa swab. You will also be given an IV by a nurse to help with the replacement of the blood loss.

"The blood and mucosal samples will be used to begin the genomic sequencing of your DNA. We know, at your current ages, your DNA fails to duplicate one hundred percent correctly each time the cells divide. Our process will figure out what the damaged genes are and what changes are needed to repair them. The issues found from these samples will add to the list of possible changes."

Charlie held up a document. "Each one of you will then sit with one of our highly trained nurses who will walk you through a checklist of available changes for you to choose from. For example, the men might want to have a full head of hair as they age instead of, well..." He gestured with one arm to encompass the bald men in the room. Everyone chuckled. "The women might want to have wavy hair or a bigger or smaller bust, for example.

"The list is more than twenty-five pages long and contains all the possibilities Twelve-Gen has discovered. The first set of items have already been checked for you. These include a strong heart, strong resistance to any form of cancer, removing the gene that causes 'Alzheimer's disease,' and removing or updating the genes associated with other diseases. All those gene-related illnesses will be automatically corrected."

He held up one finger and made eye contact with several members of his audience. "You may be asking yourselves, 'What does he mean by *corrected*?' So, let me explain the process. First, the end result is you will leave here after your stay with us with the body of a twenty-year-old. Your memories will be unchanged, but your brain will be improved. We do not know exactly what changes will occur to the brain. We only know it does change.

"All but our last twelve test subjects have been monkeys. I will tell you now, there was a problem with the last human experiment. All but one died during the rejuvenation process. The last person, who did complete the process, started to writhe, and yell about the others in his mind and how he wanted them to stop. After twenty minutes of screaming and thrashing about, he also died. Based on what we could determine, he was scared to death. These subjects were all military. This time we will be using civilians. The potential subjects are the people you see around you."

The guests looked around at the other elders in the room. One lady, clearly in her nineties, stood up without saying a word and left the room. This left fourteen test subjects, seven men and seven women.

Charlie did not acknowledge the person who left. "As I said, any of you may leave at any time. However, we will take a break every fifteen minutes to give you time to absorb what has been said and give you time to ask questions. We want you all to feel comfortable with the entire process.

"Because of the issues with the previous test subjects, part of the process has been changed. We understand what happens to your bodies though we have only conjecture of what happens to your brain and your mental abilities. We will teach you how to deal with the changes we believe you will experience in your minds as the rejuvenation takes place in your brain."

He turned toward a man in the front row. "Mr. Conway, the gentleman sitting at my right has been teaching meditation and mental control for almost half a century. He has learned techniques from his organization, the Traditional Ancient Mystical Order. We lovingly call the organization TAMO. Mr. Conway will work with each of you as individuals and as a group over the next several weeks. He will try to help you build the needed control of your thoughts to keep your minds healthy."

Mr. Conway gave the group a half wave and slight bow and turned his attention back to Charlie.

"Let's take our first break and then I will take questions and continue. The bathrooms are down the hall and to the right. You should be aware, because of the size of our organization, the government requires all bathrooms be unisex. I understand this is nothing new for most of you. I only wanted you to be aware. Also, outside of this room, we've provided a buffet with midmorning food. It is mostly soft foods you will all find easy to digest. The foods on the far end of the table away from the door are all gluten free. We have added these foods based on the medical information you gave us."

Everyone got up, half with walkers, and headed out the door to the bathrooms. One by one, the prospects came back from the break. Some carried their own food and drink. Others relied on help from staff members.

With everyone present again, Charlie stood. "Allow me to continue to describe the rejuvenation process. We will create a special organism like a virus that has the DNA of only one person. Each virus is designed to seek out a particular human cell group. Once injected into the human body, the viruses will continue to grow and flow through the body. When the virus finds a cell from the group it is designed for, it will enter the cell, find the DNA, and replace the cell's DNA with the new and improved version. The virus then dies and becomes food for the cell. As this cell begins to grow and replicate, it will spread this good DNA throughout the cell group.

"Some of the various choices you make from our list of options will cause your rejuvenation to take a longer time. These choices may require additional discussion with our psychiatrists after you come out of rejuvenation. For each of you, our psychiatrists will take time to help you to learn to be twenty again. At this time, let's have everyone take another short break and regroup outside of this room. After the break, I will take you down to the experiment room where I will provide more details and visuals about the process."

The reaction from the fourteen subjects varied. Some appeared excited. Others looked tense and worried, but no one else left the project.

The Proposal

Only one lady had left the Twelve-Gen discussions: Samantha Sampson. When Samantha left, she walked with short but decisive steps down the hall to the elevator. She did not even acknowledge the secretary at the desk.

She entered the elevator and called out, "First floor."

The elevator repeated, "Going down. First floor and lobby."

Nerves on end, she waited to leave the little box as it rushed down to the first floor. After an hour-long minute, she finally heard, "First floor and lobby. Have a nice day."

With a grunt, she stepped out. Relieved, she focused on how to leave Phoenix and fly home as soon as possible.

"Mrs. Sampson. Mrs. Samantha Sampson." Only a few feet from the elevator, the soft whispered voice called her.

A handsome young man, who looked in his late forties, walked toward her with a big showboat grin on his face. His demeaner shouted "shifty," which she kind of liked. At the same time, it irritated her. She wanted to head for the airport and go back home. Still, she paused, curious. She wondered what she could get from him.

He came right up to her and held out his hand. "Good morning, Mrs. Sampson. My name is Mario Menotti. I am a member of the Ancient Universal Knowledge Association (AUKA)." He handed her a card with his credentials. "Could I trouble you for a little of your time? Would you join me for brunch? It will be anything you want from the menu. The Down Home is a nice restaurant across the street. We could talk there in private. I have a proposition for you. I think you will find it financially satisfying."

Samantha adjusted her glasses to better see his face and almost said no. After thinking about it for a second, she figured, for the price of a good meal, she would listen to him.

"I will join you. You can talk while I eat. I walked out of a meeting where all they did was talk. I'm not overly patient at my age. In the meeting upstairs, I wanted them to get on with the process. You can tell me the short version and we will get along fine."

Mario gave Samantha a quick polite answer. "Yes, ma'am!"

They left the building together and crossed the street to the Down Home restaurant. Each table had a pleasant, black-and-white checkered tablecloth and a candle made with an electric bulb. Even the napkins were made of cloth. The murals and general atmosphere, as the name said, suggested a down-home atmosphere. It was indeed a nice-looking place. It only took a minute for the two of them to be seated. They had arrived before the lunchtime rush.

Reviewing the menu, she remembered how the restaurants in the United States had standardized on the word authentic, meaning the food was from the location and of the type they mentioned. Food made in a food factory could not be labeled authentic.

Samantha looked down at the menu items and found the most expensive authentic, but soft foods... something easy for her to chew. The restaurant offered a grilled authentic Atlantic salmon stuffed with authentic Maryland crab meat that cost 200 new dollars. Real seafood coming directly from the Atlantic Ocean and Chesapeake Bay. The authentic Brazilian coffee with authentic cream cost forty-five new dollars. She ordered them from the waiter.

"It's your time, Mr. Menotti. Now tell me what this is about. Please don't waste my time with jibber jabber."

The man pushed his glasses up on his nose and nodded. "We wanted one of our people to be part of the Twelve-Gen experiment but were unable to do so. Only prescreened people like you and the others were accepted into the project. Would you be willing to go through the process of rejuvenation and work on our behalf?"

She scoffed and reached for her purse. A mental picture of the expensive seafood made her mouth begin to water and she tightened her lips and stared at the man over the top of her glasses.

"I know your next question is, 'What's in it for me?' To save you time, I will answer it now. We will pay you 50,000 new dollars a month as long as you work for us. We will put you up in a multi-million dollar condominium at an area called The Top of Central overlooking the city of Phoenix.

"It will be your job to prepare for the rejuvenation. Once the rejuvenation is completed, you will need to use your new talents to help us find information about the other subjects and the people they work for."

She knew he had no alternative, so she adopted a stern expression and asked for the sky.

"Well, to start with, it won't be no 50,000 a month. I will require 100,000 new dollars a month, with the first payment today. I don't like condos, so you will need to find me an expensive home with a pool on the south side of the big mountain there that looks like a camel. The home must be high up on the mountain so my view will be of all the city of Phoenix.

"Also, I don't want to listen to long lectures of what changes they are going to do to me. I liked my body when I was a young woman leaving college and won't be needing anything else. If we have a deal, my friends call me Sam."

She stretched out her hand, expecting him to counteroffer.

Mario shook her hand. "We have a deal! We happen to have a beautiful home on Camelback Mountain built to look like a castle from King Arthur's time. It has every modern convenience a person could want."

He pulled out a platinum-colored card from his wallet. "Here is a debit card already containing 200,000 new dollars. You were not greedy, and I was authorized to go up to 200,000 per month. I will tell my boss you asked for that much. Your actual first monthly salary will be added to the debit card the day you move into the home."

Sam was surprised at Mario's generosity. She realized her mouth had fallen open, so she snapped it shut.

"Would you like to see the house? I can have the real estate agent meet us there. It will take a week to prepare the home for you to live in. Until then, we can offer you a two-room suite at The Phoenician Hotel in Scottsdale."

"Don't need to see the house. I went on a tour and saw it years ago when visiting Phoenix. I want to have the house furnished in Victorian style of furnishings."

A server delivered their food, and Sam tackled it like she had never eaten before. After adding a dessert for seventy-five new dollars' worth of an authentic hot fudge sundae, she raised her gaze to Mario's.

"I am tired now. Have someone pick up my bag and deliver it to my room at the Phoenician. Let's head to my temporary homestead."

He grinned, they stood up and walked outside to hail an auto-driver cab.

During the ride to the hotel, they both remained quiet. Sam felt something besides the business deal was going on in Mario's brain. It was only twenty minutes to the hotel, but she enjoyed every minute of it.

When they arrived at the Phoenician, the front desk clerk glanced around as if looking for something. "Suitcases, reservations?" His tone sounded suspicious and condescending.

Mario said nothing. He pulled out his wallet and grabbed a glowing, almost translucent, credit card emblazoned with the word *Diamond* across its top next to a big cobalt colored diamond.

The clerk turned to face Mario. "What room would be your preference, sir?" he asked quickly in a humble tone of voice.

Sam answered for him, "We want the nicest two-bedroom suite you have here."

All three of them smiled.

The clerk inputted the information into the computer. "Single entry or dual entry?"

Sam gave Mario a quick wink and smiled a pixy smirk. "Dual entry."

The bio scanner clicked at each of them. No keys. Either one of them could walk up to the room door and it would open. They had become the room keys.

The clerk pointed at a small bellboy robot. "Follow Little Jeffry. He will show you to the room."

Mario and Sam followed the robot as it led them up the flight of stairs. Once at the suite, the door opened as expected.

Samantha scanned the first room, a large living room with fourteen-foot ceilings. It pleased her. She couldn't help but smile at Mario.

Standing in the doorway, from where she stood, in the back of the suite an open door led to a large bedroom. The room appeared to have silk wallpaper. Next to the bedroom, a beautifully carved open wooden door led to a nicely furnished office with rich wood paneling. Each of the rooms had large one-hundred-inch 8K television screens. Business news flashed on the screen in the office. In the front room, the sitting area, bar area, and dining area, all contained elegant furniture. Her hand touched one of the big chairs. The softness of the leather was obviously expensive. She slid down into the chair and felt the firmness of it.

Little Jeffry enquired, "Is this satisfactory, miss?"

The sudden words from the silent robot shocked them. Both nodded their heads. The robot turned, left the room, and the door automatically closed behind it.

Mario picked up a binder from a table. "Order what you want from room service or go to any of the wonderful restaurants here in the hotel. You will be able to obtain all the authentic food you want. I realize you have only a limited amount of clothes with you. For anything you need—clothes, accessories, or toiletries—they have classic designer shops and a convenience store right next to the lobby. Charge the items you want to the room.

"It will take me a day or two to arrange things at the clinic. Here is my phone number. If you need anything, call me. I do mean if you need or want anything at all." A twinkle sparkled in Mario's eyes.

"Thank you, young man. I think it will all work out fine."

Sam led him to the door, ushered him out, patted his bottom, and closed the door. She immediately went into the bedroom, took off her clothes, and slipped into the bed under the silk sheets, and fell asleep.

She woke up and decided to have some fun—awfully expensive fun—without leaving the hotel. A call to the front desk confirmed the price of the suite, 8,000 new dollars per night. After doing some math, Sam decided to try and purchase enough to cost these people ten times what they had been expecting to pay. Being glad Mario had set up her allowance as 200,000 new dollars per month, she planned what could be done to reward him for it.

The Room

While Mario and Sam were discussing the AUKA project at the Down Home restaurant, everyone at Twelve-Gen assembled outside of the conference room. Charlie motioned for the subjects to follow him. He walked patiently and slowly to the end of the hall, opened a set of double doors, and turned on the lights of the dark room. The LEDs shone and illuminated the contents of the large room. Three rows of five tanks filled the space. Each tank measured eight feet long, three feet wide, and three feet tall.

The tank closest to the door brimmed with a light blue liquid, which covered the dummy in the tank. The dummy was quite lifelike, but with no eyebrows nor eyelashes. Wires hooked into its head, chest, stomach, groin, hands, and the bottom of the feet—probably fifty different wires. Charlie encouraged all the group to examine the tank and the dummy.

He lifted a small tablet from a nearby table and clicked a few buttons. The tank lit up with a blue glow. He became energized and excited as he prepared to talk about his brainchild, his baby. He pressed a button on the tablet.

"Each of the colors aids in several of the subject's changes and their growth. This one is sunlight and gives the individual a natural source of vitamin D."

A man raised his hand.

Charlie acknowledged him. "Yes, sir."

The man's eyes teared up. "I was a pilot in the Vietnam War in the nineteen seventies. My plane was shot down in North Vietnam. The Vietcong captured me and put me in a POW camp. Most of my time, I spent in a box not much bigger than these. Day in, day out, little light or food." He inhaled deeply and let it out to regain his composure. "I want to participate in this project. The thought of death does not bother me. I have lived a full rewarding life. The only problem is I do not think I could stay in that box for even one hour. I think I should leave."

Charlie immediately held up both hands. "Mr. Felder, before you make up your mind, please let me tell you a little bit more about the process."

He lowered his head keeping his gaze on Felder as he waited for the veteran to reply.

Mr. Felder gave Charlie a concise nod.

"On the night each of you begin your transformation, you will be given an anesthetic. It is a special formula we devised specifically for these procedures. It will totally relax you without putting you to sleep. It will allow you to feel comfortable, even though you have no clothes on.

"You will lie on a comfortable portable table. This gurney will be warm to the touch and smell like your favorite scent which you will pick out during your time with the nurse.

"After careful review of all the attachments and their data, we will begin the process. In addition to a DNA viral vector, a stronger sedative will be given to you. At this point, you will enter a state of unconsciousness, a medically induced coma, if you will. You will be maintained in this state during all your transformation time. It is only after you are stable in the medically induced coma, will you be transferred by gurney and brought to this room."

Felder thought about the explanation and wiped the remaining tears from his eyes. The look on his face went from sad to a wide grin. "Thank you, I think I can work with that. I will stay."

"I have spoken for a long time now. I am sure you all would like a break. We have more food and drinks for you outside of the conference room. Let us convene back there in thirty minutes. If anyone has any personal questions, please write them on the paper provided in the conference room and place them on the table at the front of the room. This will allow you to ask personal questions and maintain your privacy. We also placed short brochures there which may answer some of your questions."

Charlie took the time to drink a glass of juice and eat a lox bagel sandwich himself. Afterward, he motioned to the imperial grand councilor to follow him into a nice office several doors down. They sat.

"Mr. Conway, what do you think of this group?"

The imperial grand councilor grimaced. "First, even though I am sixty five, when I hear the name 'Mr. Conway' I look around for my father. So, please call me Nate."

His face relaxed into a more contemplative expression. "I have read the biographical information on all of them. Each of them has knowledge of specific sacred places around the world that relate to my organization's needs. The three women and six men who are high-ranking members of our TAMO organization, I am sure will survive. That will get you three quarters of the way to the twelve people you need to meet your military contract and the twelve needed for my purposes. The lessons I will give should help all fourteen of your subjects. I will do the classes in the days just before you begin the transformations."

He sat back in his seat and, with elbows on the chair arms, steepled his fingers. "I am going to enjoy watching all these people change. You have a great batch of nurses, doctors, and researchers to help them out. I am sure there will not be a repeat of the previous experiment. Losing twelve people to complete madness must have been hard to take. I'm glad the correlation of all of the data gave us a hint into the issue that caused the problem and the death of the subjects."

Charlie smiled. "You are right, Nate. I feel like there is success in the wind. It's going to be interesting to watch these bent and crippled elderly people become beautiful and handsome young adults again. As it used to be said, 'Youth is wasted on the young.' We are going to find out if rejuvenated old people continue the mistakes of youth." He glanced at the door. "I think it's time to get back and see what sorts of questions we need to answer. Any training-related questions, I will punt to you."

Nate nodded, rose from his chair, and left the room with Charlie.

Questions Answered

When Charlie and Nate walked in, all the prospects had assembled in their seats in the conference room. Most of them were eating or drinking. Nate quickly took his seat at the front of the room. Charlie picked up the many slips of paper with questions on them and sat next to the table. He read them all and separated them into groups. As he suspected, from the questions asked, only four needed answering.

Charlie picked up the first slip of paper and read the first question out loud, "How does Twelve-Gen make money on this project? It looks like a lot of expensive equipment."

He glanced up. "We are a big corporation; this project was preceded by ten years of research and experimental design. What you see here today *is* expensive, including materials, floor space, and staff. It is, however, a small fraction of the cost we have paid so far. A large portion of the project was paid for by the U.S. military. Other nonprofit groups like the Gates Group donated a billion dollars to fund part of the startup costs and research. Profit from Twelve-Gen's genetic testing program has also helped to fund outside research and development for many genetic diseases and issues associated with aging. Part of the checklist of "enhancements" that you may receive came from that research."

Charlie waved his arm in a gesture to include all of the people. "Each of you, after the rejuvenation process is completed, should live well beyond 2150. For those of you not good with numbers, it means another hundred-plus years. The good news associated with this is that your body will only degenerate quickly in the last ten years of your life. Fifty years from now you will still look and feel like a thirty-year-old. With a good diet and exercise, you may look and feel like you were the day you left the tanks."

The subjects beamed and nodded their concurrence with the ideas presented.

"One last group will pay for this project, that group includes each of you."

Everyone started talking at once. Their happy faces changed to concern. Charlie raised his hands in a calming motion.

"Do not worry. The way you're paying for this is not 'out of pocket.' We have secured an agreement from the Social Security Administration. They will take the value of your current Social Security payments, based on you living until 2150, and give Twelve-Gen the value today, assuming no growth in the payment. That amounts to around two million dollars the government will give to us for each one of you. The catch... You stop receiving your Social Security checks."

He picked up one of the informative brochures and held it up. "For those of you who read the details, this will simply be repeat information. We have contracted with the newly renovated Phoenix Hyatt Hotel. Their top floor, below the revolving dining room, has been turned into two-bedroom, two-bath suites. A small kitchen in the front room blends in with the living room furniture. We will continuously stock the kitchen with food of your choosing. A full bar will also remain fully stocked. You each will be given these accommodations at no cost. This benefit will continue until one year after the last person completes their rejuvenation."

The subjects started to clap. Charlie interrupted them.

"I have more good news. Also, as part of this process, you will be given a Twelve-Gen debit card with your picture and 'official' date of birth. The card will provide you with 24,000 new dollars, deposited on the first of each month starting today. You can spend it anyway you want. We are assuming you will be in the rejuvenation tank for at least six months, so your card will start with around 144,000 new dollars on it. If you are longer in the tank, your card will have more added each month."

A stooped woman in the last row stood up. "Hello all, my name is Sandra Haspure. I suffer from osteoporosis, as you can see. I used to live in Baltimore, Maryland, but came out here after selling my home, furniture, and other belongings. I flew here to Phoenix with one suitcase. I arrived in time for this meeting. What am I supposed to do until our accommodations are ready?"

Charlie held up both palms in a placating manner, then turned one of them thumbs up. This was one of the many situations Twelve-Gen had planned for.

"Mrs. Haspure, those who decide to enter the program after today's discussions, will be given a key to their hotel suite and taken there today. You will be given your Twelve-Gen card to provide access to cash. Even those who live locally can move into their new hotel home at any time. For transport, you will have access to one of our company's auto-drivers for local travel. You will also have access to our corporate air-transport vehicles which can take you anywhere in the world in less than three hours. I hope that meets with your satisfaction, Mrs. Haspure."

She returned his thumbs up gesture. "Yes, sir. It certainly does. You can drop the 'Mrs.' And use 'Ms.' My husband died when I was sixty. That was too long ago to bother about. Better yet, call me Sandy."

Charlie nodded to her amiably and picked up another slip scribbled with a handwritten question. "What I have finished describing has also answered this question, 'What will happen to me during the first year?' At least it explains the first year after the rejuvenation is completed and the next several weeks before entering the tank."

He picked up another paper slip, read it silently, then looked up at his audience. "After serious study, we now believe we know what changed in each of the prior subjects. They gained the ability to receive the thoughts of all of those around them. This made them agitated and unable to cope. To help you, the Imperial Grand Councilor Nathaniel Conway will teach you the mental teachings of TAMO." He gestured to Nate with his hand.

"You will learn how to quietly listen to the thoughts of those around you, and to block those you do not care to hear. You will learn to block your thoughts so others cannot hear you. You will attend his class four days a week during the two weeks prior to immersion in the tanks.

"We believe it was the stress of the opening of the mind and hearing the thoughts of all those around them that drove the prior military subjects to purposefully shut down their own bodies. You will have the benefit of controlling these issues. Even though you will be heavily sedated and in an unconscious state, the mind will still awaken as it improves beyond where it is now."

Charlie smiled to himself as he saw the worried looks and long faces softened to pleasant acceptance.

"This last question is an interesting one and I have saved it for last. 'If we have kids after our transition, will they reflect the genetic benefits of the changes we went through?' First, for you ladies and the one member who will be changing into a female, your uterus and all the rest of your sexual organs will be like that of a twenty-year-old woman. You will technically be able to have children. I say 'technically' because both the men and women will be given a five-year implant that will prevent pregnancy. The implants can easily be removed by a pill that contains a special virus. Once the pill is swallowed, the virus will find and dissolve the implant, render the virus inert, and your liver will flush it from your body. The changes in your DNA will be permanent. The eggs from the women and the sperm from the men will all carry your perfect DNA. Like all children, the ones you bear will be a blend of the two parents. If you want super results, have children with one of the people you see here."

"Yes!" one of the female subjects said with enthusiasm. Her response resulted in happy glints in many of the subjects' eyes and some chuckling. "This brings us to another question which many of you are probably thinking. If you have artificial limbs or joints, what will happen? For those who fall into this category, the answer is quite simple. The rejuvenation process is also restorative. It will repair joints, ligaments, muscles, bones and, as previously explained, organs. We will monitor this new growth, and the reduction of growth caused by things like bone spurs or other malformed calcium deposits or bones. This will happen automatically. Since we are working with individual DNA, the results of the rejuvenation will not make you all look identical. Instead, you all will be identically healthy. Your changes in looks will only include what you request."

Heads nodded in approval.

Charlie paused and moved his gaze across everyone in the room. "Are there any more questions?"

No one responded.

"Okay, then, as a final note, over the next several weeks, those who have not already done so should be sure to put your affairs in order. If you have living relatives, you should talk to them about what you are doing. As with all experimental medical projects, there is a chance you will not make it through the process. All of you were chosen because you do not have a spouse to leave behind. When you are finished with the rejuvenation, you will look younger than most of your grandchildren. So, you'll want to make sure they all know they probably won't see your older selves again.

"After the change, you will start to acquire new friends. Be sure to tell all in your circle of current friends you will not be back. It is best not to give anyone, including relatives, more details than absolutely necessary. Upon successful completion of the rejuvenation process, you will be given a new birth certificate identifying you as twenty-four years old with your current birthday month and day. Later, after success of the experiment, if you desire, you can be part of a press conference to announce the success of the process."

You could almost see the thoughts crossing the subjects' faces. They all seemed ready to go. "That is the end of our discussions for the day. For those who would like to continue and become part of the project, please follow me to the blood donor room where our techs will draw two pints of your blood. After some more refreshments and a signature stating you will continue with the project, you will be given your Twelve-Gen credit card and directions to the Hilton hotel along with keys to your suite. Auto-drivers downstairs will take you over to the hotel. For those who have decided not to participate, please sign the document at the back of the room and you may leave."

No one went to the back of the room. You could feel the excitement as they followed the director to the blood-donor room.

As the last subject left, Charlie blew out a long breath. It had been a long day but, this time, he felt the project would be a success.

Sam's House

Mario called Sam at the hotel in the early morning a week after she had moved into her temporary home. He said her Camelback home had been updated, and everything she requested had been purchased and put in place: security, repainting, furniture, and stocking of food.

Sam insisted Mario come over to the hotel and help her with a situation. During his fifteen-minute drive, Mario fretted that something had gone wrong at the hotel. He worried. What could it be? What could have happened?

Mario instructed his auto-driver to park itself while he ran up to Sam's room. He normally would have knocked but, instead, used his presence to unlock the door. "Open door!" he said. It opened for him and shut behind him. "Sam, what is it? Where are you?"

"In here, dear. Please hurry. Come in here and give me a hand!" Sam's voice came from behind the closed bedroom door.

Mario ran to the bedroom, still fearing the worst. He opened the door and stopped short.

Sam lay on the bed in a red saffron negligee. Totally sheer, it left nothing to the imagination. She wore red fishnet stockings, red high-heeled shoes, red lipstick, and ruby earrings with a matching large ruby necklace accenting her chest as it nestled between her breasts.

His response came immediately. "Sam, you are a stunningly beautiful woman!"

Sam gave him a sly grin, clearly appreciating his point of view. "Come here, handsome. I have a special situation you can help me with."

Mario needed no more prodding. Even though she was a much older woman, he was thrilled to help her resolve her special "situation," especially since it involved him, her, and the bedroom. He was glad he could help her with this important task in her time of need.

He finished the task after several hours, successfully completing the job. He experienced surprise at how adept and limber Sam was in the bedroom. Who knew a woman of her age could bend and act like that? In fact, he found it wonderfully delectable being with her.

"Will you do me the privilege of allowing me to be your first intimate partner after your rejuvenation is complete?"

"Maybe." She provided woman's universal answer in a coy tone.

After the pleasant morning's adventure, Mario helped Sam pack all her clothes into seven large Gucci suitcases she had purchased. He could not believe all the designer outfits she had bought. He knew that in six months, after her rejuvenation, the clothes would all be thrown out, though she would surely keep her rubies and other jewelry. Later, he learned her beautiful "playtime" outfit amounted to an investment of 90,000 new dollars. The auto-bellman required two trips down to the hotel entrance where Mario's auto-driver waited for them.

While they loaded the baggage into the car, Mario settled the 590,000 new dollar invoice with the hotel. The checkout clerk's stare and subsequent wide grin validated Mario's 1,000 new dollar tip for the maid and other service personnel.

The perfect gentleman, Mario, opened the door for Sam. She climbed into the car with slow deliberate movements, exposing her thigh. She made sure he could also see her sultry smile. He stepped in on the other side of the vehicle and had barely buckled his seatbelt when Sam grabbed his head and pulled his face to hers.

When their long passionate kiss ended, she whispered, "Yes, I will let you be my first."

Mario hummed his appreciation, then told the car, "Take us to Samantha's home."

The car whisked off, heading for Camelback Mountain. The house on the side of the mountain was only a ten-minute drive, but her added security measures required twenty minutes more to reach the front door of the home.

During the week while Sam relaxed at the Scottsdale Phoenician Hotel, a designer had updated the home on Camelback Mountain. The woman organized everything. The house had been painted to match the designer's plan, which included furnishings in the most glamorous and most expensive Victorian style available. Some pieces required expedited transport from Europe.

The designer walked Sam and Mario through the house. She explained how each room featured a panel Sam could talk into to communicate with the maid and the cook from anywhere in the house. Temperature sensors could be told exactly what temperature to make the room, and how to best illuminate the room for varying purposes. When people left the room, the panel turned off all the appropriate lights.

Sam appeared to enjoy the tour of her new house. After a tour of her new bedroom, she smiled an expectant grin at Mario and winked.

As the decorator left the room and headed toward the front door, still talking about features over her shoulder, Sam whispered, "Well sailor, shall we break in that new bed?"

They both profusely thanked the designer and tried not to act too eagerly as they encouraged her to let herself out of the house. After all, they had a brand new king-sized poster bed to break in.

Later, as Mario left, he told Sam he would meet her the next morning in the building next door to Twelve-Gen for her to give some blood. He quickly explained the experiment would start in two weeks and she should enjoy her home and money during that time.

Sam said she would call him when she needed various situations taken care of and winked at him again. He knew he would be back multiple times. He could not believe an octogenarian woman could be so sensual.

Putting Affairs in Order

Steve did not have much to do in order to follow the imperial grand councilor's advice about putting affairs in order. His house and vehicles were all paid off. Those, along with all his bank accounts and stock market accounts were part of a revocable trust. The trust was set up to transfer to his daughter and granddaughters.

The hardest part might be finding the time to meet with his busy daughter, Alisa Johnson-Weinberg, a high-powered Washington DC lawyer. She was even under consideration for a federal judgeship. Steve knew—between work, her two sets of twins at nineteen and twenty-one years old, and her husband—it would be difficult to schedule some quality time with her.

Steve made the call, and a woman answered. He always found it difficult to tell which of the four girls, or even their mother, answered the phone. Steve hoped it was one of the girls.

"Hi, this is Pop-Pop. Is your mother home?"

"Hi, Pop-Pop, this is Caroline. Mom is in the other room. Let me call her."

Caroline covered the phone and yelled as loud as she could, "Mom! Pick up the phone. It's Pop-Pop."

After only a few seconds, a mature woman answered, "Hi, Dad. What's shakin'?"

Such a standard way for his daughter to answer.

"Hi, sweetheart, I will need an hour of your time this weekend. I need some wet signatures, and I want to explain to you what I am planning."

"Give me a second to look at the family calendar. I think the hubby will be in town this weekend too." Silence filled the line for a few seconds. "It looks like all four girls are coming home from Georgetown University to get their laundry done here at home." She chuckled. "Such typical college kids. But I've cleared my schedule a bit while they're home, so I can even see you for more than an hour. We could all do lunch. I don't need to be anywhere until three p.m. How does eleven sound to you?"

He felt a flood of relief. Things would work out with plenty of time to explain everything. "I'll fly out to President Schwarzenegger Airport and take a cab to your home in Georgetown. I have one hell-of-a story to tell you and, I'm bringing along some paperwork I'd like you to sign."

☆ ☆ ☆

Saturday morning, Steve hopped on the DC flight with no issues. Thank goodness, after thirty years, the government finally had figured out how to load people onto planes safely without requiring them to take their shoes off.

Steve remembered well all the paperwork he needed to fill out to obtain the express passenger designation on all his tickets. He moved right from the front door of the airport to the gate in less than ten minutes. The plane took off from Phoenix and was in Washington in less than twenty. With no luggage to pick up, he was out of the Schwarzenegger in a few minutes more. The Washington traffic slowed him a bit and it took twenty-five minutes to get to Alisa's Georgetown home. Including his eighteen minute ride to the Phoenix airport, the whole trip had taken a little over an hour and a half. With the speed of travel, it hardly ever bothered him anymore. He used to have so little patience for waiting during travel.

He knocked on Alisa's door at exactly eleven in the morning. Her husband, Mark, opened the door. "Hi, Dad, I can hear the girls coming down the steps. Let's head outside to the patio. I'm making steaks for us, Isabella, and Tiffany. I'm grilling vege-burgers for Caroline and Evelyn." He shook his head. "How did half of each set of the identical twins become vegetarian? They certainly don't get it from my side of the family." He smiled at Steve still shaking his head.

They walked down the long hallway to the back of the house and Steve, as always, admired the fine woodwork in their home. Back in the early 1930s, they really knew how to build a home.

He loved visiting here and seeing his daughter thrive. Living in Georgetown in a house with any kind of yard was not cheap, and they had a spacious yard behind their home with its three floors, eight bedrooms, and many balconies.

"Pop-Pop is here!"

Steve pivoted back toward the voice.

"Yay!" The chorus of sound included all four girls.

He shared hugs with each of his granddaughters as they passed through the door into the backyard.

Steve turned to Mark. "How can you handle so much estrogen in this house?"

Mark cocked his head to one side. "Dad, you forgot we have more estrogen around here, even beyond those five females. Don't forget the two dogs and the cat."

Steve placed one hand against his forehead in an exaggerated gesture of mock disbelief.

"I spend a lot of time out of town," his son-in-law answered. "And, it is a good thing we have a girl who comes in to help out."

They both laughed.

Alisa strode up from a shady spot where she'd been shuffling a binder of papers. She hugged him and pulled away, still holding his arms to study his face.

"So, Dad, what's up? What's the big mystery?"

Steve studied his daughter, she was showing physical signs of her forty-six years: crow's feet around her eyes, graying hair... *She might be a candidate for future programs*, he thought. When she frowned in response to his intense gaze, it brought him back to the task at hand.

She gestured to a clean new authentic wooden picnic table with six chairs under the large 120-year-old oak tree. He pulled up a lawn chair and the family all sat around the table.

"Once I explain my plans, I would like you to read and sign these papers, Alisa." He placed the papers on the table in front of her with a pen. "I have again been called into service by my imperial grand councilor for a highly noble experiment."

He inhaled deeply and met her gaze when she looked up, clearly puzzled by his intense pause. "Do you remember all of my talk about the possibility of a rejuvenation center opening in Phoenix in 2037? Well, I was right. I am one of fourteen people who have the opportunity to participate in that innovative experiment."

"You mean the process of making people young again? But isn't that highly dangerous, Dad?"

He inclined his head in affirmation. "Yes, I will come out of the rejuvenation as a young man." He paused and met her gaze. "Unfortunately, there is a chance I will not survive the experiment. Twelve subjects did die during the first experiment with humans. Only one finished it, but he died within hours of completion. Also, when the experiment succeeds, you won't see me again. At least you won't see *this* me again."

Open mouths and worried expressions met him from around the silent table. He held up one palm to stall any comments.

"Let me finish, please. The papers make you, Alisa, my full attorney and trustee over all of my assets: money, homes, vehicles, and investments. You will remain as my medical attorney for all health decisions. The doctors on this experiment know I have a do-not-resuscitate clause in my living will." He ignored the wide eyes and sinking demeanor of his powerful daughter. "If all works out as planned, they will have fixed the issue that caused the deaths during the first round of experiments."

"Dad, we don't want you to do something this risky!" his daughter interrupted with vehemence.

Steve refused to react. He'd expected this reaction. "The next time you see me, I will have a new social security number and a new birth certificate stating I am twenty-four years old and born on October 23, 2013. I will have the body of an eighteen-year-old but still have all of my memories and knowledge. I am expecting the experiment to be a success. I have already signed the paperwork to begin the process. I wanted you, Mark, and the girls to be well taken care of if something bad happens."

His granddaughters shared concerned looks. Mark's intense stare moved between his wife and her father. Steve figured his family was all too stunned to comment. He took his daughter's hand.

"I wanted you to know what was going on, just in case. Will you support me in this, Alisa?"

She answered quickly, "Dad, I know this has been your dream for many years. You supported me when I dreamed of changing my life and going to law school to become a lawyer, though *that* endeavor was not quite as drastic." She sighed. "Still... I will support you now. I love you, Dad, and I will make sure everything works out for you no matter what the outcome."

Mark had his arms over the shoulders of two of the twins whose tears streamed down their faces.

Steve gave the young women a wry grin. "Think about it, girls. When this thing works and I come to visit, the five of us can go anywhere together and you won't be embarrassed to be seen with me. Even if we went bar hopping. In fact, you might see me pick up a young honey and leave you guys to get home on your own."

The girls' faces turned from sadness to shock. They glanced at one another and, amidst hand-covered mouths and wiping dampness from cheeks, they all burst out into laughter.

Steve's affairs were now in order. It was time to start the next phase.

Medical Preparation and Mental Training

Preparation for the rejuvenation required each subject to endure three invasive surgeries. The first would be a stomach tube to allow the direct introduction of food substances into the body. The second two were ports inserted directly into the blood system: one on the right to permit drawing of blood and one on the left to allow injecting of substances into the blood. Each of these would have, individually, been outpatient surgery. Doing all three would require only an hour of surgery and a three-day stay at the hospital to watch for complications and recovery.

The doctor doing the surgery turned out to be the son of a doctor who installed Steve's feeding tube during his treatment and cure of cancer in 2007. He still remembered the older Dr. Rotherman as pretty much a sadist. Within minutes of meeting the younger Dr. Rotherman, it was obvious he carried the same sadistic streak as his father. Steve shrugged it off with minimal trepidation. He did not expect any problems, as the doctor's despicable bedside manner did not influence his excellent surgical skills.

Each of the fourteen subjects were given a different time to arrive at the downtown Phoenix Hospital. Each appointment was forty-five minutes after the prior one. The hospital dedicated two surgery rooms to this day of surgery.

When Steve arrived, he noticed someone from the orientation meeting. He went up to the gentleman and held out his hand. "My name is Steve Johnson. I saw you at Twelve-Gen. I take it you are here to get the three holes poked into you?"

The man chuckled. "Yes. Hi, Steve, my name is Ryan Bentley." They shook hands. "My appointment is five minutes from now. I take it yours is in forty-five minutes?"

"Yeah, I'm not looking forward to it. The last time I got a feeding tube put in it was by this doctor's father. I understand they both have the same skill and temperament. This shouldn't be difficult, more of a pain in the chest. What are your thoughts on this whole experiment?"

Ryan shrugged. "I actually am—"

A nurse called out, "Ryan Bentley!"

He gave Steve a shrug and followed the nurse into the preparation room.

On the cusp of Steve's appointment time, an exceptionally large elderly Native American woman with beautiful hair down to her waist walked into the waiting room. He introduced himself, but she only had time to say her name, Cecilia Begay, before Steve was called into the preparation room.

Steve's operations succeeded with the tube and ports placed and ready. He needed to spend the next three days recovering. The hospital pretty much kept him knocked out most of the days. They woke him up for medicine and statistics. On the third day, he saw Dr. Rotherman, who poked Steve at each of the surgery sites. He made sure it hurt.

Just like his father. When released, he went back to the Hyatt for another couple of days of rest. He did not recover as easily as he used to. The feeding tube stuck out and Steve had to hold it down with clean tape so it would not flop around. The other two ports were subcutaneous with catheters to the appropriate vein or artery. He only needed to keep a bandage over the sites until they healed.

One of the nurses visited him to provide an update on the project. Apparently, several of the patients had a difficult time with their surgeries and the project could not continue until all the subjects were in approximately the same physical condition. She said everything would be delayed by two weeks because of the others' personal health issues.

Living it up in the Hyatt was not so bad. The food was delicious, the service was good, and he became acquainted with what would be his home for the next year or so. Some nights he would go to the Hyatt's top floor where its bar provided pleasant music.

He did sneak out several times to his Paradise Valley home to enjoy the quiet and positive energy of the area. It was always nice to be home. With the caretaker only coming into the home twice a week, Steve picked the caretaker's off days. He wanted to be totally alone. A high energy place like the Hyatt made it difficult to meditate. When all is said and done, home is still home.

Finally, all fourteen of the subjects were healed and settled into their new homes away from home. The subjects followed a simple schedule. Each person could eat downstairs with the others, or upstairs in their individual suites. Most ate alone. People in their eighties and nineties were not much fun to be around, but Steve always went for his meals in the restaurant. He enjoyed life and watching it happen to those around him.

Once each morning, around ten o'clock, the imperial grand councilor, who most everyone called the "IGC," held a two-hour meeting. It was Nate Conway's job to teach the test subjects how to control their minds and bodies. The sessions involved group talks with all the experiment subjects. Six of the lessons specifically taught them how to control their minds. These were spread out over the two weeks prior to entering the rejuvenation tanks. The rest of their talks were with psychologists. The PhDs shared knowledge about how to reenter society, with the mission to help the subjects learn to be young again. It would be necessary for all the subjects to learn how to fit in.

Each day after the mental training, the subjects had a full physical checkup. They each came into the examining room in their bathrobes. When it was time for them to be examined, they casually took off the bathrobes and placed them on any nearby chair. It did not matter to them if others looked on. As octogenarians, there was nothing to be embarrassed about. They had all seen many male and female body parts. That turned out to be one of the many things the psychologists needed to address with the subjects, as current-day young people still practiced a modicum of modesty. Clothing designs accented and blended with various body parts to show a lot, but the designs still made the wearer feel clothed.

For most of the subjects, the special mind-training talks amounted to a review. Nine of the subjects were TAMO members who had varied experiences to earn their statuses from the Fifth Level to the Twelfth Level. TAMO members learned about meditation and controlling their minds in the early Neophyte Levels. Those at the Twelfth Level— Steve and Rob Worthy — could probably have taught most of the classes.

Nate Conway had worked with the project director to figure out what went wrong during the first round of tests of the rejuvenation experiment. The solution required the subjects to learn how to build mental barriers, a new talent that would lead to success in these experiments. These especially important lessons must be learned by all of the subjects, or they would probably die.

Nate's biggest concern focused on the five subjects who had not been members of TAMO: Father Jonathan Ashton, Donna Andrews, Cecilia Begay, Nadia Belova, and Sandy Haspure. Father Jonathan Ashton would probably learn quickly. As a priest, it was necessary for him to meditate during his prayers. The IGC would have to work extra with the four women. He would need even more time to work with Nadia Belova as her deafness caused an extra challenge.

The subjects must be proficient at putting themselves into a meditative state since it would simulate what it would be like in the tank. There, they would have no feeling in their bodies, only their minds would be aware.

The first week's three lessons consisted of learning this style of meditation. Everyone picked it up quickly, except Nadia.

After each class, Nate sat with Nadia and her daughter, the Russian sign-language translator. Everyone else in the class was able to close their eyes and listen to the instructions. Nadia had to see the instructions.

Nate had figured out a way to make it happen. They would go into a room with no lights. Nate sat next to Nadia while the interpreter sat several feet in front of them with a dim light on her. Nate talked and watched Nadia as the interpreter translated.

The three of them spent many hours on this process. In between meditation attempts, Nate talked with Nadia about her life and growing up deaf. The two developed a strong bond. Nate even picked up enough sign language to be able to make light conversation.

By the end of the two weeks, all the subjects could create the mental image of a wall and use it to attempt to block out all but their own thoughts. Even Nadia had a grasp of what was needed. All the test subjects believed this mind stuff was theoretical in nature. They figured no one could in actuality receive another person's thoughts.

For Sandy, Steve learned, these lessons had opened a new pathway of light. She had never shown any interest in metaphysics before the training and had asked Nate if she could learn all the wisdom of the TAMO organization. After the rejuvenation, he promised she would be able to learn the knowledge of the Traditional Ancient Mystical Order.

Steve was glad the two weeks of training was completed.

"I have trained you to the absolute best of my abilities," the imperial grand councilor had told them.

Steve believed, too, all of them knew enough to survive the changes in their minds.

The Day of Entry

The day had finally come. The fourteen "Tankers," as they called themselves, arrived early in the morning for their nine o'clock appointments. Several were waiting inside in the lobby of the building at seven. Everyone seemed so excited to start the project. They did not care if they needed to wait for the doctors and nurses to arrive.

As the fourteen entered the examination room, their personally assigned day and night nurses greeted them. The patients routinely stripped down to no clothes in anticipation of entering the tanks.

Steve stood while the nurses—wearing sanitized gloves—shaved his head, pubic areas, arms, legs, and anywhere hair could grow. Once all hair was removed, he laid face down on the gurney by his station.

A quick glance showed the other subjects undergoing the same process with their medical assistants. He took a few deep breaths to keep his heart rate at a steady level. *Here we all go!*

His nurse carefully applied the first electrodes to locations on the back of his head and back, his arms, legs, soles of his feet, and one electrode on each toe.

With assistance, he was turned face up so she could set the additional electrodes on the sides, top, and front of his head. His nurse also connected the nodes to his face near the eyes, nose, cheeks, lips, and neck. When she finished with his arms and each of his fingers, along with multiple spots on the chest, abdomen, hips, legs and pubic regions, Steve chuckled. He looked like a porcupine with wires.

He noticed two of the others, Maurice and Alison, had extra electrodes added to their chests, waists, and hips. Maybe they had special diseases that required monitoring. He figured he would find out the reasons later.

His final adornment involved a pair of plastic diaper-styled pants with two tubes, one in the front and one in the back. Obviously, that would remove bodily waste. The pants were carefully put on to not disturb the electrodes. Closing the Velcro on both sides sealed the pants closed.

Finally, his assistant attached clear hoses to the feeding tube, two to the diaper, and one to each of the blood stream ports. She tested each electrode and tube as nutrient-rich liquids poured through the feeding tube. The electrodes registered his stomach beginning to digest.

A blue fluid flowed into the back of the diaper and was sucked out of the front. Steve heard several of the Tankers giggle as this occurred. The electrodes covered by the diaper were double checked for reaction. At each console where the electrodes attached, lights went from orange to green. In some cases, the lights changed from orange to red. In those instances, the nurses replaced the sensor and wire. They knew the equipment and the sensors needed to work for a long time.

When all had been set and checked, Charlie, the project director, came into the room.

"Good morning, adventurers! You are about to embark on a great advance for mankind. We are sure the preparation you have made will guide you to a successful completion of your tests. I wish you all a great deal of luck. In a minute, the sedative will flow to port one, and the first sample of blood taken from port two. Before we begin, Father Jonathan Ashton, one of our subjects who is a Jesuit priest, would like to say a few words. Those of you not wishing to participate, please be respectful and remain silent."

A skinny and fragile looking man with deep-set eyes, sat up on his gurney and bowed his head.

"This is the Prayer to St. Michael. Archangel St. Michael, defend us in battle. Be our defense against the wickedness and snares of the Devil. May God rebuke him, we humbly pray, and do thou, O Prince of the heavenly host, by the power of God, thrust into hell Satan, and all the evil spirits, who prowl about the world seeking the ruin of souls. Amen."

All the subjects joined in with, "Amen." That surprised Steve. It did not seem to matter, Christian, Jewish, or agnostic. All responded with the utterance. The prayer must have struck deep into the collective memory of all the subjects. The rest, like Steve, calmed.

Father Ashton laid back down.

As soon as Steve saw liquid pouring into port one and a sample of blood pulling from port two, he started counting. He got to thirty and knew no more.

☆☆☆

At each gurney, the day nurse and the night nurse for the patient pushed the subject out of the examining room and down to the tank room. Each team knew where their subjects needed to go. At the top and head of each tank, a lid stood open, ready to be lowered into place. Each lid provided an area where the tubes and electrodes could pass through. The bundle of electronics was connected to the monitor plate at the head of the tank. The nurses were cautious to recheck each of the connections.

The nurses carefully lifted each subject and laid him or her on the fabric material inside the clear rectangular tank. All connections were checked again, and anything that failed was replaced. After all connections were established as being in full working order, one of the nurses pressed a button and the breathing liquid started to fill the tank.

This happened to each subject at a different time.

Steve's reaction, in tank number twelve, came as a shock. His body did not want to accept that he needed to breathe liquid. His two nurses held him down in the liquid. Finally, after some choking and spitting out liquid, he gulped the liquid into his lungs and began to breathe normally as the oxygen from the liquid provided his body with what it needed. He relaxed and became totally comatose.

Others—like Sandy in tank number three, and Maurice in tank number eight—inhaled the liquid quietly with no reaction. They started calm and remained calm.

When the tanks filled to within an inch of the top, the liquid stopped flowing and the lids automatically lowered down onto the top of the tanks.

The nurses conducted a final checkout. Each of the various lights were turned on for a few minutes to test their quality. The tanks took on beautiful hues of greens, blues, and yellows, and of many other combinations of colors. At one point a white, like sunlight, could be seen in each of the tanks—a perfect simulation of the noon sun. The final color was black, causing the tanks to turn completely dark so no one could see inside.

Each subject had chosen different sounds to be heard while in the tank. Studies show that people in comas may be able to hear sounds which keep them connected and grounded. Most everyone picked beautiful symphony music or a favorite style of music like jazz, rock, or country.

Steve's request was unusual. He asked for a combination starting with two hours of Brahms or Beethoven. In alternating two-hour segments, he wanted to hear language tapes. He had been quite specific. For month one, he wanted to re-learn Spanish, a repeat of his freshman and sophomore years of high school. For month two, he wanted to re-learn French. That would reinforce his last two years before going to college. For the third month, he wanted to re-learn Russian which he'd tried to learn before he went to that country way back in the early spring of 1999. That year he met the love of his life, Natali, who passed away in 2027, a little more than ten years ago. In month four, Steve requested Latin and Italian, another refresher from high school.

He had hoped that, by the fifth month, his mind would have expanded enough to easily add a new language each month. If his transformation was not complete by then, Steve wanted to learn Chinese. The doctors expected him to be in the tank for a minimum of six months because of the bone reconfiguration of his back. For that last month, Steve had requested special tapes to replace all the language time. He requested to hear the voices of all of the great capitalists of all time. His long list included great speakers and con men: Barnum, Bailey, Carnegie, Rothschild, Ford, Nixon, Obama, Tony Robbins, Donald Trump, Arnold Schwarzenegger, Zig Ziegler, and Dr. Wayne W. Dyer.

By five-thirty that night, all subjects were secure in tanks set to black for the night. The night nurse for each subject stayed while the day nurses went home.

The adventures of the fourteen Tankers had begun.

Samantha Sampson's Day of Entry

Mario Menotti kept his word. He had talked with the Project Director Dr. Charles Swenson and asked that he add Samantha Sampson to the list of those being rejuvenated. Mario explained she asked only for the standard DNA options. Basically, she wanted her eighty-five-year-old body to look as her body had at twenty.

The director explained Ms. Sampson would need to study the lectures being given by the imperial grand councilor. Without this knowledge, there was a good chance Ms. Sampson would not survive the rejuvenation process.

She would need to go through the same process as the other Tankers. Each step would be done at a time and place separate from the other patients. This separation was Mario's request. He didn't want to have her near the TAMO members. He agreed to pay any additional costs for keeping Sam in a different location.

Ms. Sampson was given a small contract to sign to get started. Mario affixed his notary signature to the document. Along with a handshake of agreement between Mario and Charlie, the deal became official.

They started the process by drawing her blood to extract her DNA. She participated in private sessions with psychologists. All of this was done at her home on Camelback Mountain after the other Tankers were placed into their tanks.

Mario, a frequent visitor to Sam's house, had become accustomed to their special meetings. One of the times he'd met Sam, he brought a small memory stick with all six days of lectures by the imperial grand councilor. He explained to her she must learn the information in the lectures to make her rejuvenation transition a success.

Sam thoroughly studied the first four lectures given by the imperial grand councilor. When he started to get repetitive in the fifth lecture, she figured she had learned enough and did not listen to the other two. She missed the discussion about building doors and windows to allow thoughts in and out of her mind. At least, she had learned about building mental walls.

The director had set up an alternate location for a single tank in the building next door to Twelve-Gen. He ate meals at the restaurant in that building, so no one would suspect anything unusual about his coming and going from there.

The invoices sent to Mario were immediately paid so the director's clinic did not lose any money. In fact, the cost for the equipment and nurses was paid by the Department of Defense. The DOD wanted to have fifteen subjects to increase the chance of success and hoped to use the results of this experiment to make future super-soldiers. They said two military recruits were all they desired. The overhead of two out of fifteen was common for defense projects.

Twelve-Gen was thankful for the investment in the project by the DOD and the money they would receive from the Social Security Administration for the ending of pensions to the Tankers. With this money they would easily break even on their research and development costs. After the rejuvenation succeeded and the one-year continuous medical review of the Tankers, Twelve-Gen could make a fortune with the military and rich private individuals.

A month after the other test subjects were placed in their tanks, doctors at a hospital in Tempe inserted Sam's three tubes. She stayed at the Tempe hospital for three days and endured nothing more than the other test subjects. Healthy, she recovered quickly and was able to begin the rejuvenation process only a week after her operations.

The day finally came when it was time for her to enter her tank. She started the day with a call to Mario.

"Sweetie, could you come over? I'm terrified of going into the tank."

"I'll be there to support you, as soon as I can."

When Mario entered the house fifteen minutes later, he looked everywhere for Sam. He found her in the guest room on the bed with the blanket covering all of her but her eyes. Pink glitter sparkled on her closed eyelids as she pretended to sleep.

He crept quietly up and slowly slipped the blanket from her head. Her hair glowed a bit pink. Her lips, passion pink with the same glow and sparkles. He could not resist kissing her. She moaned. Mario pulled the blanket down to expose a passion-pink negligée that emphasized her best physical assets. It left no doubt about how Sam wanted to start her day, and he complied by unveiling and exploring the beautiful pink package.

After an hour of play, they showered together to thoroughly clean and prepare her body for entry into the tank.

Sam pulled her clean dress over her head, while she studied Mario's fit form.

"At least, if I die," she said, "I ended my life with a nice toss in the bedroom. Thank you, Mario." She kissed him on the forehead.

Thirty minutes later, when the elevator arrived on the tenth floor of the building next to Twelve-Gen, the director and six other people waited for them. The whole floor stood empty except for a few chairs and several cots and tables. Of course, the tank sat in the middle of the room with all its attendant electronics. This floor held none of the glamour of the Twelve-Gen center. It was spartan, but well supplied.

The director introduced Sam to two handsome young men in their late twenties. They would watch over her full-time. The director introduced the other support staff and explained their purposes.

After the introductions, her two nurses explained each step of what was going to be done and what would happen to her as they prepared to put her in the tank.

When told to take off her clothes, she thought nothing about it. In fact, she did a little striptease to prompt a rise out of her all-male entourage. She laughed at their reactions as she wriggled up onto the preparation gurney.

The six men would split the days into twelve-hour shifts with one nurse and two support staff on each shift. They had all been paid well for their long hours and continued silence.

Sam's entry into the tank followed the same careful procedure and, six weeks after the other test participants, she slipped into the silence of the induced coma.

The 4ᵗʰ Month

Almost four months passed for the test subjects in the tanks. As the rejuvenation center had predicted, Steve and several of the others became more aware of their surroundings, unlike what doctors expected for someone deep asleep in an induced coma.

Steve simply became aware of the nurse checking his vitals. He could not see her but could sense her presence outside of the tank. This sort of intuition had occurred all through his life.

His awareness grew until once, while she checked his vitals, he heard her thoughts.

Oh my god, he is starting to show the same signs as the first group. I hope he doesn't die like they did.

Steve's heart rate and blood pressure jumped from his normal 70/40 with a 40 pulse to 150/100 with a pulse of 120.

He is accelerating in all his vitals. If this keeps up, he will die. I have to press the panic button.

The training of the imperial grand councilor filled Steve's mind.

Breathe slowly, he reminded himself. Think of building a house and slowly build a wall to block the sounds in your mind. Make it a strong wall but leave a good solid door to allow you to open it when you desire.

Slowly, Steve's panic subsided as the mental effects of the symbolic wall prevented him from hearing the nurse. As he calmed, he opened the door to listen. He heard four voices. Two voices bloomed clearly in his head, and two voices came muffled through his ears.

"Dr. Swenson, I know his vitals were higher. It appears he is back to his normal blood pressure and heart rate," the nurse said.

At the same time, he heard a much clearer voice inside his head. *The director must think I'm crazy.*

The mental voice held a pattern, the same one that had scared him. Steve realized the pattern belonged to his day nurse.

The second voice in his head—clearly Charlie, the project director—did not sound as pleasant. Not at all like the calm pleasant Charlie who had informed them of the procedural steps for deciding whether to enter the program.

That nurse is an idiot. She had no reason to hit the panic button. Seconds later, after the director examined the details of the last few minutes, he said out loud, "Oh, I see why you pressed the panic button. Five minutes ago, his numbers went off the chart. The pattern shows the spike and gradual change back to normal. This must be the same point at which the last subjects failed to understand their condition, panicked, and caused their own deaths."

Steve enjoyed listening to the conversation. He especially reveled in knowing he had passed the first big test. He was alive and sane.

His body would not allow him to give the nurse any signal. That he knew, but he decided to try something. He reached out with his mind in a quiet way.

Nurse, can you hear my thoughts?

No answer. Steve figured it was only possible for him to listen. After completion of the rejuvenation, even that would be a great advantage in any kind of business negotiation. Steve began to think of the many ways he could easily turn his nice Twelve-Gen allowance into a fortune using his new gift.

In the tank, Steve had no concept of time. He knew only when his mind was awake and when it was not. He could feel his body changing, becoming stronger. His heart beats grew stronger, though remained slow because of the induced coma.

Each time Steve's mind reawakened, he listened for voices and thoughts. Because of the liquid in the tank, he found it quite easy to distinguish voices, which were a little garbled, from thoughts that "sounded" clear as a bell.

After a while, he knew the nicknames of his two nurses. Barbara Katz handled the day shift and Wendy Forbush handled the night shift. Wendy called her counterpart "Babs." When the director spoke to the nurses, he was formal and never used first names. Steve recognized individual thought patterns which differed in little ways for each person, entirely like a real voice.

Steve's mind slept for quite a while, but something forced it to reawaken. He heard a new voice in his head.

Help! Help me! I can't move. Is no one out there?

Steve automatically sent out a thought. *Don't worry. Calm down. Everything will be alright.*

Who's there?

This is Steve Johnson. I'm in tank number twelve.

Oh! This is Robert Worthy. I'm in tank four.

That surprised Steve. Robert's tank sat at the opposite end of the room, more than forty feet away.

Robert, is your nurse nearby?

Yes, she is, and her thoughts were scaring me. Thanks for your calming words. They helped me remember the lessons of the TAMO imperial grand councilor. Thanks again. Oh, by the way, my friends call me Rob. So please call me that.

Will do, Rob.

Steve contemplated the situation. He did not shield his thoughts. It never struck him that he should since he'd left up his barrier to block regular thoughts. Rob's nurse was too far away for Steve to hear her voice, but Rob's thoughts were perfectly clear. It meant that those with the ability to hear thoughts could easily listen to one another.

Rob, Steve sent mentally, *I want to try an experiment. Please, think of counting down from one hundred to one. I will do the same. Remember the last number you hear from me.*

Rob started a slow mental countdown. *One hundred, ninety nine, ninety eight...*

While Steve started counting down in his thoughts, he started to construct two new walls in his mind. One wall was created to stop his thoughts from going out of his head. It had a door. For that, of course, he imagined a sturdy solid oak door. The second wall stood inside the first one created days ago, and its door led to the other door. At that point, Steve reached fifty-three in his countdown. The minute the second wall was built, Rob's thoughts stopped at, *"Forty-eight."*

Steve continued counting until he reached twenty. At that point, he opened all his mental doors to Rob's countdown. *"Thirty-seven, thirty-six, and thirty-five."*

Steve stopped his countdown. *Okay, Rob, that's enough. What was the last number you heard from me?*

Fifty-three, then there was nothing. Did you stop counting to see if I would continue?

Sorry Rob, I didn't mean to play a mental practical joke on you. It just happened.

Steve understood he could control all incoming and outgoing thoughts. He did not yet feel willing to share this information with any of the other Tankers. After all, he was the first one to have his mind wake up and he had to figure it out all by himself.

During the remainder of the fourth month, every one of the twelve other Tankers' minds woke up. Steve had kept count. As each new person developed, he needed to change the makeup of his wall that blocked out thought. He could still hear the thoughts of other people only if they walked close by his tank. The original wall and door kept their thoughts out.

The second wall, blocking the Tankers, needed to be reinforced each time a new person's mind awakened. Each time, after reinforcement, Steve would create a new door. In this way, he could decide who he wanted to listen to and when. It also meant when he shut a specific door, the rest of the Tankers could not hear him.

Apparently, no one else came up with this idea. When he tuned into any of the others, he always heard a variation of, *Can you all think to only one person at a time? It is hard to concentrate with so much going on!*

A Day for the Caretakers

The first daily task for each nurse involved one hour of detailed review of the prior twelve hours for their patient. If any of the readings appeared even a little off, a doctor would be called in to review the same materials. If something needed to be done, a change in formula or chemicals, the nurse implemented the doctor's requested change. They made changes in diet for those losing or gaining too much weight. Some Tankers required adjustments to the DNA-altering viruses as bodily changes took place.

Once a month, the medical staff raised the tank lids. They lowered the level of the liquid in the tank to about two inches over the head to maintain the liquid breathing ability. The lowered liquid made it easy for the nurses to shave the Tankers' bodies. The liquid in the tank made for a good lubricant. Sharp blades did their job quickly. Each sensor had to be removed, the area shaved, and the sensor replaced. This required a full check of each node. Once completed, the staff exchanged the old tank liquid by completely replacing it through the filtration system.

The process took the nurses most of a shift. It provided a change of routine for them.

After the first five months, the Tankers could hear all that was happening to them through the thoughts and discussions between the nurses. Most of the nurses' thoughts were quite vivid. Each of the Tankers told the others what was going on with their own nurses. They were able to understand one another's progress based on the nurses' thoughts and discussion.

Aside from the monthly shaving and the first hour of data analysis, the nurses had little to do but talk amongst themselves. Some of the individual nurses led interesting lives—like soap operas. The Tankers waited for the next installment as a particular nurse came on duty. When a Tanker heard something interesting, they would pass the information on to the rest. This continuous drama kept the Tankers mentally busy in between mental quiet periods.

Steve's day nurse, Babs, had gone through a nasty divorce before the project began. The work gave her a way to escape the ugliness of the divorce and to participate in the excitement of this new experiment. She was twenty-five years old and would be of the same generation the Tankers would enter. As the last few months had passed, Babs' thoughts about Steve became prurient in nature. In fact, Steve had not heard of such ideas except in his youth in the 1970s, the era of free love.

Babs dared not express any of her thoughts out loud. If anyone heard what she was thinking, she would be removed from service. Ever since he had scared her at the end of the third month, she had watched him change slowly but magnificently. She shaved Steve and knew every inch of his strong masculine body. During the sixth-month shave, she realized his physique was complete. His body looked like a well-developed gymnast to her. Not massively muscled but with that wonderful young man's six-pack stomach. In her mind, she dreamed of the time when Steve would leave the tank. She hoped he would take her away and ravish her as a means of saying thank you.

Babs was not alone in her secret interests. Almost all the "twenty-something" nurses, both the males and females, had similar thoughts about their changing subjects. Some of the Tankers, Steve included, figured that some mutual rediscovery of the sexual side of youth would be in order once they left the tank.

The Days Changed

With one day left in the seventh month of rejuvenation, a loud alarm went off on tank number twelve. The nurses all knew what it meant, but apparently had not expected it.

Steve became aware of the loud sound outside of his tank and the racing thoughts of his day nurse, Babs.

OMG, number twelve is done! His request for fast rejuvenation has helped him leave the tanks first. I can't wait to see him fully awake.

Steve's heart rate picked up. He had reached the end of his rejuvenation!

Babs turned off the alarm and examined the various printouts. While she did that, one of the other nurses called the support team to help with the "de-tanking."

There will be a lot going on today. I hope all the commotion doesn't scare him. Babs's thoughts grew quiet and calming.

That helped, even though Steve felt more than ready for his awakening.

Within a short time, seven new people arrived in the room near his tank. Hearing those many thoughts all at once after months of only a single nurse's thoughts quickened his pulse. Steve practiced his mental wall building and pulled himself under control within a minute.

Once his nurse saw his heartbeat had normalized, her first step was to super-oxygenate Steve's blood. He followed what was happening by opening his mental door to Babs's thoughts.

She noticed the tank's blue liquid becoming lighter blue as more and more oxygen entered the liquid, and the two ports continuously exchanging blood: one port removing blood, the other replacing it with highly oxygenated blood. Eventually, he experienced the liquid draining from the tank through Babs's thought processes. He could feel his face was still covered.

A rumbling near the tank signified the arrival of more equipment. Perhaps a gurney? The touch of gentle hands on his legs felt odd, then on his arms and under his hips. He sensed a set of hands on each side of him in each location. Another person cradled his head.

The group of seven flipped him face down. At that moment, Babs induced a drug into his blood stream to take him fully out of the coma.

The team waited several seconds, then lifted Steve out of the tank so his head remained down with the rest of his body higher. One member of the team started slapping Steve on his back. Another person inserted a device forcing Steve's airway to remain open.

He started coughing, choking, and his body spasmed as the blue liquid left his lungs. In only a few minutes, the hellish spasms stopped, and the team laid him on his side. Babs affixed an oxygen mask to his face. He breathed deeply and painfully for several minutes until his breaths came regularly and felt normal.

He projected to all the Tankers, *I'm out and alive! What a great feeling to be out of the tank. See you all when you get out. What a day!*

Steve listened in on the thoughts of the recovery team and learned his exit from the tank had been the first for the recovery team. No amount of training could have taught them what to expect until it happened, but they handled it well. Even though some of the team members were large strong men, they'd found him much stronger than expected. Some of his thrashing around had bruised several of the team both physically and mentally. The care providers considered his reentry difficult, but they had learned what to do. They expected the process would grow easier for them as each new Tanker went through recovery.

He was whisked away to his private recovery room, where he was given a shot and immediately fell asleep.

Steve awoke later when he heard Charlie's thoughts. The director was congratulating himself on the decision to avoid any physical contact between the Tankers until the subjects had been completely reviewed by the physiologists and psychologists.

Steve learned he would be kept incommunicado until he had been given a complete positive review. This final checkup would happen only after he moved to the Hyatt hotel. While in his Twelve-Gen private room, he was told he would be observed 24/7.

☆☆☆

Steve mentally chatted with three other tankers as they finished their time in the tanks during the same month as him. Tank number two, Ryan Bentley, was the second Tanker recovered. Next came number thirteen, Father Jonathan Ashton. The last in month seven was Daniel Wright in number one.

Communication with Daniel Wright during his recovery gave Steve an idea why the man experienced a little more difficulty in the waking process than the other three. When the recovery team tried to help, he became fully conscious much faster than any of the others. He thought he was being captured by the Vietcong during the Vietnam War in the 1970s. Every bit of his military training kicked in and he fought hard to stop the recovery team from doing its job. Dan required a strong sedative to stop him from fighting.

From his private room, Steve kept track of and mentally talked to the other Tankers. Things quieted down for a few weeks after the second three left the tanks. In month eight, Rob Worthy left tank number four with no issues. Rob's recovery was so easy he continued to chat with Steve until the doctors insisted Rob focus on them.

Their New Bodies

Out of the tanks, Steve experienced a fresh start. He was like a baby, unable to control his muscles, his bladder, or his bowels. So, he stayed in a special hospital bed initially, clothed only in special adult diapers. The diapers had sensors constantly checking for liquids and solids. When the time came for clean diapers, the system notified the nurses to take care of the changing process.

Steve had his own private room with his own bathroom in the Twelve-Gen building. The staff explained to him that, for two months following his extraction, there would be no privacy. Even the bathroom had multiple cameras. They locked the showers until the staff could come unlock them to help wash him. This lack of privacy and indignity would continue until he left this accommodation and went to his permanent suite at the Hyatt hotel.

His room had been locked from the outside to prevent him from wandering and going places he shouldn't go. The staff told him it was for his own safety, and to avoid meeting the other Tankers accidentally. They never told him what the dangers were outside of the room. Only that he needed to be kept from leaving.

The private recovery rooms had no mirrors or any reflective surfaces. Part of his training included the lack of knowledge about what his rejuvenated form looked like. It was the psychologist's opinion, he needed to be eased into seeing his new face and the full visual impact of viewing all of himself at one time before he was psychologically ready.

He could not see the full visual of himself. But he could see pieces at a time. Just seeing the muscular six-pack on his stomach, his hands cleared of dark spots and unwrinkled, and the swell of his biceps made him want to see it all at once.

Steve's original nurses had been replaced by male staff. Initially, his room was kept warm since the doctors did not want him to grow cold while lying there, almost naked.

The doctors talked with and examined him multiple times a day. Each time the doctors came into the room they drew blood from the port and took urine samples. Not only did medical doctors check internals, but physiotherapists visited often. He was subjected to physical therapy to exercise his new body and muscles. Bending arms and legs, head tilts, and back stretches occurred at the beginning. Once he was ready, several times a day, he was taken up to the gym area to walk and exercise with the gym machines. Even though other Tankers had recovered, the staff made sure he would not see the other Tankers. He, like the rest of the patients, was expected to be in tip top shape as soon as possible.

After two weeks out of the tank, the surgeon who put in the feeding tube, Dr. Rotherman, came by to visit Steve. The doctor sat with him and quietly and calmly explained he would be removing Steve's feeding tube. Right in the middle of the explanation, he simply pulled on the tube, and it came out of Steve's body. The sneak attack was sudden but effective. Before Steve could worry about the pain, the tube was out.

With it removed, he needed to teach his stomach to digest food again. Dr. Rotherman put him on an extremely strict diet. For the first several days, three times a day, he would consume a liquid drink containing vitamins, nutrition, and probiotics. That first step began to prepare his stomach for solid foods. Several hours after he finished his first drink, the doctors came in and took a blood sample to make sure his new body digested it and brought in the vitamins and nutrients.

For Steve, each day was new. He went from a liquid diet to soft foods, and onto solids over the course of the two months in the private room. Once his body adjusted, he went from adult diapers to loose-fitting clothes.

He and all the Tankers needed to learn to cope with their new bodies and at the same time, how to become a twenty-four-year-old in 2037.

Month nine began and Steve already looked forward to his move from the recovery room to the Hyatt at the end of month. During the beginning of the month, the first of the women Tankers, Cecilia Begay in number eleven, arrived. Like Rob, she had no physical issues. She told him and the other Tankers about her recovery experience. Her first request before she even left the tank room, while still on the gurney, was for some food. Starving, she did not want some vague food offered by the doctors. She wanted something very specific.

I wanted a Deli Special with lots of corned beef and sauerkraut on marbled rye bread with Russian dressing. She explained to the other Tankers, as the took her to her room

Steve was sure Cecilia made the same request orally. When her thoughts of disappointment came to him, he knew the doctors had kindly denied her request.

The end of month nine completed Steve's time in the recovery room at Twelve-Gen and they finally took him up to his suite in the Hyatt. The hotel staff explained to him, each of the suites in the hotel and the elevator had been set up so no Tanker would be able to leave their room or enter the elevator up to the floor while another Tanker was in the area. This allowed them to maintain their distance from one another.

Steve had something special waiting for him in his suite. Laid out on the bed were clothes fitted perfectly for his new body size and shape. The high-fashion outfits were made of authentic cotton and other authentic materials, prized possessions in the world. He was happy to discard the baggy clothes they made him wear for two months.

During the time in their private rooms, and for months after in the Hyatt suite, Steve and the other Tankers led solitary lives. The study protocol for the Tankers required that they not see one another. The doctors didn't realize the Tankers continuously talked mind-to-mind.

They all learned skills associated with their new mental abilities. None of the medical doctors or psychologists could teach them what they needed to know in that area of training. They had to learn from one another. Steve, who figured it out first, finally decided to impart some of what he had learned to the other Tankers.

The imperial grand councilor had taught them all how to build walls and doors. "Normals," those who did not have the gift, built their walls and doors crudely at best. Steve learned to build magnificent walls in his mind. The two levels of ability could hardly compare—like the difference between an African hut and a San Francisco skyscraper. Steve learned to block thoughts, emotion, pain, smell, sound, taste, images, and varied combinations of these and more. He helped the others learn about much of it too.

Steve had lived in his Hyatt suite for almost a month. Near the end of that tenth month the two Russians left their tanks. Andrey Petrov in tank number five, when recovered by the team, did not fight. But as soon as his lungs cleared, he started screaming Russian profanity. His mental words projected even stronger profanity. If the Tankers had not lived for so many years, they might have experienced shock.

Andrey made a mental apology when he finally calmed down and understood where he was.

Nadia Belova, in number seven, left her tank in month ten, only a day after Andrey. As she became conscious, she said not a word, but transmitted an image to all the other thirteen Tankers. They received a mental picture of American Quaker artist Edward Hicks' famous *Peaceable Kingdom* painting from the 1830s. Nadia knew the Tankers would be loving lions among the lambs of humankind. She knew, ultimately, the Tankers would be in charge.

Nadia needed to learn to fully speak for the first time. She had not been able to hear since the age of four. She was so excited to hear and talk, she wanted to talk to everyone. The imperial grand councilor came to visit her often, more than any of the other doctors. He showed up to chat with Nadia at least once a day. Some days he would visit her for hours.

Nadia most easily recognized smell, taste, tactical feel, and images. In fractions of a second, she could mentally project things to other Tankers using these traits while others would take many seconds to explain the same items. Her long-time deafness had accelerated these other senses. However, the method to relay thoughts about sound were new to her. She needed to learn to use them not only in her mind, but with her voice and ears.

She shared how much she enjoyed it when the imperial grand councilor came by each day to help her learn what everyone else had known since childhood. She wanted his human contact. The contact with the IGC seemed so much more personal. The two became close enough for him to ask her to call him Nate.

Everyone who came into her recovery room always wore gloves and a mask. They touched her, but not skin to skin contact. It actually depressed her. Even Nate had to follow the same protocols as the others.

Unbeknownst to her fellow Tankers, Nadia always experienced a special deep joy inside her when he visited.

In the first weeks, when they sat and talked, she could read his tender thoughts, and she would respond verbally to them. He could not hear her thoughts. So, she encouraged him to speak his thoughts out loud. He knew she could hear what went through his mind but made no attempt to block her out. He said he felt very close to her, as if she and he belonged together.

After four weeks of the clinical touching, Nate was the first person who came into her room dressed as a normal person without a mask or gloves. Nate told her he wanted to be the first person to touch her, skin to skin. He sat down beside her and picked up her hand.

I am so happy it is you who gives me the gift of your touch, Nadia thought.

Nate drew back and his mouth opened in slight surprise.

He read her thoughts! An unexpected tear rolled down her cheek and he leaned in to thumb the dampness away.

I love you, Nate! She sent the message before consciously thinking about it. She gasped and tightened her lips in anticipation of his reaction.

"I love you too, Nadia!"

Nate pulled his hand away, clearly realizing he'd just read Nadia's thought. *Did that just happen?*

When she didn't respond, his brows knitted, and he shook his head back and forth quickly. He grasped her hand again and repeated his question. *Did that just happen?*

It did! Her heart pounded against her ribs.

And you really love me?

She squeezed his warm hand. *I truly do, Nate!*

Nate's face lit up. "I hear your thoughts when we touch!"

She only nodded but stretched her lips into a shy smile.

He took both of her hands in his and held them tight. *My beautiful lady, I have loved you from the time of our first meeting to teach you meditation.*

She inched her face toward his with her gaze locked on his eyes. He hesitated slightly, then gently lowered his mouth to hers. She closed her eyes and savored all of the sensations firing through her system. A knock sounded at the door. The two lovers separated, and the doctors came in.

With their physical disconnect, she knew Nate could no longer hear her thoughts, though she heard him clearly.

I hope you will be mine and we'll find an opportunity to continue where we left off.

She nodded and winked to let him know she agreed.

☆☆☆

The eleventh month remained quiet until the day when four women needed recovery. The number three tank alarm went off for Sandy Haspure on the third day of the month right after lunchtime. Before the recovery team had moved her onto the gurney, the alarm went off in Briana Goldsmith's number six tank. Her day nurse simply turned off the alarm. She expected a wait while the recovery team settled Sandy in her new quarters. Then they could take Briana.

Before the team returned with the gurney for Briana, both alarms sounded for Lindsey Banks in number nine and Donna Andrews in number fourteen. All three of the male nurses waited impatiently as the recovery team took the next person in line. It took until almost ten that night to deliver the four Tankers to their individual recovery rooms.

Month twelve brought the recovery of the last two: the subjects who went through gender reassignment changes. Martha Felder, as she now called herself, recovered from number eight at four in the morning in the middle of the month. They recovered the new Albert Sanders in number ten the following day, one hour before lunch.

☆☆☆

Martha, having changed from a man to a woman, experienced new things every day. She loved her new body and could not believe all the wonderful changes. During her doctor's exams, expert gynecologists came in to examine her. Her complete physical change from male to female required extra time in the tanks and extra care once extracted. She had never been poked and prodded so much but was delighted when they told her everything was in working order. After the coming years on the birth control implant, she would be capable of becoming pregnant.

Albert experienced his transition from female to male quietly. Alison had always felt trapped in a woman's body. The change to being a male with all its new body parts, he found rewarding.

The doctors and psychologists spent extra hours with Albert. With his new alpha male body, learning his place in the world would become an adventure. He looked forward to exploring how to interact with others in his new identity, especially women. Having been on the receiving end of men's attention in his former female form, he already knew some social skills he would always, or never, use.

Identification, Please

It was the first night that the center allowed the Tankers to leave the hotel. Incognito from each other still was the rule. Steve decided to go and check out the local nightlife. He undressed in front of the full-length mirror. What he looked like now continued to amaze him. The full head of hair, the muscles, the youthful look, it was all his.

He went to the closet to see what might be appropriate to wear. He picked an outfit that the psychologists had been talking about. It was a one-piece stretch pants and shirt combination. The top was a dark mesh with a solid piece of cloth running from right shoulder down to his left hip. If a person came really close, they would be able to see his left nipple. The black color of the outfit seemed appropriately conservative.

When he examined the back of the outfit in the mirror, he realized that it really wasn't all that conservative. The dark mesh went down the whole back of the outfit. He did admire his own muscular butt. The rejuvenated body was more than he ever expected.

On this first night, he planned to wander in downtown Phoenix. He made a short review of "Hot night spots, near me" on his phone. He picked a bar. The Watering Hole opened at eleven and appeared to be frequented by a younger crowd. His older self would have never gone in, but the psychologists had recommended it as a first step in finding a rhythm to their new lives. The loud music bombarded Steve's ears as soon as he walked into the nightclub. With a shake of his head, he grimaced and moved farther into the club. He needed to do this to help acclimate to his new self and new life.

"Drambuie on the rocks with a water back, please," Steve told the bartender over the boom of the music's bass line.

He could not wait to see what his favorite drink tasted like. It had been more than a year since he had drunk any alcohol.

The forty-something bartender smiled and asked if the drink would be on a tab or a credit card.

He reached into his wallet, pulled out the Twelve-Gen card, and handed it to the bartender with a smile. "I'll only have this one, thanks."

Steve immediately opened the door to let in the bartender's thoughts.

The server reviewed the card and looked up to compare its photo with Steve's face. *Yeah, that's him. Twenty-four and legal.* "No problem, young man. I'll get your drink." He turned away. *What a stupid kid. I think I'll run his card twice for this drink and give myself a big tip too.*

The bartender ran the card and returned it to Steve.

"You're all set," the bartender said.

He did not give Steve the receipt. The charge was small enough to not require a signature.

Steve held out an open palm toward the bartender. "I need a receipt to claim my expenses at work. Could I have it please?"

The bartender's eyes widened. "I'm sorry. I put the receipt into the trash when you didn't ask for it."

Steve picked up his drink and looked the bartender in the eye. "Don't worry about it. When the bill comes, I will refuse to pay for the second drink and your big tip."

Right after Steve said it, he regretted it. No sense in giving someone knowledge they might be able to use against him.

An expression of confusion lit the man's eyes, and his mouth gaped. As he began stuttering unintelligibly, Steve took his drink and wandered through the crowd. He kept the doors in his mind wide open for thoughts from everyone. The mental noise from the crowd sounded as loud as the music. He found an empty booth in a corner, sat, and proceeded to look and listen.

He thoroughly enjoyed his favorite drink. The taste of it did not disappoint. When he had sipped it down to the "rocks," he sucked on the ice cubes to savor the last of the Drambuie's sweetness.

That guy in the corner is a real cutie. I wonder if he is marriage material.

His attention focused on two attractive young women coming his way from the dance floor: a blonde and a brunette. He was sure one of them had made the mental comment. He stood up as they approached and offered them a place on the other side of the booth. The brunette sat down on one side and the blonde slipped in where he had been sitting.

The young woman who sat in his place gazed up. "Hi, my name is Jane, and this is my bestie, Veronica. You aren't leaving, are you?" She looked at his empty glass while broadcasting a strong mental image.

I hope he's not leaving. Up close, he's even more handsome and courteous. How wonderful. We'll see if he offers to buy us drinks, or leaves.

Not needing to be anywhere, Steve scooted back into the booth next to the blonde and asked the ladies if they would like a drink. They agreed and he drew the attention of a waitress, who came over.

"Good evening, my name is Nancy. How can I help you?"

Focused on her work, Nancy projected no extraneous thoughts. Steve ordered the drinks the two young ladies requested and a tall cranberry for himself. The "chit-chat" rules suggested by the psychologist came into his mind.

"Jane, do you and Veronica work for the same company or are you only friends?"

"We work as tellers at the World One Bank building on the first floor. We have been friends for years and share almost everything. What do you do for a living?" She smiled at him.

Jane had responded quickly for both women, and clearly wanted to be in charge.

Veronica's thought, short and clear, flooded through the door in his mind.

We may share things, Jane, but this is one hunk I'm taking home, and I'm going to have my way with him.

Veronica's thought made things twitch on his young body. Steve worked to keep his face calm and friendly. "I'm in real estate. I invest in houses, clean them up, and resell them for a profit."

This was sort of true. He had not flipped a house in twenty years but, even then, he only did one house a year to keep himself busy. He knew it would sound good.

Steve was right. Jane shifted in her seat to look sexier. Her change in position included a very clear thought. *This guy is good looking, probably rich, and may be good marriage material.*

When the waitress came by with the drinks, she was a little anxious when she gave him the bill. *I hope this guy is a good tipper. I really need to pick up food and some diapers for my little baby girl.*

Steve gave her his Twelve-Gen card. She accepted it graciously and handed him the receipt.

The women at the table glanced at the card's jet-black color and knew it was an incredibly special card. Black was still the color bankers used for their clients with the highest credit lines. These young tellers knew instantly.

Steve signed the receipt to pay for this part of the evening, he made sure to give the waitress an extra-large tip—one hundred dollars. He winked at her. "Nancy, keep the drinks coming until closing time."

The thoughts from the women came in simultaneously.

Jane took on a more serious pose, looking at Steve. *Definitely marriage material. I need to learn more about him.*

Veronica "accidentally" allowed the neckline of her blouse to slip lower. She continued along her previous vein. *A rich hot guy. I am taking him to bed tonight if I can get rid of Jane.*

On his first night out, Steve was not planning to go anywhere. He considered this training on how to deal with women. It differed greatly from when he was a young geek in his previous life. Plus, his mind-reading abilities didn't hurt the situation. These women were interested in him for two different reasons.

The three of them talked about a lot. The two young ladies had attended different schools. Jane went to the University of Arizona in Tucson. Veronica studied at Arizona State University in Tempe. They discussed how fun and free those college days were. Steve told them about his time at the University of Maryland in College Park. Though it all happened in the 1970s, he left out any details that might indicate the timeframe. They all became great friends.

By the time the place closed, the women had downed three more drinks and were quite drunk. Each one had been trying to outdo the other all night long. At this point, Steve noticed their thoughts slurred as much as their voices. He had always been sensitive to things like that. The two women felt to him like large objects covered in oil, like greasy slimy oil right from the ground. Their minds and auras felt plain ugly.

Being a gentleman, he asked the waitress to order an auto-driver cab for the young women and paid for their ride home. He gave Nancy another large tip—three hundred dollars—for all her help.

With a large smile that made her face glow, her thoughts and voice coincided. *He has been a Godsend. I'm so glad I took good care of him.* "Thank you so much for the unbelievable tip. You don't know what a godsend you are!"

The first night away from the hotel turned out to provide quite an education. After the young women left, Steve walked the four blocks back to the hotel. As he sauntered home, he decided to close his mind off to the thoughts of others around him. At this time of night, hearing the thoughts of drunks, bad guys, and hookers ranked low on his list of good things to do.

Steve arrived back at the hotel safe and sound. The bar in the revolving restaurant at the top of the hotel was still open. Restaurants could stay open later than bars. Steve decided to go upstairs for a nightcap, a double Drambuie. He thought about his night, finished the drink quickly, and realized he was not high from the alcohol. In fact, he felt no effects. None.

That information may come in handy someday.

Meeting Someone Familiar

Steve's second night found him wandering from nightclub to nightclub. He did not find any place with music he liked. On his walk home, he passed a door sporting a small sign, *"Best Jazz."* No one stood outside, so he opened the door to reveal steps leading down. Black lights illuminated the old, yellow-painted stairs. Quiet blues emanated from below.

The bottom of the steps opened out into a large room with a small bar hosting probably ten small tables with two chairs each. Up on the stage, three people performed: one man playing a sax, another softly playing a drum, and a beautiful dark-haired woman singing a sad song.

Steve ordered a Drambuie on the rocks and sat down at a table at the side of the room. The table had a full view of every person, every table, and every barstool in the place. With his mental walls still up from his walk outside, he had not paid much attention to the other patrons.

"Is this seat taken?" The woman's voice broke his attention from the singer. She did not wait for an answer and sat down next to him.

She appeared around his age, maybe around twenty-five years old with nice long blonde hair, blue eyes, and an hourglass figure. Her perky young breasts mounded out of the top of a tight-fitting blue dress. She gave him a big smile showing beautiful white teeth. "You look familiar. Are you from around here?"

That was one of the dumb lines a geek like him could have said to gain the attention of a young lady. It had never worked for him. Apparently, it was going to work for her.

Steve opened his mental doors to the young lady's thoughts.

He doesn't recognize me. I watched him go from a shriveled old man to a handsome hunk over the last six months, and all I got was one thank you as we pulled him out of the tank. Maybe I can convince him to give me a proper thank you all night long.

Steve didn't let his surprise show on his features. "Please sit and tell me what you want to drink. To answer your question, I live at the downtown Hyatt. My name is Steve. What is your name?"

He almost felt guilty about taking "advantage" of her.

"I would like a vodka martini, shaken not stirred. I'm sure you know who drinks it that way. My favorite movie character from the old movies, James Bond. I guess I am a little like a secret agent. My birth name is Barbara Katz. Most of my friends call me Babs. My closest friends call me Kitty. You know like 'kitty cat.' You can call me either..."

Her sentence trailed off as though it was not complete. Her thought, however, finished the sentence. *When you take me to bed, you stud!*

The two of them talked for a few hours. At one point, Kitty got up to go to the lady's room. As she walked away, Steve noticed the five-inch heels that matched her blue dress. It was also difficult for him not to notice her ample and well-shaped backside. The back of her dress was virtually nonexistent above her waist. In the fold in the material at the dress's hemline, the top of a garter belt peeked through.

The guilt he experienced thinking of her sexually made him decide to confess and let whatever happened happen.

As she walked back to the table, he found her walk and the bounce accompanying it even more spectacular. His guilt increased.

She sat again and placed her chin in her hand and stared at him with an expectant upturn of her lips.

Time to come clean. He swallowed. "Kitty, I know you know who I am. It took me a few minutes to recognize your voice." His gaze lowered to his glass as his fingertips touched the condensation on the glass surface, then raised his eyes again. "Each time I heard your voice, I thought of an angel, even though the liquid in the tank distorted sounds quite a bit. I hope you will forgive me for not admitting I knew you were my day nurse. I wish I had told you sooner."

Kitty sat back and lowered her eyes. "I hope you are not mad at *me* for not telling you I knew who you were. I took care of you for so many months and the transition is so remarkable that... Well, I fell in love with you..." She leaned in again, her arms flat against the table, but still didn't look up. "Maybe that's not the right term. I fell in love with the idea of you. I wanted to have you and didn't care if I had to trick you into bed."

She glanced up then.

Steve laughed heartily. Kitty didn't quite understand what the laugh meant. She pulled back, bit her lower lip, and her eyes began to glisten with tears.

Steve put his hand on hers. "Kitty, I have not had sex in twenty years. I am technically a virgin again. Would you like to go back to the hotel and teach me how your—I guess, now, *my*—generation does it?"

Kitty perked up and intertwined her fingers with his.

"I was going to do this as a last resort to convince you to take me home with you. I must admit I did something naughty when I went to the bathroom. Will you hold onto these for me?"

She reached under the table handing Steve a pair of bright-red satin and lace panties. He could not mistake her intentions. He dropped some new dollars on the table. She stood, grabbed his hand, and eagerly pulled him to the door. They left together and headed back to the hotel.

About a block away, one of her tall heels caught in a sidewalk crack and broke off. She toppled toward him. In an instant, he grabbed her and kept her from falling. He was able to lift her up into his arms. The new strength surprised him. She seemed as light as a feather. That certainly had never happened to him in his previous eighty-six years, even when he was in the best physical shape. He'd just lifted some 130 pounds and barely noticed it!

Kitty leaned into him and kissed his neck. "Thank you! You are such a gentleman... my knight in shining armor."

He carried her into the hotel and to the clear glass elevators. Up they went to his floor and suite.

Steve's palm print was sufficient to open the door. All the while, he held her with one arm. Again, the innate strength of this newly designed body impressed him. He carried her into the room and moved to set her down on the couch.

"If you put me on that couch, I'm leaving. The bed is where we deserve to be."

She wasn't sure if she should make a suggestion on how to make things move along more quickly, as she desired. *I want him to take this dress off quickly, I should tell him about the difficult zipper on the right-side, hidden by the Velcro panel.*

Steve sat Kitty on the bed and eagerly helped her out of her clothes. He removed her shoes, reached to the right side of her dress, opened the hidden panel, and unzipped the dress down to her hips with little effort. The dress literally fell off her, revealing a red-satin lacy push-up bra that emphasized the beauty of her young breasts.

Her eyes lit up in surprise and she gave him a joyous passionate kiss. *You can read my mind! That must be the gift the director kept talking about. All I have to do is think about what I desire for you to do with me, and you'll do it?*

He removed her dress from around her hips and set it aside. "Yes, my sweet Kitty Cat, there will be no need for claws tonight."

Kitty did not talk for the rest of the night, she simply directed Steve with her mind.

That contributed to the most incredible night Steve ever experienced in his life. Early that next morning he called the Twelve-

Gen office and told them he was taking care of a sick friend and would miss his appointments for the next three days. Kitty called her employer to say she was under the weather. They never left the room. The wine, the food, the desserts... everything came by room service.

Even though he experienced the most spectacular sex ever, and he cared for Kitty, something about it didn't completely fulfill him. He finally asked her to go home, though he promised to call her in a few days.

In their time apart, Steve realized he needed more than what Kitty could give him. The woman was beautiful and intelligent, but something was missing. He knew what he had to do. When he did as promised, and called her, he expressed his feelings. To let her down a bit more easily, he shared lofty praise about her sexual prowess and how deeply he appreciated her care of him for so many months. But he also explained how he needed to know more about himself and his new role in life before he could commit to any serious relationship.

To her credit, even with the sadness he heard in her voice, she told him she understood and hoped they could connect again sometime at a later date.

He thanked her but made no promises.

A Stranger's Mind

It did not take long for Steve to visit all the downtown Phoenix nightclubs suggested by the psychologists. Steve had enjoyed his evenings for three months. He honed his skills for picking up women. He could meet any woman and, in a matter of ten minutes, walk out of the nightclub to take her to her home for sex. Basically, it was too easy. What was the old saying? "Like shooting fish in a barrel."

Steve had gotten used to the music at the "Watering Hole." Aside from the quiet bar at the top of his hotel, it became his favorite place to go. One night, Steve went in and looked for his favorite waitress, Nancy, who always took good care of him. She saw him and waved.

He probably wants his regular Drambuie drink with water on the side. I like giving him good service, he is always polite and gives me great tips.

Steve heard her mental commentary in his mind, relaxed, and waited for his drink to arrive.

Nancy came over with a tray containing the Drambuie on the rocks with a water back. "Mr. Johnson, do you want your 'regular'?"

He nodded and Nancy placed the two glasses on the table.

While Steve took care of setting up his charges for the night, he focused totally on Nancy and her good thoughts. Positive and negative mental thoughts abruptly hit him from all around the room. Even Nancy felt it and they both looked up. Steve glanced away almost immediately but Nancy nudged his shoulder with an elbow.

"That is Katia. She is really a nice girl. She is twenty-eight, so you might think she is too old for you, but you do act very mature. Would you like me to bring her over here for a drink?"

Steve nodded.

The voices of the guys in the room registered with things like, *I really want her to fall in love with me,* along with other more graphically sexual ideas. One woman nearby spit out venomous thoughts. *Anyone have an ax? This chick needs to die.* Not a single pleasant thought came from any of the women, except the one wishing the same thing as most of the guys.

With Steve's eidetic memory, he remembered exactly what Katia looked like without staring at her again. As he sat quietly and patiently waited for Nancy to return, he played the memory back in his mind and blocked all the thoughts in the room except hers. She would have qualified as a Madonna look-a-like. He remembered the famous singer from the 1990s who disappeared from the public eye around thirty years ago.

Katia's long blonde hair flowed halfway down her back. She wore only a black bustier to emphasize large supple breasts popping out from under her golden hair. Her skirt could barely be called a skirt. It looked more like a pair of black mini shorts overlaid with a filmy miniskirt of lace. A golden belt left a small bit of flesh exposed between the bustier and the skirt. Like Madonna might have chosen, long black satin gloves covered three quarters of her arms. Black fishnet stockings held up by garter straps disappeared under her shorts. Her slender gracious feet looked sexy in black six-inch heels.

Steve brought himself into the present when Katia arrived at his table and Nancy introduced him.

Katia offered her hand in an almost standoffish manner and yet a smile brightened her face. "Hello, Steve. My name is Katia Poklonskaya. Nancy says you would like to buy me a drink. Since you are the only man here not staring at me indecently, I would like to share one drink with you."

Her face was perfect and her eyes a deep blue. Perfectly rounded lips framed flawless teeth. Steve stood and gestured to the seat on the other side of the booth from him. "Happy to meet you, Katia."

"Thank you, Steve. You seem to be quite the gentleman."

As Nancy winked and went on her way, Steve opened his mind up to hear what Katia was thinking. He found he needed to control his expression. He heard nothing from her mind. A complete blank. Steve had never experienced this from a non-tanker, 'normal', before. Even the imperial grand councilor could not prevent all thoughts like Katia could.

Amazed, Steve wanted to learn more about this gorgeous woman. To be sure about her, he let down all his mental barriers. The crescendo of mental noise was incredible and almost all negative. Not only were the women negative, but the men too. The guy in the next booth wished him a horrible death because Steve sat there with the woman of the guy's dreams.

Still not a mental sound from Katia even after he built up the walls again to keep out the other patrons' mental gyrations.

Steve and Katia drank their drinks slowly, chatted pleasantly, and listened to the music. Even though she appeared to be four years older than his modified age of twenty-four, she was young at heart.

After about an hour, a slow dance song came up. Steve stood and held out his hand to her. "Would you care to dance, my lovely Katia?"

She smiled, rose, and placed her gloved hand in his as they walked over to the middle of the dance floor and began to dance slowly. Others on the dance floor sent them negative glares.

One couple came close, and Steve swore the woman put her foot in Katia's way. When his dancing partner started to fall, Steve's quick reflexes kicked in and he safely caught her. The angle of the grab brought his hand against the skin on her back between her bustier and skirt. Only a quick touch.

That witch purposefully tripped me. Oh, but gallant Steve! I almost feel sorry he is my mark for the night. I have picked his pocket. She grinned to herself. Steve could not see the grin but clearly heard what she was thinking. *Now that I've got his wallet, where is Alex for the turnover?*

Steve brought her up in his arms and she wrapped hers around his neck. He purposefully moved his hand to a new position to only touch her clothes. Her thoughts were gone, like turning off a radio.

With her arms around him, Steve knew his wallet was in one of her hands. He quickly bounced her up, leaving one hand free. He reached over his shoulder, found the hand with the wallet, and grabbed it. He dropped it back into his front pocket.

Steve carried Katia over to the booth and sat her down a little roughly. He slid in beside her, pushing her into the corner of the booth where she could not escape. He took off the glove on the arm closest to him and put his hand firmly down on it. "Let's talk!"

She started to cry and whimper. "They made me do it. Don't turn me in to the police, please!"

Touching her skin, he knew what she had planned. *A good cry and the innocent girl line always works.*

"I'm sorry, Katia. I can tell when a person is 'fake' crying. You might as well turn off the waterworks. I'm not going to turn you in. In fact, I may need your services in the future."

She stared at him until one side of her lips quirked upward. *Now this is an interesting turn. What could he want?*

Steve didn't know exactly what the imperial grand councilor of TAMO had in mind in order to pursue the Dragon Prophecy. He did know it was TAMO's goal to retrieve the treasure of humanity's ancient knowledge. The expenses they had already paid in order to create fourteen rejuvenated "super" humans with the gift made the project of vital importance. A mission of this kind could use a talented and highly distracting female. It would be an excellent tool to keep in their toolbox to help in the eventual quest.

They talked over several more drinks. Steve kept his firm grip on her hand the whole time so he could tell what she was thinking and if she lied. It took a while to convince her she could not lie to him, without him revealing he could read her mind.

Steve ended up putting Katia on retainer. He transferred 10,000 new dollars to her right then, double the amount she had been offered by her Russian mobster boss to retrieve his wallet. Each month, he agreed to send her an additional 5,000 new dollars to keep her available. Steve got Katia's special phone number, a special blind communication method, and a drop location. He explained he did not need her services right away and the monthly retainer was to continue for the next year. If he needed her, he would call her or put an ad in the "Singles Wanted" web site. She agreed to respond.

They continued to make like two young lovers until Steve motioned to Nancy for the bill. He paid it and added a 1,000 new dollar tip, since Katia had assured him, the waitress had nothing to do with the thieves.

"Nancy, that tip is for the introduction to this lovely creature." All three of them laughed and the two women smiled at each other. Steve did not need to read Nancy's mind to know the money would go to good use.

The couple left together holding hands. Near the entrance, Katia looked at a man, shrugged, and thought, *Sorry Alex, this one didn't work out the way we planned.*

Steve held back a smile. He now also knew who Alex was.

They walked aimlessly for a while. He continued to chat with her until they reached her seedy hotel. It did not look like a nice place. With all the evening's excitement, Steve wanted Katia, but did not even want to go inside the hotel.

"Let me find you a nicer place to stay, Katia."

This guy can't be for real. I was after his wallet for the job. Now, I really want him.

She thanked him profusely and leaned close against him as they walked down the street to a nicer hotel. At the reservation desk, he reserved a suite. It cost 30,000 new dollars for the month. Steve gave the desk clerk his black Twelve-Gen card and told the clerk to use the card to pay for the room and an additional 10,000 for room service with any remaining balance going to Katia when she left.

The desk clerk handed over the key.

Katia held Steve's hand firmly, reversed roles, and literally pulled him to the elevator.

You aren't going to get away that easily. You will be mine by morning.

Steve did indeed find out how amazing Katia was. Late the next day, wearing a hotel bathrobe, she gave him a final kiss as he walked out the door.

Steve ran a finger along her collar bone. "We shall definitely be in touch." He pivoted and left.

Striding out of the hotel lobby, he reflected on how every woman he had met, including Katia, bent to his will. Maybe because he could read their minds, he could supply what he thought they needed. He "pressed all of their buttons" until they succumbed to his charms.

Still, the triumphs left him hollow. With no challenge and no deep meaning in the relationships, he had tired of each of the women after several days.

Samantha's Changes

When her mind awakened, Sam lay alone in her tank with no other Tanker to talk to. She could hear everything flow into her mind from the three people in the room. It disturbed and scared her until she remembered her lectures. She built the wall as recommended by the imperial grand councilor. She was not sure exactly what to do, so she made the wall double strong and succeeded in blocking the thoughts of those around her.

Even though she had not listened to the rest of the training tapes, Sam figured out how to let a single person's thoughts into her mind, one person at a time. This kept her sane as the nurses and various people came and went from her private tank location next to the Twelve-Gen Center.

Two months after the first of the other tankers had left his tank in the building next door, her own exit from the tank was completely uneventful. When the alarm sounded from her tank, her nurses called in the support team from over at Twelve-Gen. That team knew exactly what to expect.

Sam was cleaned, wrapped from head to toe in gauze, and taken to a convalescent home in north Scottsdale where she would become familiar with her new body. The recovery time would give her a chance to adjust to breathing actual air too. The rest home would also allow her to begin to regrow her beautiful hair and look, again, like she had at age twenty.

She left the convalescent facility to return to her luxurious Camelback home two months later. Mario met her at the door. She grabbed his hand and took him directly to the master bedroom. There she changed her "maybe" into a continuous "yes" for three days of lovemaking. They stopped only for food.

She continued to enjoy many a rendezvous with Mario. Even though he had a much older body than hers now, he was highly skilled, and she enjoyed their lovemaking. She especially loved playing tricks on him when he thought about something erotic. She pretended she did not know what he wanted but always ended up in whatever situation he desired.

He was such a good man. She came to appreciate his tender care of her. Sam pretty much never left the house unless she was escorted on Mario's arm to a restaurant or a theater far away from downtown Phoenix. She loved listening to the jealous men and women. They all thought he should not be in public with a woman young enough to be his granddaughter. Those were fun times.

Finally, upon satiating her younger body's initial lustiness, she began work with her benefactors from the Ancient Universal Knowledge Association. They had access to copies of TAMO books and other ancient translations of long-ago legends.

Her goal was to learn as much as possible about the Dragon Prophecy, the meaning of which the two organizations held directly opposite points of view. The TAMO documents described the goodness that would come to the planet when the Dragon's Teeth were found. The AUKA documents described how the Dragon's Teeth would be the end of humanity and explained how they must be destroyed or at least hidden from humanity.

Sam learned a lot about both organizations, but the AUKA propaganda convinced her she was on the correct side of this situation. Everything pointed to danger if TAMO had their way, which made her more and more anxious about what she could do to undermine the TAMO group's success.

Her young body, beauty, and strength would allow her to do many physical tasks. But would it be enough?

She continued her learning and training with several "support" people from AUKA. She realized early on they were simple thugs there to do her bidding.

A Special Meeting

Twelve-Gen had made it clear their rejuvenated subjects could either join the military or simply serve as a test subject for a year. Steve opted not to go into the military. It meant many nights, he found himself totally bored. To ease his boredom, Steve went upstairs to the Hyatt lounge. Dark, with pleasant soft music, the venue played jazz some nights and old classical songs from the 1970s or 1980s other nights. Almost all the women were escorted so he did not need to worry about being "hit on." The unaccompanied few were hookers, judging from the clothes they wore. Steve never needed their services, but he did enjoy talking to them and listening to their thoughts as they tried to convince him to join them for only a couple of thousand new dollars.

One of those nights, a few minutes before midnight, Steve sat in the lounge drinking his second Drambuie. A young woman walked into the room. She looked about eighteen years old or maybe a little older. Steve knew appearances could deceive. After all, his body might look the same age as hers, but he, no doubt, was much older than her in mind and spirit.

Her pleasant outfit most definitely did not look like a call girl's. Her long beautiful red hair complemented a particularly strong physical look.

She found a table on the other side of the lounge and Steve listened to her simple thoughts. She was enjoying the music and reminiscing about earlier times with friends. Her thoughts came across as lonely and subdued. He did catch one positive note from her.

Interesting man over there. I wonder what his story is.

Steve had used less information to pick up other women at other nightclubs. When he noticed the woman's drink was almost empty, he asked the waitress to take her another one and to tell the lady the drink was from the nice guy across the room. He tipped the waitress an extra fifty and off she went.

When the waitress delivered the drink and explained who it came from, the lady at the table turned, smiled, and raised her glass to say thank you. Steve caught her thought.

What a pleasant gesture. He does seem nice.

With that response from her, Steve rose and carried his Drambuie to the other side of the room. As he approached the woman, he noticed clear and beautiful dark-green eyes sparkling in the light of the table lamp. The lady's genetics appeared healthy. Even with red hair, her face bore no freckles on her light ivory skin.

He looks even nicer up close.

Steve held out his hand as he came to the table. "Good evening, my name is Steve Johnson. May I join you?"

"Of course, please sit down." *I really was hoping you would come over here.*

Steve gave a slight bow of his head, smiled, and sat down opposite her. As he asked about her and listened to both her oral and mental answers, he felt more and more comfortable with her.

Throughout the discussion, none of Steve's thoughts went in the direction of sexual innuendo. All his thoughts had been positive about himself and about her. He did hedge a little about what he did for a living. He used the real estate business line, but secretly wished he could tell her he was a wealthy Tanker.

When the waitress asked for last call, Steve realized it was closing time.

"I know we are going to have to leave soon. It has been so wonderful talking with you. Would you mind telling me your name?"

Her big smile showed those perfect beautiful white teeth he'd admired all night.

"My name is Sandy Haspure, and you should guard your thoughts like I do."

As the name made a light bulb light up in his mind, Sandy fully opened her mind to Steve. He could not believe all the information she was able to transfer to him in that split second. It provided answers to all the questions a polite person would not ask. He literally knew all about her. She even revealed she wore a wig still because of the transition. She wanted him to know, in time, her real hair would appear as long and as beautiful as the wig.

As her information poured into Steve's mind, he reciprocated. With the exception of the forbidden transfer of TAMO knowledge, he opened his mind directly to her and told her all about himself. The communication took less than a minute, a glorious moment for both of them.

Sandy turned her big smile on him again. "Well, are we going to your suite downstairs or mine?"

Though stunned, he was not too taken aback to answer her question. "Your place. It is the gentlemanly thing to do."

They laughed. Steve knew he would be near the other Tankers as he went down to her room. He shut all the doors and windows in his mind, except for the one to Sandy. On the way down in the elevator, a grandmotherly person rode with them. Sandy and Steve stood beside her, staring at each other in silence. Behind the quiet gaze, the two linked in a mental connection neither had ever felt before.

As they stepped out of the elevator, the grandmother said, "You two make a cute couple. I hope you stay together."

They both nodded a thank you to the woman as their internal conversation continued.

When they arrived at the suite, Sandy opened the door and pulled Steve inside. They both knew exactly what the other wanted, and each was willing. Steve had been with a good many women since the transformation, but this was different. No other women, though they might have been beautiful of body, could compare to the magnificent form of this woman and her gorgeous mind link with him.

At eight o'clock the next morning, they had not slept. They had come together so many times neither could remember the count. The love and intertwining of minds made it difficult to tell who was experiencing the orgasms.

Sandy sat up in bed to show off her perfect porcelain-colored body one last time. "Steve, I am never letting you go. We are one." She placed her hands on either side of his face and stared into his eyes with regret. "I will order us some breakfast but will need to shoo you away so I can prepare for my nine a.m. meeting with my psychologist."

Steve rubbed a thumb along her lower lip. *I am yours forever and I promise to never let you go.*

Later in the day, Steve felt compelled to share his thoughts. *Sandy, I can't stop thinking about you. I know we have only known this version of ourselves, together, for a few hours. Somehow you have become the woman of my dreams, physically and psychically. This direct connection to you wherever you are makes this even more intense.*

Within a second, he heard Sandy's reply. *I have let my guard down so I can always hear you. I am all yours.*

I, too, have built a special window in my mental wall so I can hear what you need to say to me and me alone.

From then on, Steve and Sandy were almost inseparable. Together, they shared tips for keeping out the thoughts from other people. They refined how to block their own very personal thoughts from other Tankers living near them in the hotel. The couple wanted to have their own kind of mental privacy.

☆☆☆

The days and weeks became fairly routine for all of the Tankers. A full ten months had passed since the last Tanker's extraction. In the last three months, all of the Tankers were finally able to interact with one another. Most of them still kept to themselves.

Sandy's hair continued to grow, as did the hair of all the Tanker women and men. Each person's body was making final adjustments to its new self. Martha, no longer Maurice, and Albert, formerly Alison, enjoyed having the bodies they thought they belonged in. Each day, they met with their psychologists to help them adjust to their new genders and ages.

Nadia continued to be tickled she could hear both the thoughts of all the Tankers and their voices. She spent most of her days working with speech therapists since she wanted to develop perfect English and a full vocabulary as soon as possible. The rejuvenation gave her a young body and mind, fully healed from several strokes experienced in her last years as an old woman. The marvelous changes made her upbeat and excited.

She was the only one who did not participate in many group activities. She refused to talk with her fellow Tankers unless they verbally spoke in English. The one exception involved her unique ability to mentally communicate in images. She spent hours with many of the Tankers, using her skill to teach them how to share images. Visualization provided a much faster way to communicate mind to mind.

Nadia continued to enjoy her interludes with Nate. Each time they came together, they always touched each other so Nate could make the most of their unique connection. Though Nadia had the opportunity to touch the skin of many other "normals", no one except Nate could hear her thoughts. She cherished her relationship with him, and their love only grew stronger.

Each person had a set of classes they attended at the downtown Arizona State University campus. The director had cut a deal allowing each of the Tankers to pursue a refresher in their desired field over a period of a few weeks. This would allow them to receive their college degrees under their new identities. With new social security numbers, licenses, birth certificates, and passports, the college degrees put each person on what appeared to be an equal playing field with the rest of the young people of Phoenix.

Dan and Ryan left Phoenix and headed out to spend their time at the Air Force academy. The military gave them full credit for their prior lives. When they completed basic training in San Antonio, Texas, their next assignment was the Pararescue Specialist Team, the most elite group in the Air Force.

During their tank time, without their knowledge, the military had added tapes that explained about all the modern aircraft and weapons at their disposal. They also learned all about hand-to-hand combat. They both listened to tapes and became fluent in Russian while in the tank.

No one on the team of eighteen and nineteen-year-olds could compete with the "twenty-four-year-olds'" physical strength, dexterity, speed, and military knowledge. Even on that elite team, Dan and Ryan had to keep themselves as separate as possible. Hearing the bad thoughts of their jealous comrades made them uncomfortable. Those envious thoughts of their teammates did not stop the pair from outperforming everyone in almost every way.

The two men were inseparable. They enjoyed hitting the bars around the base while on furlough. They took turns playing the "wingman" for the other, though they quickly found out that wasn't necessary. Surprise! When you can hear what a woman thinks, it makes it easy to give her what she wants.

One night, in their regular hangout, they ordered their third beer. Neither one worried since one of the standard DNA adjustments included a metabolism which broke down alcohol before they could get drunk. Two young women walked into the bar, each beyond stunning. One was blonde and the other brunette. Their blouses and skirts were as minimal as one could get and still be in high fashion.

Dan and Ryan glanced at each other at the same time, having caught what the women were thinking, even though their thoughts were in Russian.

The young ladies walked right up to the guys' table and, in perfect English in tandem, asked, "You flyboys want to buy a couple of girls a drink?"

The blonde blinked rapidly at Dan. *I want the hunky black man!*

He easily understood her Russian-language thought.

I want the hunky white boy, the brunette thought.

Ryan also understood her Russian.

Each young woman pushed herself into the booth beside her desired partner.

Dan and Ryan listened carefully to the women's thoughts as the four carried on a perfectly normal verbal conversation in English. The two women talked about their time in college and how they were born and raised in Omaha, Nebraska.

A thought from the blonde made both men wary. *These guys are so easy. I'll never betray my mother country Russia.*

Dan and Ryan decided to play along with their game. The young ladies cooed and snuggled, and soon were kissing the men. They asked if the guys wanted to come up to their room.

The men knew the rooms would be bugged, based on the thoughts of the women. Instead of taking the women to their motel, the airmen took them to the most expensive hotel in San Antonio and purchased a suite with two bedrooms.

The young women forgot all about their mission to get some "goods" from a couple of pilots.

Of course, the night was unforgettable for the women. About midway through the night, Dan started talking to his date in fluent Russian. He lied to her about him being part of a sleeper cell dedicated to destroying America. That made the woman even more passionate. Dan found out the next morning that Ryan had taken a similar approach with his date.

After a light breakfast, the four comrades said their goodbyes. Dan and Ryan obtained the young women's special phone numbers and promised to give them a call if they ever needed any help. They separated friends.

Only the two airmen knew they had completely outsmarted a couple of undercover Russian agents. Dan took the information from Ryan and contacted his superior officer giving him the names, numbers, and details about the Russian agents.

Fortunes Change

All of his life, Steve prided himself on his self-sufficiency. He had thousands of new dollars in the bank—not to mention the money he'd stashed in his daughter's care, which he never planned to access again—he wanted to try to use his new mental gifts to acquire more money.

Steve had always been a gambler of sorts, the first place that came to mind, Las Vegas. After all, it was only a thirty-minute trip from entry at the Phoenix Sky Harbor airport to exiting the McCarran International Airport. He made a plan.

He obtained permission to travel to Las Vegas with Sandy for the weekend. Steve cashed out 240,000 new dollars from his Twelve-Gen card and wired it to the MGM Grand Las Vegas. The cash he wired guaranteed them complimentary rooms for the weekend and tickets to the best seats for any show on The Strip. The hotel also flew the two of them, first class, from Phoenix to Las Vegas. It took more time to reach the plane than the actual fifteen-minute flying time.

When they arrived that evening at the Las Vegas airport, a man from the MGM Grand waited for them outside the gate. He took their luggage tags and explained the bags would be delivered to their room later. As they left the building, a large stretch auto-driver vehicle sat at the curb to take them to the hotel and their complimentary room.

In no time, Steve found himself involved in a card game of Texas hold 'em at the MGM with Sandy at his side. He knew his ability to hear thoughts would give him an extreme advantage over the other card players. Having Sandy there only added to the joy.

Steve did not want anyone to recognize him as one of the Twelve-Gen Tankers, so he wore a false mustache, a hooded University of Michigan Law School sweatshirt, and a pair of dark sunglasses.

Sandy's disguise went all out to reveal as much skin as legally possible. She added make-up and dressed like a forty-year-old, 1,000-an-hour hooker. They made the perfect couple: a young stud with an older woman. No one would guess the age of these decades-old Tankers.

For the first time in Las Vegas, Steve played at the high-rollers' tables. The next evening, he had already agreed to enter the 200,000 new dollar table stakes Texas hold 'em card game at ten o'clock. Sandy played her part of the older woman.

His current competitors included eight fairly normal looking people. Six men of varying ages and two women in their early twenties. Both women were stunning and dressed to kill. One rocked a bright-red dress with a low-scooped front to show off her prominent breasts. The second woman, no less beautiful, wore a dress meant to discourage the concentration of the other players. The blue number barely even had a front.

Watching and listening to the minds of all the players convinced Steve the plan of the two women was working quite well.

Sandy stood behind Steve, who sat at the table to the right of the dealer. She provided the six other men with additional "eye candy" to covet.

Steve and the rest of the players gave the dealer their markers for 20,000 new dollars and each received several stacks of chips. Each stack of a different color indicated its chips' values of 100, 500, and 1,000 new dollars.

When everyone had their chips, the dealer paused and looked each player in the eye. "Alright, ladies and gentlemen, let's begin this game of Texas hold 'em. We will continue playing until one person has all the chips or five hours have passed. Please ante up one hundred new dollars to start."

What Steve heard from the thoughts of the dealer was quite telling. *Yes, gentleman, ante up. Soon my two girls will have all your money.*

Steve now knew the women were shills for the casino and they would try to distract everyone.

The game began with the antes, then the dealer dealt two cards to each person and five cards face down in front of him.

Steve listened carefully as each player looked at their cards and thought about what they might be able to do with them. He knew what everyone was playing with.

The first hand of the game, the two shills had nothing. One of the guys had an ace. Steve had a pair of twos. The man with the ace threw in a 1,000 dollar chip, each person around the table followed, calling his bet. They all wanted to see the "flop."

The last play was Steve's. "I'll see you and raise you a thousand."

Everyone went for the raise. The pot was at 18,900 new dollars and no one had seen any of the dealer's cards. The dealer rolled the first three cards: a king of spades, a jack of hearts, and a two of diamonds. At this point, Steve knew he had everyone beat. One of the girls had a jack of clubs so she matched it up with the jack of hearts in the community cards. Everyone checked, except the girl with the two jacks. She threw five of the 1,000 dollar chips into the pot and shook her breasts. "You gotta stay in to see 'em!"

Steve could not believe the thoughts of the six men. Sandy mentally giggled and shook her chest too. The guys were so totally focused on the woman's breasts, they thought she had said, "If you stay in, I'll show you my breasts."

Steve chuckled to himself as he threw in the chips but did not raise the bet. He couldn't believe every single guy threw in chips even though they had no hand.

The woman with nothing folded.

The dealer flipped "fourth street" and it was a king of diamonds. It meant everyone had a pair of kings and Steve held a full house. Everyone continued to bet wildly, hoping the last card would match with something in their hands. The woman in the red dress kept flaunting her breasts at each turn of a chip into the pot. Somehow, this first hand had gotten out of control.

The "river" card was flipped, a two of hearts. It appeared to give everyone two pairs from the community cards. It meant whoever held the highest card in their hand could win it all. In seconds, everyone had put all their money in the pot. One hand for 177,900 new dollars. Steve had never seen anything so crazy.

The dealer indicated for each person to show their hand. One by one, each player turned over a card a little higher than the previous.

The woman in red flopped her cards down and puffed out her chest. "I've got you all beat with a pair of kings and a pair of jacks." The way she bent over the table made her breasts even more visible. She grinned, thinking she had won.

Steve held up a hand to stop her move toward the pot. "I have the same pair of kings, but I also have two pairs of twos. The cards play themselves."

The dealer smiled at Steve as he pushed the stack of chips his way but flashed an angry mental thought. *This young fool is ruinin everything!*

Steve had almost all the chips available on the table. He flipped a 1,000 dollar chip to the dealer. "Can we stop now? Only the house shills and I have any money remaining. I have a show I want to see."

The woman in blue stood up and walked away. The woman in red cozied up to Steve and glanced up at Sandy. "Would you like to come up to my room for a nightcap of milk and a three-way with your girl?" She rubbed her breast against Steve's arm.

Steve might have agreed, with Sandy's approval, except he caught the shill's thought. *Yeah, you two come up to my room. I'll get half naked and give you a mickey and take all of your money and hers too.*

Steve chose an easy polite tone. "No thank you, ma'am."

He picked up the chips and walked away with Sandy on his arm, both laughing at the nasty mean thoughts the woman spewed at them.

The Big Game

Steve knew he had enough money to enter the big game with the 200,000 new dollar buy-in. His current clothing did not meet the standard of a real high-roller game. But, since the game didn't start until ten that night, they had time to shop, dress, and eat dinner.

He and Sandy wandered down the Las Vegas Strip until they found the shops at Caesar's Palace. They planned to show up at the big game showcasing the style and flair of James Bond. He purchased a fantastically fitted black designer tux with diamond buttons and cufflinks. He also picked out a big pinky ring with a diamond in the middle.

While Sandy shopped to find her outfit, Steve slipped away to a nearby jewelry store and blocked her from his thoughts. It took a little bit of talking and a lot of mental listening, but Steve finagled the owner into showing him the best five-carat diamond in the store. It was only 125,000 new dollars, and he used the credit on his personal MGM account to pay for it. Steve added another 5,000 to get it mounted immediately. As the owner placed the diamond ring in a small black felt box, Steve contemplated how he probably could have purchased the same thing in Israel for one third the price. He did not care.

Sandy, tired of looking like a forty-year-old call girl, bought clothing to make her look like an eighteen-year-old rich kid. The dress was formal, but young in style. While checking out, she told the salesperson she was buying it for her younger sister who had the same build.

The salesgirl nodded her head in halfhearted agreement, but thought, *good thing. That outfit is not appropriate for an older woman like you.*

The comment deserved a comeback. "Well, sweetie, if you had remained nice, I would have given you a nice tip. Instead, let me leave with this derisive smile." Sandy gave the girl a "snarky" smile, as promised, and left.

The expense of the outfits didn't matter much since the money for them all came from the winnings of the first poker game.

Sandy thought to Steve, *I'm almost ready, you can come back and stop your window shopping.*

Be right there, my love.

Since Sandy knew he hated waiting around as a woman shopped, Steve was sure his little side trip went unnoticed. He needed to be extra careful about what he thought though. He didn't want her to know about the ring.

He met her outside the shops at Caesar's. They returned to the hotel room and took a shower together. Their amorous shower play led to some additional playtime which totally messed up the bed sheets.

After another shower, they began the transformation for the card game. Sandy colored his hair with grey sideburns, and added makeup which made him look like he was in his forties.

As he dressed, he watched as Sandy put on her outfit, one definitely not intended for an older woman. Its bodice, a jet black bustier, barely covered her nipples. Attached below the bustier, a long silky skirt flowed. Slits down both sides exposed her long, beautiful legs wrapped in a pair of fishnet stockings. It reminded him of the attire the thief Katia had worn that night he met her in the bar, months ago now, sporting the Madonna look which had been all the rage in the 1990s. Was the risqué style coming back as high fashion?

Sandy slipped her perfect-sized feet into a pair of five-inch heels to complete the look. Steve realized her attire presented a more beautiful and sexier version of the outfit Katia had worn. He made sure Sandy saw the image of her and the image of Katia, side by side. There was no comparison, beyond the similarity of the clothes. That resulted in a wickedly sexy smile directed at him.

They took a cab to the best restaurant in Las Vegas. Normally, reservations were required three months in advance. The MGM concierge knew Steve had entered the high-stakes Texas hold 'em card game, along with a 500 new dollar tip, the concierge did not hesitate to find them a table.

As the couple entered the restaurant, they enjoyed some of the thoughts from the patrons. Most of them centered on the fact that a man in his forties shouldn't go out with a woman who was barely old enough to be his daughter. Sandy enjoyed the compliment, for she was technically really seventy-three years old.

Dinner tasted excellent, as expected. Steve had an authentic Angus New York strip steak that came from a real cow rather than a meat production factory. Sandy enjoyed her grilled authentic salmon, especially because she knew it had come from the streams of the northwestern United States. They split a bottle of fine wine. Steve paid the bill of 5,000 new dollars without a thought.

As ten o'clock approached, they willingly slipped into character. He as a forty something businessman, and her as his flighty eighteen-year-old date.

☆☆☆

The table at the MGM sat within a special area for high rollers. Sandy had to show proof to the pit boss that she was of age to be in the casino at all. Seeing she was twenty-four, the pit boss simply nodded to the others to allow her to stay.

Steve, again, sat at the right of the dealer. There were no shills this time, only nine hardcore players. Each expected to win all of the money from the other eight players. Steve knew he could win any bluff if he held a better hand.

Each of the players handed the dealer a note worth 200,000 new dollars for the buy-in. The dealer passed out the chips: new dollar stacks of 1,000, 5,000, 10,000, and 20,000. When everyone received their chips, the dealer expertly shuffled the cards.

"Ante-up, please. One thousand dollars."

That began a long night for Steve and Sandy as his mental support. The game was based on chance to some extent though Steve had the advantage. It was like playing the game with everyone but the dealer's cards showing. He found it easy to calculate what remained in the deck, and what chance the cards other players needed remained in the community cards.

Steve lost some hands and won some hands. The amount of money on the table made the play serious business. Each of the players, one at a time, attempted to bluff and buy the pot. If Steve had them beat, he would play it cool until the last round of cards had been shown, all the time watching the pot grow.

Steve played with 20,000 new dollar bets. He won almost all the hands when he stayed in. Only he and one other player remained by three in the morning. Each sat on a pile of chips worth around 450,000 new dollars.

Steve knew this could be the last hand. The dealer dealt cards, and Steve had drawn two aces. The other player had drawn two kings. Steve could tell by the eagerness of the man's thoughts that he was planning to go all out. Before the first flop, the man bet 100,000 new dollars. Steve matched it. He wanted to see the flop as there was always a chance the other player could end up with a better hand.

The cards flopped: two aces and a king. The man held three kings and two aces, a full house. But only Steve knew there were no more aces, and the last two cards didn't matter because the man would never think Steve held two aces. Maybe a king or another pair in the hole, but not the two aces.

The betting began, first the other player, then Steve. That went on until the other player pushed all his chips into the center. He was all in with two cards left to flop. Steve matched him. The dealer rolled the next card: a nine of hearts. This was followed by the last card: a seven of spades. The dealer looked at the two players. "Show me what you have."

The other man rolled his cards. "Full house, kings and aces." His smug expression showed he thought he had won.

Steve rolled his cards. "Four of a kind, aces."

A grimace lined the other man's face momentarily, but he quickly schooled it into a gracious smile. He held out his hand and Steve shook it. "Well played, sir." A similar thought crossed his mind.

He was a good gambler but did not lie to himself that, sometimes, others might win.

The dealer put away all the chips and sent Steve a certified receipt for a deposit of 900,000 new dollars to Steve's bitcoin MGM account.

Steve's smile went from ear to ear as he watched Sandy stare at him in disbelief. He picked up from her thoughts that his winnings were more money than she had ever seen. She cocked her head, perhaps listening for his thoughts, to hear his reaction to winning so much money. Of course, she heard nothing because he was blocking his thoughts. He wanted her to be surprised.

He knelt on one knee and pulled the ring box from the inner pocket of his tux. He held out the ring, gazed up into her eyes, and asked softly, "Will you marry me, Sandy? You are the love of my life, and I want to be your other half forever."

It took no mind reader to see how her face lit up. "Yes, you sexy lecherous old man, I love you and I will marry you." At the same time, she thought, *I love you more than I can say. I can't imagine life without you.*

He placed the ring on her finger, kissed her soundly, and wiped tears of joy from her face.

Of course, they heard thoughts of jealousy and disgust from those around them even more strongly than from the restaurant patrons. Sandy and Steve simply closed their minds to it all. The joke was on these people.

They went up to the room to celebrate their engagement. Though it should have been fun and spontaneous, some niggling idea kept Steve from reveling in the moment. Something was not right. Not sure what to do, he asked Sandy to give him a few minutes to meditate. He wanted to be fully present with her before they moved into the bedroom. She kissed him lightly and mentally shared, *I would wait for eternity for you. Do what you need to do so we can celebrate properly.*

He excused himself to go to the other room and, as always, closed his mind to everyone as he meditated. As he listened with an open mind, that slight, almost imperceptible, thought clarified into a concrete concern.

The money I won was not won fairly.

He continued to allow his mind to calm, and a solution came to him.

I will donate all my winnings to TAMO.

Decision made, he felt much better. He rose and went to find Sandy who was waiting for him in the main room of their suite. With his mind still closed to others, he sat next to her on the couch.

"I have made a decision. However, Sandy, my love, I want to hear your advice." His face became very serious. "I feel uncomfortable about the way we won tonight. I am thinking I should donate my winnings to TAMO."

Sandy leaned into him and hugged him hard. *I feel the same, my love. I didn't know how to ask you to dispose of it.*

The topic was closed, both satisfied everything would be well.

She pulled away and gave him a seductive smile as she twisted the ring on her finger. Steve picked up his fiancée and carried her to the bedroom and they enjoyed themselves until nearly dawn.

Days of Relaxation

Steve and Sandy called into the Twelve-Gen office even though it was only five in the morning. With a little convincing, the answering service rep allowed them to ring through to Charles Swenson. Though the director initially balked at their request, they pleaded with him to allow them four more days in Las Vegas to celebrate their engagement. Charlie finally agreed.

For the rest of their time in Las Vegas, they went to the casinos only to pass through to a specialty restaurant or a great show. Sandy had convinced Steve to sit out by the pool during the day. In his last marriage, his wife drove into his mind that sitting in the sun from mid-morning to late afternoon was dangerous to the body. Sandy had to remind him their rejuvenation process literally made their skin impervious to cancer at any time.

Steve quit complaining when he saw Sandy in the bikini purchased at the MGM swim shop. He could not believe she would wear it in public. The conservative suit's minimal material absolutely covered everything but hugged her frame like skin. Steve realized he was no slouch either and wore the skimpy Speedo bathing suit she'd purchased for him; it did show off his new "six pack" quite nicely.

The two of them looked the part of their actuality: young, beautiful, twenty-something kids in love, with their whole lives before them.

They sat at the pool all day for each of their remaining days at the MGM. They drank and ate all their meals poolside.

The one area Steve had withheld from Sandy during their multiple mind connections with each other, was the level of his affiliation with TAMO. She knew he was a twelfth-degree member but had never asked for details. He'd told her he would explain more when the right time came. Though no one suspected it, Steve spent his time at the pool teaching Sandy to meditate and to learn about TAMO's Neophyte degrees.

On the last day at the MGM pool, Steve and Sandy mentally discussed the final monograph in the Neophyte series which involved the workings of the human body. They had literally paid no attention to the people around them. No one could hear their mental conversation anyway. But Steve had left a sliver of his meditative mind to become aware of anyone who came too close or too interested.

A flash of hate came to Steve's mind. He opened his eyes in time to see a man in disheveled clothes run toward them.

The man screamed, "All those of the Traditional Ancient Mystical Order must die!" He carried a long sword and rushed toward them.

The man's mind was not right. Steve could feel something very wrong in him. The man's voice made sense, but his thoughts came through all jumbled and confused.

Sandy jumped up and started spinning cartwheels and flips toward the man. Steve was shocked as he watched her accelerate closer to the crazy man. *Remember, I was a cheerleader once and this body is able to remember the stunts. Do not worry. I can handle this!*

Her last flip took her to the feet of the crazed man and a twist of her legs between the man's shins caused the man to fall. He smashed his face into the concrete and the sword went flying into some nearby bushes. The man lay still. Sandy had knocked him out cold.

By the time the man woke up, the Las Vegas Sheriff's Department was putting handcuffs on him. The man remembered nothing. Steve listened to his thoughts and the man did not know where he was or what he was doing.

Before the authorities arrived, when the few other pool patrons were talking excitedly with Sandy about what happened, Steve surreptitiously found the sword and wrapped it in a towel to sneak it up to their room. He reappeared with a first-aid kit to help with Sandy's scrapes and bruises as a reason for leaving the scene.

The sheriff asked what had happened and everyone supplied a different answer. Even Sandy indicated the man must have tripped over her legs and hit his head. The sheriff recorded everyone's names and took the man in for questioning.

Later, Steve and Sandy examined the sword closely. Though ancient, its blade was sharp enough to cut through paper or steel. Its most remarkable feature was the Chinese writing on the blade. Steve had learned enough Chinese language to translate.

"The song of this blade shall end the life of those who desire to misuse the teeth of the dragon."

This event had triggered something important and dangerous. They agreed Steve should pack the sword and express mail it to the imperial grand councilor.

Afterward, Steve and Sandy quickly packed and headed for the airport.

In forty minutes, they arrived safely back in Steve's suite and tried to forget what had happened earlier. Tired, they called down for room service for their dinner, but only made it through half of the meal. They crawled into bed and fell asleep in each other's arms.

The next morning when they woke, Steve told Sandy she should go back to her room. He explained to her he could feel something was about to happen. Nothing heard orally or through his mind, it was an intuitive thought.

When Sandy left, Steve went into a deep meditation. It revealed to him the Tankers were about to be called to service. Their one year of close observation had ended, and it would have been the time for the Tankers to normally begin their new lives as young and independent people. Instead, they would be called to work for TAMO. Help was needed to complete the tasks related to the society's very reason for existence: the hunt for the Dragon's Teeth, the "keys" to the treasure heralding mankind's future. Because of this, the "Dragon's Teeth" became shortened to the "Ancient Keys" or simply the "keys."

A New Call to Service

Steve was right, two Tankers did have additional work to do. The next morning, he and Rob received text messages on their phones. The notice from the imperial grand councilor invited them to come to Canada to participate in the Thirteenth Level Initiation of TAMO. Very few TAMO members knew a Thirteenth Level even existed. The imperial grand master of all TAMO would preside over the initiation.

Steve and Rob took a standard airline to Toronto Canada and landed at the Lester B. Pearson International Airport. The flight from Phoenix lasted only an hour so they had spent more time in lines than on the plane. A member of TAMO met them in Toronto. She would tell them nothing, and was obviously well trained in blocking her thoughts, for neither Steve nor Rob could catch a single thought from her.

She took them by auto-driver to the private plane terminal. The car dropped them off at a small jet. She left the car, boarded the plane, and sat in the captain's seat.

Another young lady, dressed as an airline attendant, ushered them to their seats for the flight. She made sure the two Tankers remained comfortable during the additional one-hour flight.

Rob couldn't stop looking at the attendant. *There is something about that woman, Steve. She makes me think she might be the final one for me.*

Steve couldn't help but chuckle. *Rob, I think she is the fourth one you have said that about today.*

Rob flashed his friendly smile to the attendant. She smiled back. *Steve, I'm sure she is the one.*

That was it. Rob and Steve just relaxed in their seats for the rest of the trip.

They arrived at the small airport, knowing only it was somewhere in Northeast Canada. Imperial Grand Councilor Nate Conway met them as they descended from the plane.

"Good afternoon, and welcome to the Center of Silence." Nate shook the hands of both men. "You will be taken to your separate cabins shortly. There, you will find a change of dinner clothes and a map of the grounds of the center. It is five in the evening, local time. We will eat at seven. After dinner, you will be given some materials to read thoroughly. Meditate on the information, then sleep. You will be awakened an hour before dawn for your initiation into the Thirteenth Level of the Traditional Ancient Mystical Order."

Steve and Rob went their separate ways to their assigned cabins but kept in touch mentally.

Steve found a white tuxedo lying on the bed in his one-room cabin. He made a mind image of the room and mentally delivered it to Sandy. He also sent a wave of melancholy at being the farthest distance away from her than ever before, and for the longest time.

She rewarded him quickly. *Your room is lovely, and I am sure you will look quite handsome in the tuxedo.*

His loneliness lessened. Sandy was still available to him.

Steve took some time to take a short nap. When he awoke, he realized how late it had become. He jumped into the shower, increasing the temperature of the water to give himself a long hot soapy wash. While drying off afterward, he looked at himself in the mirror and sent the image of the new young handsome man to Sandy. She didn't respond. Five minutes passed with no answer. Steve started to think they had reached their communication link distance.

It took ten minutes longer for Sandy to respond. *You are such a tease!* She sent an image of her in her hotel suite in Phoenix. She had dressed up in his favorite lingerie. It showed off her perfect young body.

He couldn't stop the lascivious thought. *Now there's a sight to make a man homesick. Thank you, my love.*

It took him almost half an hour to tie his bowtie. In Phoenix, Sandy always tied it for him. A glance at himself in the long mirror brought a rush of satisfaction.

In a split second, Sandy received the image too.

You are a cutie pie! she immediately responded, along with some imagery of what she desired to do with him.

After a suitably appreciative response, he sent how much he regretted the need to leave for his evening event as the time was six-forty-five. He walked with a swift pace to the hall indicated on the map. It also showed "The Temple of the Dragon" but, in the dark, he saw no building where the temple should have been. When he arrived at the hall, a young lady opened the door for him, the attractive pilot from the plane.

She bowed as he entered and whispered, "Supplicant, you are welcomed here for your last meal."

A table sat in the middle of the room. Rob sat at it, along with two other women in white formal dresses. One looked thirty-something, small-framed, and plain. Steve figured the other's age as early fifties. She looked quite beautiful and fit for her age. The imperial grand councilor also sat at the table.

The woman at the head of the table looked ancient but strong in body. She wore a golden hooded robe with a red sash. Around her neck, on a strong golden chain, hung the cross, star, and flower symbol of TAMO.

She gestured him toward a seat. "Come in, come in, sit, and enjoy your final meal. I am the Imperial Grand Master Julie Bernard. In the morning, your death shall proclaim life for the world."

Steve felt his brow furrow.

Rob delivered a thought. *Those are the exact words she used when I came in.*

The words must be the beginning of the preparation of the ceremony for the Thirteenth Level. Feeling slightly better, though still wary, Steve sat.

☆☆☆

As silent servers delivered food, the talk at the dinner table became very normal, though Steve realized the thoughts of everyone except Rob were totally closed to him. Discussions about everyone's occupations and general life activities interested their hosts and other guests.

They learned the imperial grand councilor would be the guardian who Rob, Steve, and the two women would meet in the morning. The woman at the door would be in the position of the sacred speaker. Of course, the person doing the initiation would be Julie, the imperial grand master. No one provided specifics on the nature of the ritual to take place in the morning.

The meal was totally authentic vegetarian. Steve, a steak lover, found the delicate flavors bound into the meal of twelve different dishes quite surprising. The dinner's grand finale came in the form of a large slice of vegan chocolate cake with chocolate icing.

After the dishes had been cleared, Julie stood to quietly show Rob, Steve, and the other two women a package wrapped in a red cloth.

"Before giving you supplicants these packages for the Thirteenth Level, I shall number each of you." She counted out from one to four as she pointed to each person. "This package and your number are your lifeline. Without this information, surely you will die by the hand of the dragon. Study well and you may live to eat and love another day."

The imperial grand master handed them each a package.

Steve, Rob, and the two female supplicants received their packages, bade farewell to their hosts, and quietly walked back to their cabins.

Even in the three-piece tuxedo, Steve shivered as he strode toward his cabin. The temperature had dropped, yes, but it wasn't the cold causing him to tremble so much.

The TAMO Temple

Beside the bed in his cabin stood a large hourglass, probably two feet tall, with its sand all settled in the bottom. The piece had not been there before dinner, but he ignored it for the moment.

Steve sat on the bed and opened the package that he had received at dinner. The expansive red cloth revealed an ancient-looking book and a black silk scarf. A simple single page of instructions floated out of the package.

It read: "Here is the cloth of the blood of the dragon. Wear only this in the morning to protect your body. The sights you may see could be terrifying. Bind the scarf into a blindfold. The guardian will come for you before dawn. Study the materials carefully and meditate upon them. Turn the hourglass and only study while there is still a grain of life in the top of the hourglass. You may communicate with no one after you turn the hourglass. Each grain of sand is a piece of your life fleeing to its final resting place. Your voice and mind shall be silent to all except those who will physically be with you."

Steve immediately alerted Sandy with the information. *Sandy, my love, I will be incommunicado until sometime tomorrow. Do not worry if I do not respond to your thoughts. Remember I love you no matter what happens.*

I understand the importance of this for you, Sandy replied. *I wish you well. I love you too!*

With that, Steve sat comfortably next to the bed on the floor. He placed the hourglass next to him. When satisfied with his physical comfort, he put up all his mental walls. He mentally could hear no one. As he started to focus on the world around him, he heard no sound anywhere. No birds, no insects, nothing made a sound.

He carefully turned the hourglass upside down to let the sand flow to the bottom. Each grain made a small almost insignificant sound as it went from the top to the bottom of the hourglass. Steve continued as the instructions had required. He opened the book and began to read.

The allegorical story talked about a great dragon with fierce glowing eyes and sharp glistening teeth of gold. It told about the life of the dragon as it grew large and strong, of its death at the hands of mankind, and the removal of its twelve razor-sharp teeth. Each of the twelve priests of the kingdom received one.

The priests decided to hide the dragon's teeth across the world so they never would be found. The dragon would never become whole again and terrorize mankind. Upon completion of their task, the priests were to return and talk of their journeys. Some priests came back quickly. Others never returned. Only centuries or millennia later did the ancestors of the priests return to tell their tales. The details of the stories were incredible.

Steve knew it was but a story based on the Dragon Prophecy. The actual story happened more than 30,000 years before. Some parts of the story, like the dragon, were obviously fiction. Other parts talking about teeth he knew existed as real objects that priests held those many thousands of years ago.

The hourglass had run half its course. Steve mentally told himself to come out of meditation to watch the last few grains fall. Having given himself a mental reminder, he used his well-practiced breathing technique, and immediately entered into a deep meditative state.

Two hours later he opened his eyes. The light in the room showed the hourglass with only a few grains of sand left. He watched and listened, satisfied to see the grains glisten as they fell into the bottom of the hourglass.

As the last grain entered the base, the atmosphere in the room changed by the smallest degree. The top of the hourglass started to turn bright red. From the beautiful color it took on an evil dark red glow.

A few seconds later, a flame leaped upward from the top of the hourglass, almost to the ceiling. The flames expanded wider. As they almost touched him, Steve quickly turned the burning fountain of fire upside down into the metal trashcan beside the bed. No smell came from the flame, nor smoke, as it extinguished.

Had Steve mistimed the end of the hourglass, he would have died in a fire. The idea sent a shiver down his spine. He had passed the first test.

A loud scream burst into his mind. It might have been the sound of someone dying. He had not fortified the walls in his mind enough to withstand such horror. One of the other three supplicants would not be going to the temple in the morning.

He climbed under the covers telling himself to wake in time to dress for the initiation in the blood-red loincloth. His sleep was fitful. He tossed and turned. The sound of death haunted him. Finally, sleep overcame but lasted too short a time. He woke himself, quickly brushed his teeth, showered, and shaved.

He wrapped the red cloth around himself like a toga. He wore nothing underneath the toga, as instructed. He wore no shoes. He sat in the simple wooden chair by the door, folded the silk scarf into a blindfold, and put it on.

A few minutes later, several loud knocks sounded on the door.

"You, number four," said a ceremonial voice from the other side, "I am the Guardian of the Gate. If you have prepared yourself, then come to the door, open it, and join our silent parade to the Temple of the Dragon. You, like these others—number one and number three—are not worthy of more than a number. You are one of the many anonymous beings on this planet."

The cry he had heard the night before had come from the woman assigned to number two. Though her loss wrenched his heart, he was glad it was not his fellow Tanker. Steve could feel his presence. Rob had obviously followed the instructions.

When Steve opened the door, a stream of ice-cold air hit him. The red cloth provided no protection from the cold. His feet and legs grew even colder from the new snow. It covered his feet and a portion of his lower legs almost up to his knees. Apparently, it had snowed about two feet during the night.

A strong hand abruptly gripped Steve's left hand and placed it on the left shoulder of the person in front of him. Judging from the smaller height and size of the shoulder, he thought, *The fifty-something woman. The one who said very little last night.* His right hand was placed on her right shoulder.

The man instructed them to march on the count of three. They did so as he gave instructions, "We shall come to the entrance of the cave of the dragon. We shall walk silently down eleven-times-twelve steps, plus nine then three more, to bring us to the magic multiple of twelve. Stay close and make no sound for the dragon detests the voice of man. This stairway echoes back to where the dragon sleeps. Dare not speak while walking lest the dragon be awakened and ye be devoured by his fire."

The group left the protection of the cabin. The cold wind picked up. He might as well have been naked to the world. In the biting cold, the red cloth was nothing.

Steve mentally reviewed the layout of the compound. The temple should have been only about fifty yards from his door. Even though the walk was short, his cold feet began to turn numb. Using his early teachings with TAMO, he drove the energy from the core of his mind and body to build an impenetrable cover over his whole body. He started to feel warmer, and his feet were no longer numb.

Within several paces, something new took the place of the cold. The warmth of summer crawled over his skin, making his mind control over the cold unnecessary. He dropped it.

Combined with the warmth came an acrid smell of sulfur in his nostrils.

"We are close to the stairway into the cave," their guide said quietly. "I will place your left hand on a rope. It will keep you on the right path. Walk carefully. There is a two-hundred-foot drop to your right. Some of the steps have broken and provide nary but a small ledge. Do not make a sound lest you wake the dragon. The dragon seeks to have his teeth returned so he may grow strong again. I will hand you a symbol of one of the Dragon's Teeth. Hold it in your right hand. Hold it high with pride. I shall be at the bottom, ready to open the door for you."

The other two supplicants were making their way downward slowly and at the same time as quietly as possible. A gasp sounded in front of him and within seconds, the thud of a body hitting the bottom of the cavern far below reached him. It must have been the lady in front of him. She must have slipped. Then the mental onslaught of her death broke into his mind. It was the same as the feeling from the lady in the night. It left him shaken and worried.

Steve's time came. He focused on his task, driving the thought of the poor woman out of his mind. The guide placed Steve's left hand on the rope and placed something into Steve's right hand. The guide had said it would be a tooth of the dragon.

Feeling the symbol in his hand, Steve realized it was a TAMO symbol the same size as the one worn by the imperial grand master. Based on its weight, he figured the symbol was probably also solid gold.

Steve held the rope with his left hand and held the symbol in his right, high in front of him. He started counting the steps. When he reached one hundred, the rope became very slack. He sensed the wall to his left was gone. The width of each stair had become only inches wide. They smelled damp and oily, and it felt like walking in a shallow stream. He slipped a little but caught his balance.

This must be where she slid off!

He strengthened his resolve, focused, and used his sense of touch to carefully place his feet.

At the next full step, the wall was back, and the stench of sulfur and heat increased to an almost unbearable temperature, probably more than 120 degrees. Internally, he chuckled to himself. The temperature was like a dry summer day in Phoenix. He remembered a day—on June 26, 1990—when the temperature hit 122 and no plane could fly until the temperature dropped. He continued down the stairway and the heat began to wane as a cool mist covered him and soaked his flimsy robe.

When Steve reached 132, the temperature had cooled to around sixty degrees, and his robe was soaked. He inadvertently bumped into number one, Rob. The touch of the fellow Tanker's back against his chest felt like skin on skin.

Rob's garment must be sopping too.

In front of them came a sound like soft metal and cloth striking a giant door knocker.

"Please allow me to enter," their guide intoned. "I bring two nameless ones bearing the gift of the symbolic Dragon's Teeth. May we enter in safety?"

"The dragon sleeps. Bring the supplicants if you deem them worthy." A woman's voice called from inside.

"These two are worthy, open the door that we may enter."

The scraping noise filling the space sounded like a massive door opening.

"Supplicants, I shall meet you at the bottom where I shall give you the sacred word to allow you to enter without harm into the cave of the dragon," their guide reminded them. "If you are unable to repeat this to the sacred speaker, you will surely die at the hand of the dragon."

Steve grabbed the rope with his left hand and counted the nine stairs. As he reached step four, his foot touched water. He continued to walk down, holding the rope. As he moved forward, the water rose higher and higher. By the time he reached the second group of nine stairs, the water had risen up to his waist. He trusted in the rope to guide him to a level path. He walked slowly, expecting to reach the last three stairs at any moment. The rope took a steep angle up as his toe touched the front of the first of the three. It rose to twice the height of those encountered before.

He hefted himself up the last of the three and someone grabbed at his right hand.

"Give me my tooth," a gruff voice sounded near his ear. "I want to be whole again."

Steve held on tight and did not let go.

The voice had turned quiet and calm. Steve recognized the voice of the guide.

"You have chosen well to hold onto the tooth. The secret is the tooth is not a gift nor a treasure. While valuable to some of mankind, it is only a key to unimaginable treasures. Remember the password to this level: 'The tooth is a key.' Remember always the sacred way in which I lightly scratch the back of your hand with my nails. It is the second part of the password."

The guide steered Steve forward into a large open space where the sound of his footsteps reverberated. A great cave?

A small soft female hand touched his left arm. "Give me the password," the voice whispered. "Give it to me wrong and ye shall die by my sword. Give it to me right and ye shall be allowed to see again. Now hold up the tooth high away from your face that I may hear the words whispered in my ear."

As she pulled him close to her, Steve whispered, "The tooth is a key." He gripped it with strength and lifted the symbol high in the air. With his other hand, he reached for hers to scratch the back of it.

A sharp object touched his breast. A knife no doubt. He worked to control a flinch. Had he misunderstood the password or the special physical contact?

The back of his blindfold was cut loose. The silk fell to the ground. It was the sacred speaker, the woman attendant from the plane, who held the knife. She was draped in a golden hooded robe with a red sash and golden boots.

Rob, the remaining supplicant, appeared to be soaked in blood from head to toe. A look down at himself revealed his own bloodied state. The mist on the stairs must have contained the blood.

The sacred speaker who had asked for the password looked at the two men. "You are covered in the blood of those that have failed the journey to Level Thirteen. May you keep this in mind as a warning to you. Follow faithfully."

Inside the Temple

The sacred speaker wore a symbol overlaying her heart which featured the six-pointed star of the twin Trikona of Sanskrit. When seen, most would recognize it as the Star of David. One at a time, the sacred speaker quietly guided them to a chair marked with their number. When they sat, the sacred speaker returned to a position behind Steve to the left.

The large hall's stone ceiling spanned the room maybe fifty feet above them. On the right and left, pillars reminding him of ancient Egypt, lofted up to the ceiling. Between the pillars sat maybe thirty people, fifteen on each side.

The imperial grand councilor, who apparently had been their guide, sat in a chair opposite the sacred speaker. He also wore a gold hooded robe with a red sash and golden boots. On his breast showed the symbol of the ancient Hermetic. Each of the four tips of the golden cross appeared to blossom like a modest flower.

In the center of the room stood a rectangular altar table. It held the symbol of TAMO, the Hermetic Cross with the Star of David with interleaved triangles, and the flower of life centering it. An exceptionally large ruby glittered in the very center of the cross's flower. The symbol, more than three feet tall, appeared to be crafted of solid gold. It stood tall in a special socket.

Strategically placed unlit candles on the table mimicked the shape of the star, cross, and its central flower. Individual candle holders attached to the edges along the figurative horizontal beam of the cross kept the wicks at table level.

The room was so quiet. All those who sat on the sides of the room turned to face towards the great chair in the east, three small steps above them. *As with all the TAMO temples, the central focus of the assembly of people is in the east where the main speaker would be,* Steve remembered from his own experiences. *Facing east seems to represent an essential element of all our religious and metaphysical ceremonies.*

The chair held a person with the head of a dragon, robed in gold with a red sash, and golden boots. A beautiful golden flower with a large dark red ruby in its center graced the wearer's chest.

The person stood abruptly. "Who dares to come into my lair! Have you come to return my sacred teeth?" The voice sounded female.

The sacred speaker rose. "These are but seekers who desire to help you to find your missing teeth. They carry the symbol of your teeth. Help them carry the symbol always and tell them where to find your sacred teeth."

She moved quietly to the front of the altar table, picked up the large symbol, turned it around, and placed it flat on the table with the top of the cross pointed eastward toward the great chair. The sacred speaker carefully nestled the symbol between the unlit candles. She returned to her seat.

The "Dragon" walked slowly down the steps from the great chair, continued clockwise around to the western side of the altar table, faced east, and lit incense in the burner. Smoke drifted up into the room.

"This is the heart of the flower, the star, and the cross. From its light, all other lights shall come. Each light is a guide to the location of my hidden teeth. Find the number of twelve keys and make me whole."

She picked up a slim unlit candle and held it inches above the burning red candle in the table's center until the little candle burned bright.

"The fantastic, protected spot of the czar. In the far east lies the main point of my teeth." With this intoned, the dragon lit the first candle on the eastern side of the center of the symbol of TAMO.

"One tooth lives with the oldest of the living priests of old. He is one who renews all with each of his lifetimes, has a home at the top of the world, and is one with God."

She lit the second candle near the western center side of the flower.

"Above the giant altar stone, and by each of the two pillars, you will find the next three of my teeth."

She lit a triangle of three candles for these three teeth. The tip of the triangle pointed toward the great chair in the east.

"As below, in a shower of water lies my tooth in the south. The Lion Man hides my tooth in a secret place. It is hidden from all including the pharaoh. The holiest of Fathers, the highest of our priests of the dragon, keeps a book. It tells all." For these three teeth, she lit the triangle of three candles which pointed west toward Steve.

"My star and flower are full of light. The cross shall now sustain me at its four points, one for each of my remaining missing teeth. My ancient children in the land to the west, who have lived for many generations, protect one of my teeth." She lit the southern candle of the cross.

The Dragon walked clockwise around to the western arm of the cross. She brought the little candle and lit the next part of the cross. "In the land to the west a burial took place where my tooth is an idea."

She walked clockwise to the northern point of the cross. "In the west and far south, a man the size of a mountain holds a tooth in his hand."

She walked to the last candle in the east and raised her arms high in the air. With a powerful voice filled with happiness, "My final tooth, if it still exists, was given to the priests of David for their new temple."

With all twelve candles lighted, she doused the thin candle with a golden candle snuffer.

The Dragon came forward from the altar walking clockwise until she arrived in front of the two supplicants. One at a time, she asked them to open their right palm. She took up the symbolic tooth and attached it to a chain. She placed the chain with the symbol around the man's neck.

The woman returned to her eastern chair and removed the dragon's head. She placed it to the side of the massive chair and, still standing, turned toward the supplicants. "The symbol that I have given to you shall always remain with you. It will tell others you are searching for my teeth. This now shall be one of your missions in life. You shall always be in service."

She ceremoniously walked down the steps from the great chair to the west end of the altar and quietly snuffed out all the candles in the reverse order that she lit them. She left only the red candle lit.

"May this remaining light, the heart of our order, ever remain lit in our hearts." She made eye contact with each initiate in turn. "You all have done well. You are all now proud seekers of the teeth and a priest of TAMO as are all those here today. Please follow your guide. He will take you back to where you will receive your new clothes."

She walked clockwise again back to retrieve the dragon's head and left through a previously unseen back door.

The sacred speaker followed in the same clockwise pattern down to the east and out the door in the back.

The guardian whispered, "Follow me. For the day has begun! All shall circle the altar table clockwise then return to the land of the living."

They followed him, walking with him around the altar and finally arriving at the door in the back of the hall.

He opened the door into the room. It revealed an anteroom and an elevator to take them up from the great temple hall. It rose three floors.

As they exited the elevator, the guardian held up a hand to detain them. "We are above the dining hall you were in last night.

Use the two washrooms to wash up and don your new golden robes. Then come down the stairs to the dining room and join us for brunch, where you may again communicate with all. The details of this ritual you shall never reveal to anyone who has not been through the trial of the dragon. Reveal this ritual and, surely, you will die."

He left them and took the stairs to the dining room. Voices and the scents of food traveled up the stairway past him.

Steve cleaned up, changed quickly, and went down for a meal. The stress of the morning left him tired. Rob looked drained as well.

During the meal, the other TAMO members were friendly and congratulatory.

After everyone ate their fill of food, the imperial grand master approached the newly initiated.

She shook each of their hands. "To begin with, please call me Julie. You have earned the right to call me by my first name. Tomorrow morning, you two, the imperial grand councilor, and I will share an early breakfast, then study part of the original Dragon's Prophecy. Until then, feel free to go back to your cabins or explore the grounds.

"I want you to know the person who screamed last night, and the one today are not dead. They are special people who know how to emulate the anguish of death verbally and mentally. They have left the compound, for their job has been completed."

Steve felt much better knowing that the deaths had not been real but only part of the pageantry of the initiation. He decided to go back to his cabin after brunch. The return walk was a much different experience than the morning walk to the temple. The new golden hooded robe provided comfortable warmth as he left the dining hall and entered the outside. The golden boots, though thin as fine paper and made of the same material as the robe, kept his feet warm even in the snow.

When he entered the cabin, he found a second set of clothes, a golden robe, red sash, and golden boots. The garments waited for him on the bed. Steve removed his clothes, turned on the shower, and steamed hot water poured over him. He washed from head to toe and stood in the flowing water, thinking of the exhilarating ritual. At last, refreshed, he toweled dry. His mind was finally at ease. He went out and placed the new temple clothes next to the bed, pulled down the covers, hopped in, and covered himself up.

He communicated with Sandy for the first time in almost twenty-four hours. *I love you. I have passed the ordeal and am initiated. I am going to sleep.*

The response came right back. *Wonderful news. I love you too. Sleep well.*

When Steve woke up the next morning, a thought came into his mind.

Sandy, do you know what a quantum entanglement is?

Even though it was still the early hours in the morning, Sandy replied immediately. *No, what is it?*

I think it explains how we can communicate at any distance instantaneously. Like certain subatomic particles, all the Tankers linked their minds individually and collectively. It doesn't matter if we are separated by a few inches or thousands of miles, we can feel and hear one another.

Steve, how scientific of you... and so romantic. This subatomic particle is going back to sleep. Love you. See you in a couple of days.

Love you too, Sandy.

Return to Toronto

During the ensuing three days after the initiation into the Thirteenth Level, the Center of Silence leaders filled Steve and Rob's time with reading and translations of various mythologies and copies of the Dragon Prophecy. Steve and Rob were given access to a great deal of material they never knew existed. With help from the imperial grand master, imperial grand councilor, sacred speaker, and other members of the center, they gained an understanding of the various manuscripts which today make up the Dragon Prophecy. With this information the gifted ones would help TAMO achieve their ancient goal of finding the keys and the treasure for mankind.

Steve examined much of the material by reading the pages and turning them as quickly as he could focus on them. Later, he could review the material from his eidetic memory and turn the information into knowledge. Discussions with the others came down to knowing with high confidence the location of seven of the twelve Dragon's Teeth. Sometimes the writings referred to these differently as the keys.

These seven keys, based on the Dragon Prophecy, were located in various places all around the world; at the Vatican in a secret library, on the Nazca Plains in the hand of the spaceman, at the center of the Siberian Tunguska blast, at Stonehenge in England, in Zambia behind Victoria Falls, high in the Himalayan Mountains at the Drepung Monastery of the Dalai Lama, and the last tooth they were sure of was in the eye of the Ohio Serpent Mound.

The Center of Silence leaders would focus on the location of the other keys while the team of gifted ones located these seven. The one admonition, repeated over and over by the dragon in the texts, read, "Ye must understand my ways to seek my teeth. If you do not follow my instructions, ye shall surely die."

They had gained a great deal of knowledge about the Dragon Prophecy and the location of the teeth. On their flight home, Rob and Steve mentally conversed about the challenges ahead. Back and forth, they reviewed the knowledge they had learned.

Unlike the flight to the Center of Silence, the first leg of the flight was not hidden from them. As new Thirteenth Level members of TAMO, nothing was hidden from them. Even so, they only knew they would end up back in Toronto when they landed. The same woman piloted the plane. The young stewardess, they now knew, was the sacred speaker. Rob and Steve knew no one on the plane could read their thoughts.

During a break from their mental discussion, the sacred speaker came by to ask if they wanted anything to drink. As she retreated down the aisle, Rob, being single, studied her closely.

She is such a beautiful woman. I want to spend my time on this short flight trying to get to know her better before we land at the Toronto airport.

You said something like that on the way to the center. Steve looked at her and wondered what Rob saw in her.

Rob bit his lower lip. *She is definitely my type: metaphysically oriented, shorter than me but not too short, blonde hair, and those ocean-blue eyes. Not to mention her rockin' body!*

Rob, I honestly hadn't noticed her looks. How are you going to find out anything if she won't let you in?

Rob's gaze met Steve's. *We each have been learning about our Tanker abilities and how to better communicate with those who do not have our gift. Believe it or not, when I was younger, I was particularly good at conversations with women. One of the things I have learned since our minds opened, even though you cannot read their thoughts, skin contact allows us to receive at least their emotions, and sometimes everything is open to us. Most "normal" have not learned to block that level of information from us.*

Steve nodded, recalling the woman in the bar he was able to read once he made physical contact with her. He chuckled. *I will watch and learn, oh, great master!*

Though the woman was a petite cutie, Steve had no interest at all in bedding her. She could not compare to the love of his life.

The sacred speaker came by to deliver their drinks. Rob took his drink and put it in the armchair cup holder.

"Excuse me, miss. We have seen you in a stewardess uniform, in a formal gown, and in the golden hooded robe of the sacred speaker. We have talked about the keys with you, the imperial grand master, and the imperial grand councilor for several days. Yet, no one has ever formally introduced us. So, if I may... My name is Robert Stanley Worthy. My friends call me Rob. My companion is Steve Henry Johnson. And your name is..."

Rob paused and waited for her to answer.

The woman's white skin turned a pale pink. "I'm so sorry... Rob. In all of the excitement, everyone assumed we all had been introduced. My name is Nancy Elizabeth Cromwell, from the British Cromwell line. My friends call me 'Nan,' except when I'm in my spiritual garb, when I am only addressed as 'Sacred Speaker.'"

She held out her hand for Steve to shake, which he did with a firm grip. She turned from pink to an even darker red as she also shook hands with Rob.

Rob gestured to the seat next to him. "If you don't have other current duties, would you like to sit with us and become better acquainted?"

Her eyebrows lifted along with the corners of her mouth. She immediately sat and began absentmindedly to buckle her seatbelt. Rob reached over, pulling both of her hands away with one hand while he used his free hand to buckle her seatbelt.

Nan reddened an even darker red. Even the center part in her blonde hair turned crimson.

Rob was succeeding. The obvious connection between the two lightened Steve's heart and made him miss Sandy.

He mentally contacted and opened a full link to his mind, eyes, ears, and nose so she could experience the whole adventure.

"Nan, we know so little about you," Rob commented in a quiet voice. "You know I am a Tanker, one of the gifted ones mentioned in the Dragon Prophecy, and I know you have read my dossier. You know all about me. So, would you please share more about you? I am interested to know how you came to attain your position with the center at such a young age. Where did you come from? Tell me all you are willing to tell."

Steve noticed Rob had dropped all his mental walls of protection, at least as far as Nan was concerned. Rob had done the same for Steve. Nan's thoughts could now reach both Steve and Sandy.

The touch of her hands when Rob helped her buckle her seatbelt must have done the trick because, right now, almost all her walls were down too.

Steve could feel the positive thoughts flowing from her.

"Well, my family is from Britain. My distant ancestor was Oliver Cromwell. Few knew it, but Oliver Cromwell was deep into metaphysics." *And wizardry.*

Her thought came clearly through to Rob, so Steve and Sandy must have heard Nan's internal commentary too.

"The imperial grand master of that time taught him a great deal about the laws of nature. Needless to say, Cromwell used them to his advantage as he rose to power. Part of his power can be attributed to my ancestor, his secret mistress." *Rumored to be a witch.* "They never married. Back then, it was common for great men not to marry their 'commoner' girlfriends."

Rob touched her hand and left his hand there as he nodded his understanding.

She glanced down at their hands and her cheeks became rosy again, but she didn't pull away. "Down through the ages, the women in my family were aligned with..." *Witchcraft.* "Uh, metaphysics. Someone from TAMO would help teach each generation of children in the family. The teachers paid special attention to anyone in the family with an aptitude for—*the magical arts*—metaphysics.

"Everyone in our family tree learned to read at a young age. Even though it was not legal for a woman to read in many of those generations. When my grandmother grew old enough, she moved to the United States. She fell in love with the master of the New York Albany TAMO Lodge. He taught her about the Dragon's Teeth, at least a little anyway." *Should I reveal how much he actually taught her about the keys and what was known about them? Probably better not.* "Like her ancestor, she became pregnant. The master loved her so much he married her after my mother was born.

"My mother followed in the family tradition. She learned all about the Dragon's Teeth from Grandma and, like all of the female first-born in my family, she got pregnant, and I was born out of wedlock as the daughter of a TAMO master." Nan looked down at the floor away from Rob. She seemed embarrassed about that part of the family history. Changing the subject a little made her cool down and focus on her story.

"She, like most of the females in my family, had fallen in love with a TAMO master. Her love hailed from Toronto. When she found out she was pregnant, she convinced him to marry her. She moved into his home in Toronto where I was born, just weeks before the wedding. She learned as much as she could about TAMO and climbed up through the ranks of the organization. She continued to learn more; she became indispensable to the organization. To help me in my growth, she also legally changed my name to our ancestral name of Cromwell."

Nan separated from Rob. She rose and went to the back of the plane. She returned with a drink of her own. Without even thinking she sat down, put on her seatbelt, and placed her hand back on Rob's and looked at him with great regard and a soft smile.

"When the dollar collapsed in the United States, TAMO lost only a small portion of their money. They had, for years, hoarded gold, silver, and gems... also stocks. My mother realized the world was becoming volatile. She felt the necessity to hide TAMO's headquarters to save it from prying eyes. Somehow, she knew the time to use the Dragon Prophecy to discover the keys would come soon. TAMO bought ten square miles of property in a location I cannot tell you."

Nan didn't specifically think about expressing where the Center of Silence was located, but a map of Nova Scotia, following mental images of an older resort some two hundred miles north of Halifax, popped into her mind. It looked like a precursor to the reconditioned facility the Tankers had finished visiting.

Nan abruptly stopped talking. Her mental walls came up in a flash and her lips tightened in worry.

Rob saw her concerned facial expression. Even with her Thirteenth Level training, the pleasant chat had her anxious about what she might have revealed. Her eyes went down, and she stared at his hand on hers.

Rob softly stroked her hand. The more he lightly touched her, the more the walls in her mind again descended.

"What's wrong, Nan? Why have you stopped talking?" he asked in a soothing tone.

I've liked this Rob since I first saw his handsome face. I want to tell him everything. She tingled as he spoke.

Rob tilted his head and raised his eyebrows in question to her. "Please go on."

Nan smiled a big smile and shook her head slightly. "My mother found the location—an old, dilapidated resort. With help from Thirteenth Level lodge masters from all over the world, the Center of Silence was renovated with the addition of the dragon's temple. All of the lodge masters had known my mother for many years and were sworn to silence about the location of the temple. You two have also met my mother...Julie, the imperial grand master."

Both Steve and Rob were shocked. They looked at each other with eyes wide in disbelief. When they calmed down, they looked at each other and then they turned to see Nan. They now looked at Nan completely differently.

"That is how I became the sacred speaker. I, too, have worked in many of the positions of TAMO and finally achieved the Thirteenth Level. As you know, the mysticism which is part of our organization goes back more than 30,000 years. Our knowledge even precedes the rise of the Egyptians. We all feel we are now approaching the time of the Dragon's Teeth and the great treasure that will become available for mankind. The rejuvenation has given us the 'gifted ones' talked about in the Dragon Prophecy. TAMO is ready to begin the search. All the signs are evident."

Rob gently stroked Nan's hand and spoke to her in a relatively low voice. "Yes, Nan please tell us more about you. Tell me about your early life."

"Oh, I guess I am getting off topic about me. You asked about me rather than the organization. Let me go back a few years. I mentioned being born in Toronto. That was twenty-six years ago. My mother's husband originally came from a French-speaking family. As I grew up, I became fluent in French. Even as a young child, I enjoyed playing in the Toronto lodge when no one was there. I pretended I was the master of the lodge."

Rob gently squeezed her hand. "That's somewhat of a harbinger of your family's future. How did your mom become the imperial grand master?"

"Well, my father was wealthy in his own right. He had taken his family's meager resources and used the metaphysical tools of TAMO to turn it into a fortune. When he died and went through transition, ten years ago, my mother became the master of the Toronto lodge and a very wealthy woman. Then, when the former imperial grand master started to lose his health, my mother grew close to him. Perhaps because of her intelligence, foresight, or simply her intense involvement, he considered her a likely replacement for him. Her fortune didn't hamper the situation either. So, he taught her all he knew about the Dragon's Teeth. When he passed through transition, the lodge masters throughout the world voted her in as the new imperial grand master. While I could not read people's minds, I could sense what they felt." *Like now, I can sense you want me as much as I want you.*

Nan moved her hand but held Rob's hand firmly for a moment. They both smiled that *I think you are special* smile at each other. Nan gently separated her hand from Rob's, unbuckled her seatbelt, and stood. She put up all her mental walls, at least she thought so.

"Rob, I have to prepare the meals for the captain and the rest of us. Would you give me a hand?" *Come with me now so we can join the mile high club together.*

The two of them left hand-in-hand. When they entered the galley, they pulled the curtain closed.

Once Steve heard Nan think to Rob, *Take me! Take me now!* His gentlemanly instincts required him to raise his walls to give them some privacy. Even so, he had to smile. The sounds coming from the galley were definitely not cooking sounds. At least not food cooking.

Sandy caught the thought from Steve and replied with a mental chuckle. After that, she sent a mental image of what little she was wearing. Steve smiled to himself and closed his eyes to dream of his lady love.

Needless to say, no meals were served before landing in Toronto. The last time Steve saw Nan was after disembarking. Back up the stairs, Rob was giving Nan a kiss for the ages. Within his arms, she stood on one leg with her other leg "popped" at the knee. Classic.

Phoenix Bound

On the flight from Toronto to Phoenix, Rob told Steve, "I can't explain it, but Nan seemed to know almost everything I was thinking. Sort of like a person who can see shapes and colors without their glasses but cannot see details. She is different. When we made love, something changed between us. While physically touching, my thoughts were plain to her. It was like she was a Tanker. When we stopped touching, though, my thoughts and senses muddied up. But I could still sense a lot from her."

Steve had not heard of this happening between a Tanker and a "normal." But, then again, Nan's ancestry did not quite make her a full-fledged "normal." From beginning to end, Steve had left a mental door open to Sandy so she could stream all her thoughts and other information.

Steve's mood soared as the plane landed. In minutes, he would see her.

Sandy made a very emphatic mental call. *Get out here right now! Our limo is waiting, and we are taking the long way home. Tell Rob to find his own way back to the hotel.*

As Rob finally came down the stairs from the plane, Steve slapped Rob heartily on the back. "Fellow, you are going to have to find your own ride back to the Hyatt. I have a private limo waiting with my fiancée in it."

Rob gave him a thumbs up and walked the other way to find a vehicle for himself.

At the outer door of the airport, a black Mercedes stretch limo awaited Steve. Attached to its side, a stylized hand-printed sign read, "Limo of Love for Steve Johnson." He opened the door and a slender black-gloved hand held out a glass of champagne.

"If you are ready to ride, your ride awaits," said a sexy voice from the inside. "Driver, take us to Carefree, please, and do not go fast. Take the most scenic route."

Steve stepped into the car, took the glass, and shut the door. Sandy wore the same outfit she had imaged to him at the Center of Silence. He glanced at her with narrowed seductive eyes. He knew this was going to be a long and welcome homecoming ride.

☆☆☆

Nan flew down to Phoenix every other week for the weekend. On alternate weeks, Rob flew to Toronto. Everyone who saw them together over the previous couple of months found it quite obvious the pair was in love. Per Steve, the new couple's connection was the same as Sandy and Steve had experienced, with the exception that, with Sandy's permission, Steve could read his partner from miles away. For Nan, the link happened only when they touched. At those times, she could hear, see, feel, and smell all the things Rob did.

One of her weeks in Phoenix, Rob acted and felt distant. Aside from the first night, they had not made love and barely even touched. Nan's heart dropped a beat every time he withdrew from her touch or closed down her advances, even to just talk seriously. Something he refused to share with her was causing his actions and she didn't like it one bit.

At the end of the weekend, he opened up only a little just before leaving. With his last touch, he relayed, *Nan, I must focus on the predicament I am in. I don't want to block you out, but I must. The person I am working with has a strong mental image of themselves and is attempting to force thoughts onto me. You'll need to find another ride to the airport.*

Nan called Sandy to talk about her distress. They had become great friends since she and Rob had been dating and, when she was in Phoenix, they double dated. With Rob holding her hand, the link between the four of them was complete, like four Tankers together. During one of these double dates, Rob had promised to love her until the end of time and never to block her from his mind.

Sandy came to pick up Nan. After Rob broke his promise to her, the two women sat in Sandy's car for her sob session.

After crying herself out, Nan grabbed her phone and broke it in half. "I never want to speak to that horrible man again!"

Feeling consoled enough by her supportive friend, Nan actually found the desire to make her flight back to Toronto.

As Sandy drove her toward the airport, she said, "Rob has a good reason to shut you out. Trust him and give it some time."

Completely drained, she gathered her luggage from the trunk and hugged and thanked her friend. Before entering the terminal, she turned, half raised her hand, and simply mouthed, "Goodbye."

Treasure Ritual

The imperial grand master, the imperial grand councilor, and other students of archeology had spent decades trying to interpret the meaning of the Dragon Prophecy. They had many false starts due to misinterpretations. The Dragon Prophecy had been written over multiple centuries by priests in different cultures and various countries. Their purpose had been to tell the story about where the keys could be found but hide the knowledge in various allegories.

All who had examined the Dragon Prophecy knew it alluded to a treasure for the advancement of mankind. The current team was trying to work out the location of the treasure talked about in the Dragon Prophecy.

An intern who enjoyed her hobby of being an astronomer gave them a clue. She had been looking at old images from various space satellites and ran across notes and images of Phobos, a gray-surfaced moon orbiting Mars. Satellite images SPS252603 and SPS255103 had been taken around 1998 by the Mars Global Surveyor. The space exploration leaders of the day had planned to land on Phobos and examine what they called a "monolith."

The flight never happened. The young intern theorized the "Hand of Mars" mentioned in the Dragon Prophecy was one of the moons of Mars. When the Dragon Prophecy talked about how Mars coveted the treasure and looked at it every six hours, it became plain the prophecy meant the moon Phobos which circled Mars every six hours. In the article about the satellite, the scientist notated a boulder eighty-five meters across like a towering obelisk. This combination of information made it plain to the team they had probably found their end goal. The location of the treasure.

An earlier Russian scientist theorized Phobos was a hollow moon. Later, scientists indicated it was probably large pieces of gray rock held together by gravity. Either scenario might yield a positive result for the TAMO searchers.

The imperial grand master dispatched the imperial grand councilor to Phoenix to assemble twelve of the fourteen gifted people. Nate had requested only Nadia come to greet him upon his arrival, based on the strong feelings they still harbored for one another. He had a professional TAMO reason to single her out as well.

Nadia had learned English but preferred to remain quiet. Most of her life she had been deaf, so speaking was not a habit. For that reason, Nate wanted to talk with her and her alone.

Of all the Tankers, she was the only one who could be thought of as a "quiet one," as mentioned in the Dragon Prophecy.

The relevant phrase read: "The quiet one shall be the center of the sign in a place of death. Along with eleven companions, the group of seekers shall lift up from the Earth and fly near to the hand of Mars. There, they will dare to awaken the dragon in a loving manner at the time of the Dragon's Teeth. Come to the dragon in love or surely ye shall die."

Over dinner, Nate touched her hand and quietly explained the passage to his quiet one. He described the plan to perform a ritual from the Dragon Prophecy. Since it was being done for the first time, they did not know the exact risk. He told her of his love, and he felt they could do the ritual correctly. TAMO's plan, which included only twelve Tankers, including her as the primary.

Over dinner, Nate touched her hand to set their private mind link.

My sweet woman. I love you so much. He gripped her hand with gentle strength. *This is our first attempt at following the instructions of the Dragon Prophecy. As with hunting for the teeth, the passage ends with "surely ye shall die." If we don't do the ritual correctly, your life could be forfeited. Because it says to do this in a "loving manner," we shall succeed. I love you and I just know that is what will make it all work. Love.*

Nate, I love you too. I believe all of your knowledge of the prophecy will keep me safe, and I trust you too. I agree to play my part even though I might not survive.

☆ ☆ ☆

The following morning, the team would fly out to Death Valley and prepare the ritual to happen at high noon. Rob was still not answering the call to service, and Lindsey was still in Paris on her modeling photo shoot. In addition to the twelve Tankers, Nate invited the intern who had interpreted the passage to come on the trip.

Nate made sure the team left the hotel at five in the morning to fly to their destination by helicopter. Dan Wright piloted the two-hour trip from Phoenix to Death Valley in California. He landed the team near the lowest point in the valley, 282 feet below sea level.

Upon arrival, everyone ate a light lunch with lots of liquids to keep up their strength and hydration.

The imperial grand councilor and the intern who had made the discovery, went to the lowest spot using a state of the art GPS and marked the point. They cleared all the brush, stones, and other debris within an approximately forty-five-foot radius. From the center point, they unraveled twine thirty feet long to help draw a circle. The young woman stood at the point holding one end of the twine while he pulled the line taught and carefully walked 360 degrees around her while marking the circle in the dirt with a rod.

He used a compass to find true north and created a north-south line which started from the northern point of the circle through the center point and back out to the circle, making a perfectly straight line. He did the same process to create an east-west line which touched the edge of the circle on the east and west sides. With the designation of east as the top of the drawing, he drew an extended line eastward ten feet. The imperial grand councilor also extended, by ten feet, the north and south lines from where they intersected the circle. He treated the west line in a different manner. It extended twenty feet from the circle. Nate observed the first symbol of his work. A great cross had been formed using perfect geometry.

Inside the circle, using a similar process, the team of two created a six-sided polygon with north and south as points of the polygon. East and west bisected a side of the polygon, creating six points as a reference. With the six points of the polygon touching the circle, the two diagrammers created a six-pointed star made up of two triangles. One triangle pointed east and the other pointed west. If they flew above the diagram, Nate knew they would see a design similar to the TAMO symbol.

All prepared, the imperial grand councilor was sure he had made the design correctly. It was time to assemble the team for the ritual.

When they returned to the lunch area, the leader called the Tankers together. He instructed each of the participants to stand at a specific point marked on the physical diagram just created. Nadia went to the center point.

The imperial grand councilor and Steve went into the helicopter and changed. When they came out, they both wore gold hooded robes with red sashes and gold boots. Nate walked to the northeast of the design. Steve walked to the point west of the center near Nadia.

The imperial grand councilor held up a hand until he had everyone's attention.

"Under the auspices of the imperial grand master of TAMO, I bring you hidden knowledge. I will not be able to hear your thoughts, but you should be able to hear mine. I will start the thought and direct it to Sandy in the eastern-most point."

He laid out how the thoughts were to be transmitted from one member to the next and back again. Each was to repeat what Sandy thought, then pass it along to the next in order.

He was specific that no thoughts should be directed to Nadia until the ritual end point. When the conclusion of the ritual came, all were to direct their thoughts to her, and she was to direct her thoughts up and out.

"Let us begin."

The imperial grand councilor pointed at Sandy and produced the strongest thought and image he could.

From deep in the Earth, pull the strength of the love of Gaia into your being and send it to the next in the chain. Each time the thought returns to you again pull the love energy from Mother Gaia. When the chain has traveled twelve times to you, link with all of your brethren and send the energy to Nadia.

It took less than five minutes. As Sandy received the end of the twelve rounds, Nate watched as Steve walked forward to surround Nadia with his arms and robe. He concentrated along with the other ten.

At that second, Nadia opened her mind to Nate with the thought, *I shall love you forever!* She started again but only sent the one thought out: *Love.*

That single word made things happen.

Nadia lit up bright red. Steve's golden hooded robe glowed the brightest gold the imperial grand councilor had ever seen. Red light streamed out of Nadia's head for almost thirty seconds. The energy powered straight up like the beam of a tightly focused laser beam.

After the light stopped flowing from Nadia, nothing happened for more than six minutes. At that time a blue beam of light shot down along the same path the red light had risen. Nate watched the beam go into Nadia until she turned a solid glowing blue. Then it spread from Nadia to Steve and out to all the remaining participants. An indescribable sense of Love filled and overflowed from the team to him, causing every nerve in his body to sing with his own love for Nadia.

As abruptly as the blue light arrived, it ended. Nadia collapsed.

Steve caught her and picked her up in his arms.

Nate couldn't contain his fear, "Take her to the shade!"

Steve carried her to the shade inside the helicopter. Nate followed closely and could see she was still breathing, but barely. He yelled for everyone to board the aircraft as quickly as possible. Dan Wright hopped back into the pilot's seat last, and the chopper took flight toward Phoenix.

The takeoff happened less than five minutes after Nadia's collapse. While Nate held Nadia's hand, he heard nothing from her. No thoughts at all. As they flew back to Phoenix, Briana Goldsmith put her nursing skills to good use to give Nadia oxygen, plasma, and liquids.

None of the Tankers said a word or released one thought about the energy they had received during the ceremony. They concentrated on directing their Love energy to their unconscious comrade. Nate didn't know how they knew, or decided, to do that but through his connection to her, he felt the energy of their love sent as one accord.

After about half an hour, Nadia blinked awake and glanced around. She smiled at Nate. "What happened, did it work?"

He pressed her hand, gratitude nearly bursting his heart. "We'll know soon."

The Kitt Peak National Observatory outside of Tucson had not contacted the team with any news. Once he knew Nadia would be okay, the imperial grand councilor made a call to check in.

The observatory had been watching Mars the whole day and said it would be an hour before they could see Phobos again.

Almost exactly an hour later, the observatory called back. The group's leader listened briefly, then put the call through the copter's headphones so all could hear.

"It's not there!" the man on the other end nearly shouted. "It is as if a cloak has been lifted. Where the grey rocky globe of Phobos used to be, there is a metallic silver sphere. Plainly not a natural, nor human-made object. This is not going to be easy to keep quiet."

The imperial grand councilor asked a couple of other questions, thanked the scientist, and ended the call.

So, the location of the treasure has been found. Now we only need the twelve keys. He was sure the whole team heard his thoughts through his connection with Nadia.

With Nadia's hand in his, he smiled for the rest of the flight to Phoenix.

The New Phobos

The man at the observatory had been right. As night came to different parts of the world, observatories noticed the big change to the moon of Phobos as it circled Mars. The once dull-gray moon now shone bright in the Sun's reflection because its surface appeared metallic silver. The Canary Islands observatory on the island of Tenerife started an international frenzy as its astronomers posted continuous images of Mars and Phobos on the internet.

The photos of what had been called the giant Stickney Crater on Phobos, looked like it could now be a giant opening like a landing bay for a giant spacecraft. Just like the face seen in satellite pictures of Mars, this change to Phobos prompted people throughout the world to believe in aliens. The metallic-looking orb of Phobos made them believe there was absolute proof showing itself in the night sky.

Throughout the world, governments were trying to decide if any action needed to be taken. No individual government had any idea of what should be done. The United Nations convened an emergency Security Council meeting to discuss the revelation, but it would take weeks or maybe months for the international organization to act.

Several groups, including the Traditional Ancient Mystical Order, knew what had to be done and began starting their preparations. One group TAMO had been watching for centuries, the Ancient Universal Knowledge Association, had a large contingent in the Phoenix area, and TAMO conjectured that Phoenix might even be AUKA's headquarters.

Both Steve and Rob had spent several days after the Thirteenth Level Initiation with the imperial grand master discussing the Dragon's Prophecy and what was known about the keys. Members of the Center of Silence in Northeast Canada acted as the support team for this venture. The imperial grand master had explained to Steve and Rob how TAMO had spent centuries building a fortune in funds to locate and find the mystical treasure of knowledge. She explained how, over the years, hundreds of billions of dollars had been spent. Even though it was only a fraction of their current wealth, those billions had been used to maintain contacts of all types with people, companies, and religious organizations throughout the world. It was time to call in favors from those in their network.

The imperial grand master knew the keys, or the dragon's teeth as they referred to them in the Dragon Prophecy, were really relics kept after the destruction of Atlantis. She expected something to happen to the moon Phobos following the desert ceremony. Only after others at the observatory confirmed the discovery of how Phobos' appearance changed from that of a small moon that orbited Mars to a created silver object did she recognize a hint about the purpose of the keys.

She started a two-pronged venture. First, find the keys. Second, find a way to travel to Phobos to use them.

Finding the keys would be an adventure in itself. In addition to the prophecy, myths and legends added to the material associated with the prophecy. The first key would require talking to the current pope and gaining access to an ancient book kept deep underground in one of the many secret Vatican libraries.

The imperial grand master remained on speaking terms with the current Pope, who had risen from a humble American Cardinal to the most powerful man in the Catholic Church.

In prior years and centuries, some of the religious politicking issues had been handled by an imperial grand master of TAMO, which led to positive resolutions for various popes. The current Pope understood what had to be done and had previously agreed to help when and if the time came.

The imperial grand master and the imperial grand councilor agreed two of the new gifted ones, including a Thirteenth Level initiate, should visit Rome. They decided Steve Johnson should go with his fiancée, Sandra Haspure, who made a good team. Both had the gift, and their love for each other would make them more cautious.

The imperial grand master called Steve directly.

"Steve, this is Julie Bernard. It is time to start your service in search of the Dragon's Teeth."

She explained the mission for him and Sandy to pursue the Vatican key as a team.

Steve's heartbeat quickened. *A quest!*

"I am honored, and am sure Sandy will be, as well. Shall we use our TAMO credit cards for our travel and expenses?"

"I have already sent two special credit cards via express delivery to you. They should arrive within the hour. During everything you do for this venture, do not be cheap. Travel first class all the way.

"You must fly to Rome as soon as possible. While you are on your way, I will request a special note from the Pope that will be delivered to your hotel. The note will gain you access to whatever you need. Once you arrive in Rome, you must retrieve a specific book from a special Vatican Library."

The imperial grand master described the book based on information the center had retrieved over the years. She told Steve to photograph the information in the book and send the photos in encrypted files to the Center.

Steve made mental notes and passed them to Sandy, along with Julie's request to team up with him on the mission. Before ending the call, both enthusiastically agreed to help, and thanked Julie for her confidence in choosing them for the important project.

★★★

The imperial grand master's next big issue involved securing transport from Earth to Phobos. Even this was associated with some lucky guesses TAMO had made back in the beginning of the century.

Around 2010, Sir Richard Branson declared he would go into space with his company Virgin Galactic. His company was later renamed, The Spaceship Company. TSC designed and built the craft which would eventually reach space. Branson needed money because he wanted to be the sole owner of TSC. The other partners of the company were bought out in 2012. TAMO's connection with Sir Richard Branson made it happen. The organization was willing to put up all the money for the buyout and become a silent partner.

In the years since 2010, the dream of passengers traveling into sub-orbit had been achieved. Even when the world economy crashed and the dollar dropped to one one-tenth of its original value, people still wanted to go into space. When the new dollar was issued, the multi-billionaires still had plenty of money and happily paid the 200,000 new dollars for those early rides into space. With additional money from TAMO and the success of the sub-orbital flights, TSC built crafts that could go into orbit and safely return.

By 2030, the world economy had again begun to prosper, and TSC built its first hotel in space. Travel to the hotel had become reasonable. The trip cost only 40,000 new dollars to fly from the Colorado TSC space center to the space hotel in low Earth orbit. For a twenty-four-hour stay in the hotel, the price was only 5,000 new dollars.

The hotel venture went well. The orbiting hotel profits, and more infusions of cash from the TAMO organization, allowed the creation of a space shipyard for building heavy spacecraft. These crafts were destined to remain only in space. They did not need to deal with gravity to leave Earth's atmosphere, so did not need a streamlined design. Only landing craft had to be able to climb out of an atmosphere on their own.

Those new crafts would be used for travel to the moon where the Virgin Moon Group had set up a permanent colony. Personnel and supplies were brought up from Earth. The lower gravity meant people would not have as many issues as they grew older. First-class engineers about to end their careers on Earth because of age could move to the moon for a second career. Also, the lower gravity, and a simulated vacuum, allowed certain kinds of manufacturing not possible on Earth. Things like semiconductors could be created without the flaws induced by heavy gravity.

As the various Virgin Groups prospered, so did their silent partner TAMO.

The plan for a Martian landing had been in the works since Sir Richard first proclaimed it in 2015. When the holograms which hid the real Phobos were removed by the TAMO ritual, the need to reach it became urgent. However, it would take a great deal of convincing for the Virgin Mars Group to change their first destination. Instead of going to Mars they would have to change the destination to Phobos.

The Library

Sam's days in the Camelback mansion consisted of studying the information about the two organizations and details of the lost keys. Of course, she also enjoyed a great deal of shopping. Her frequent distractions with Mario to show off her purchases, and other pursuits, had stopped recently. She missed him.

Finally, only days after the Phobos news, Sam received an unexpected mental caller. The Tanker delivered a mental thought. She was not familiar with any of the Tanker's mental signatures so she couldn't even guess who it could have been. The thought was clear and precise: *They are going after the first key. It will be found in a Vatican secret library as part of a book hidden by the librarian. Find the TAMO team and get the librarian to talk, any way you can.*

The person transmitted a mental image of a note of introduction. Sam took out a notepad and wrote down what she saw in her mind. A minute later she took a photo of it and sent it to Mario.

He called her right back. "Sam, be prepared to head to Rome and the Vatican in the next several hours. I will make sure a team is in place to help you locate and capture the information we need."

"I'm packing some clothes right now. I will take the first flight out. Set up my hotel at the Gran Mélia Rome near the Vatican. I think it is the best in the area. Will I see you there, sweetie?"

Sam remembered the many nights with Mario since her rejuvenation. She had not seen him in several weeks, aside from his digital image on phone calls. She wanted to be in his presence and show him how nice a young Samantha could continue to be.

Mario didn't look angry when he spoke to her. His voice was still pleasant. Yet, an underlying edge to the tone did not sound like his normal sweet self. His image on the phone also showed him crinkling his brow in worry.

"No, I won't be there when you arrive. If you succeed in your mission, I will try to be the one to pick up the book from you. Talk to you soon."

He hung up.

That was it, short, terse, and not very emotionally satisfying. But Sam had a plane to catch.

I'm going to bring home the goods. I will personally give it to Mario.

She giggled at her double entendre.

☆ ☆ ☆

Steve and Sandy's flight from Phoenix to Rome was nonstop. Two hours after takeoff, the couple arrived. They stopped at the hotel only to pick up the note and drop off their backpacks containing a day's worth of clothes. They expected a short stay in The City of Fountains.

The Vatican held many vast hidden libraries and only select people were allowed to enter them. The imperial grand councilor had produced and delivered to them the proper introduction letters. Steve's ability to speak and read Italian, and his ability to read Latin, would be particularly useful at the Vatican. A short cab drive brought them to Vatican City, the Pope's residence. The pair presented their special paper to one of the Swiss Guards at the first gate, where the cab dropped them off.

A runner delivered the papers to someone deep in the hidden center of the great church nation. They waited almost an hour before a positive response came back.

The guard escorted Steve and Sandy into the sub-subbasement by way of more than one-hundred-forty-four marble stairs and one-thousand steps through marble hallways. They finally came to a large door, ornately carved. The guard, who had said nothing, used a key to open the door. He indicated for the visitors to enter, then locked the door behind them. Steve found it slightly unnerving.

The large room offered very little light, though unlit lamps lined multiple rows of old tables. As his eyes adapted to the dimness, he could make out ancient markings on the tables from ancient readers and scholars of the past. Bookshelves lined the walls surrounding them.

A man walked up. "I am the librarian. How may I help you?" His English sounded perfect.

Steve listened for any of the man's thoughts. Nothing.

He responded in perfect Italian, "Sir, my name is Steve Johnson, and this is my friend Sandra Haspure. We are in search of some of your oldest information. We are told you have ancient manuscripts with information about the Dragon's Teeth and where they are located."

It wouldn't have taken a mind reader to know what the librarian was thinking but it came in loud and clear. *More stupid treasure hunters. I'll give them some old false books and let them think they are real. I won't let them know about the handwritten copies.* His mental imagery showed a book cover with gold-leaf and pearl inlay.

Sandy glanced at Steve, who nodded.

She spoke to the librarian in a concerned voice. It was obvious by her rigid stance and half squinting eyes that she was serious. "We are looking for a special volume of information. It is a small book. Handwritten on pages edged with gold leaf. We are told the front has a beautiful pearl and gold inlay of the symbol of the Traditional Ancient Mystical Order. That would mean the front would be embossed with the Hermetic Cross with the Star of David in the center. Within the star is a flower with a ruby center."

The librarian's eyes widened slightly, and he bowed. "You two must be of the gifted twelve the Dragon Prophecy speaks. I will retrieve the book you seek."

No negative thoughts emanated from the librarian. He went off into one of the many heavy-laden bookshelves and climbed a decrepit ladder to reach the top shelf. He reached behind the stacks of books and pulled out the book they had been asked to search for. The librarian climbed down and handed the book to Sandy.

"I am honored to let you read this book about the prophecy. It is in Old Latin. I wish you luck in deciphering it."

Sandy accepted the book and nodded thanks to the man, who gestured to a table, then wandered away.

She sat next to Steve at one of the research tables, turned on the lamp, and started to examine the book cover. It was incredibly old, possibly 500 years. At the center of the symbol of TAMO emblazoned on the front, the large stone looked like a ruby carved in the shape of a rose.

Carefully opening the cover, Steve held the book while Sandy photographed its pages with her phone. She transmitted the photos of the manuscript to the TAMO Central Office in Northeastern Canada for review.

While waiting for a response, Steve read the cryptic Latin and translated it for Sandy. He hoped the central office could add something to make things easier to understand. When given enough information, Steve's stream-of-conscious thinking often took him to the answer. If he could understand only ten percent of the information as he read it in the book, he was sure he could formulate the remaining pieces in his mind. Unfortunately, his translation did not even give him five percent.

The answer came instead from the central office in the form of a phone text.

"Lift the TAMO symbol off of the book by turning it counterclockwise until the symbol is upside down. Then lift it away from the book."

Steve did as they suggested. The front cover opened like a second book. The first page contained a map of the southern part of

Peru. As told in the old stories, a single mark, an X, graced the page. An arrow pointed from one corner to the symbol on the map. The TAMO symbol was drawn on the handwritten map's lower corner. Latin text in the upper corner translated easily: *"One quarter of the twelve and a priest bringing their gifts together will lead to the Dragon's Tooth."*

They photographed the map but did not send it off. Its obvious secrets were too valuable. Common knowledge would entice a lot of people to fly to Peru on the hunt for the teeth of the dragon.

Steve closed the cover over the inner page with the map and resealed the cover, so it looked like a simple ancient book again. He suggested to Sandy they wait to find a more private place before contacting the TAMO Central Office about the map.

Steve called for the librarian. No one answered. The two listened for noise or thoughts but sensed neither a sound nor a thought. In the absolute silence, only their breathing sounded. They mentally talked about their situation. Something was not right. They shared a worried look of furrowed brows and pursed lips. They knew whatever had happened to the librarian was putting them in danger too. Steve decided to hide the book.

He quickly picked up the volume and ran into the stacks to the ladder. He turned the ladder around and backed it up against the next bookshelf, climbed up, and placed the book behind other titles on the shelf. He noted the number of books lined up from the end of the shelf. He climbed down and returned the ladder to its original place.

They went to the door they'd come in, but the door remained locked. They searched for a while to find another exit but found no obvious door. They decided to call for help. Earlier, when they had transmitted the handwriting of the book, their phones had a strong signal. Unfortunately, their phones could not access any signal at all in their moment of need.

Sandy mentally called out, *Rob, this is Sandy. Send a team to the Vatican Library to unlock the door we're behind and let us out. Contact Nate and explain. In case Steve and I don't make it, we hid the TAMO book behind books on the shelves across the aisle from where the librarian found it. Look for it on the twelfth stack of shelves on the top shelf, fifteenth book in from the wall side of the bookcase.*

Rob responded, *Got your message. Help is on its way. Be down there in one hour.*

Steve received the mental response as well via her mental door being open.

Right after the message came to them, unfamiliar voices rose from the far end of the library where they had searched but found no door.

The couple hid in a corner behind a short bookcase where they could just see the research tables. Four people walked into the room. Three burly men with gruff looks like thugs, and a young woman probably in her early twenties. Steve sort of recognized her. She looked like the woman who left Twelve-Gen during the first discussion. It couldn't be her, though, as she was the only one who did not enter the program. This woman must be a great-granddaughter.

The woman and the three thugs started by searching all around the research tables where they expected the book had been examined. They turned over every table to look for the volume and broke open any drawer or hiding place they could find.

Steve and Sandy cuddled closely behind the small book cart hoping not to be found. The others were not particularly looking for them. As the men and the woman ransacked the study area, the couple kept trying to maneuver their position so as not to be seen. When the men came to the right, Steve and Sandy shifted left, hoping the book cart would hide them. Unfortunately, their last move made things worse, the young woman spotted them.

"Boys, look what we have here. Two quiet little birdies hidden in the corner. Bring them out, strip off their clothes, gather up any electronic devices, then tie them up. The book isn't out here in this study area. Let's see if they will tell us where the book is. Maybe, I will just read their thoughts. In case that discussion doesn't work out, Mark, start searching the stacks for the book near where the librarian told us it would be. John and Alan take care of our little birdies."

Ms. Sampson took up a position to watch the men do their dirty work.

Mark looked disappointed that he wasn't going to get to do the physical interrogation. "Yes, Ms. Sampson."

So, she was likely *not* the great-granddaughter but, in fact, the lady who had left the program. Steve and Sandy glanced at each other and shared the same thought: *How did she get rejuvenated?*

"No last names, you idiot!" she shouted. "Now we have to be sure these two won't talk!"

When Mark didn't find the book in the open area, he walked down to the twelfth stack, apparently confident as to where he would find the book they wanted.

Steve caught a thought from the thug. *That librarian described the book exactly, and where it has been hidden in the stacks for years. Too bad he won't be around to clean up this mess.*

The shock on Sandy's face showed she had heard Mark's thoughts too. Steve's heart pounded. *This might be the end of things,* he thought as John grabbed him and pulled him up out of the corner.

Steve tried his best to protect Sandy. John must have been a body builder. He easily dragged Steve out into the middle of the floor and ripped off his clothes. John tied him to the top of one of the tables that remained standing, on his back, with each appendage tied to a different leg of the table. This left Steve naked, spread eagle, and totally vulnerable.

Alan stood blocking Sandy while John tied down his captive. When finished he scowled at Alan. "What are you waiting for, permission? Strip her while I sees if I can get this one to tell us where they have hidden the book." He then punched Steve in the ribs.

Alan examined the woman in front of him with a depraved look. "Now, I'm gonna enjoy *this* work."

The mental image of what he planned to do shocked even Sandy.

John hit Steve again, and the room reverberated with the sound of a rib cracking.

Alan laughed as he lifted Sandy out of the corner with one hand. He ripped off her shirt with the other.

"Don't touch me! Leave me alone!" Sandy took the opportunity to knee Alan's groin. With a groan, he bent slightly but held her even tighter.

"You bitch!" He punched her in the face so hard she went limp in his grip. "Well, now she's in the same condition as the girls I play with at the club." He chuckled.

Steve watched helplessly as Alan disrobed her slowly. First, he removed her bra. "Nice fun bags, they are definitely the right size." He squeezed and played with her breasts.

Steve struggled to break his bonds. He wanted to help his love. "You bastard! Leave her alone!"

John had made the bonds too tight for Steve to do anything but yell.

John grabbed Steve by his hair. "You gonna to tell us where you hid the book, fancy pants?"

Steve didn't say a word. John punched him multiple times in the face until Steve tasted blood on his lips. He couldn't see out of his left eye because it swelled so much. The punching continued.

Sandy had awoken but said nothing while pretending to still be unconscious. *This guy is disgusting. I can't believe what he is trying to do to me. Don't worry. I will survive this indignation.*

Relief flooded through Steve. *I love you, Sandy! Play possum as long as you can.*

Steve also went limp. His head turned slightly toward Sandy so he could see her. Beyond her, Ms. Sampson stood studying their phones. With the thought, *Has she somehow gotten past our passwords?* he pretended to black out. Steve hoped it would end the interrogation for a little time to allow him to regain his strength.

Alan licked Sandy's body wherever he removed a piece of clothing. It did not take long until Sandy lay naked. He tied her hands to a single table leg, stood up, and unzipped the zipper on his pants.

Mark had gone up the ladder on the bookcase where the librarian had said the book was but, of course, didn't find it. He started clearing all of the books one at a time and throwing them on the floor. Finished with the first bookcase, he went down the ladder and moved it to the bookcase on the other side of the aisle. Climbing to the top, he again started throwing books onto the floor. "Found it!" Mark called out from the top of the bookcase, holding the prize in his hand.

"Bring it over here!" Ms. Sampson yelled. "John, flip one of these overturned tables and grab me a chair. Alan, you zip it up and keep it in your pants. I think we got what we came for."

Beyond Sandy's table, John righted one of the research tables, found a lamp, turned it on, and held a chair for the woman. She sat down and Mark brought her the book. She looked it over, turning the book round and round.

"Without that note in your phone, I would never know to lift this symbol on the front to open the secret hiding place. There it is. See boys, we have the first key, a map to the next key, and some interesting text which might tell us more."

As she proudly raised the book and the map in the air, the gem in the middle of the TAMO symbol glowed a bright red. It was definitely one of the keys.

"Steve! Sandy!" The grating of a large metal key in the door lock followed a woman's voice. *Are you in there and are you okay?* Steve recognized Martha's thought.

The woman inside the room held up the book. "Well boys, we are going to have to cut your playtime short. We got what we need, so let's skedaddle."

The four headed out the hidden door they had used to enter the library, leaving Steve and Sandy's phones on the table. She must have figured she got from them what she needed. At almost the exact second, the main door opened.

Sandy opened her eyes and twisted herself up, still reeling from her physical molestation. *That man acted like an animal in heat. Ugh! Surely, I could have done something, somehow to stop him?* Tears threatened, but she held them back. Still, her shame at almost being raped made her need to hide as much of her nakedness as possible.

The Swiss Guardsman quickly came into the room and scanned it rapidly from side to side to locate the perpetrators.

Steve struggled with his bonds. "They went out the back way."

The guard headed in the direction Steve indicated.

Martha Felder stepped forward into the room, sizing up the situation. Her gaze landed on Steve still strapped to the table. "I can see what enhancements you had them make. Nice."

Sandy scoffed and Steve blushed from head to toe.

Martha giggled as she untied Steve's hands and legs. She attempted to clean his face with a handkerchief from her purse, but he resisted. The pain caused by his twisting away made it clear a rib was broken.

The guard came back, shaking his head. "I couldn't find any entrance back there."

Steve could not believe the guards knew nothing about the secret entrance!

The guard took off his jacket and covered up Sandy as he untied her hands. With this little bit of privacy covering her torso, Sandy rose to dress herself in what was left of her clothes.

Steve peered down at the floor, dejected. "We lost the book and the first key to the treasure. The book had a map of the location of the next key, and those thugs and that woman—with the same skills as the Tankers—they walked off with it. Damn, I'm sorry! We photographed the map, though, so we have a record of it."

Martha waved off the predicament with a hand gesture. "We can figure it out later. You should probably get dressed so we can head out of here as quickly as possible. We need to try to beat that other crew to the next key."

Steve nodded and started dressing. Even as he pulled clothing on, his wounds started healing on their own. He was glad the doctors had been able to figure out how to make him heal quickly.

Sandy finished dressing, handed the guard's jacket back to him, and thanked him in Swiss. Clothes could be replaced. It would be a while before her injuries would heal.

The three Tankers and the guard traveled slowly back down the hall and up the many steps. When they arrived at the outside wall, the guard simply stepped back into his place by the gate, silent and unmoving.

Once the team walked out of earshot, Martha turned to Steve and quietly whispered, "Project the image of the map to Albert. He is at the airport and can get things going for us. He can prepare everything for the flight and have a medic available to attend to any unhealed injuries. We will be ready to take off the minute we get there. You may have to project the map image to him multiple times."

Again, she giggled, then hailed a cab.

Sandy called the hotel as they drove. She requested their belongings be returned to Phoenix and the shipping bill be paid via the card number on file with the hotel.

It had been an hour since Steve had been injured. Even now, the bruises were fading, and he could feel his rib mending. Changing his DNA to quickly heal turned out to be a real life saver. Sandy did not have the same adjustment to her DNA so it would be several days before she would heal.

Andrey and Lindsey

Lindsey had been one of the last people out of the tanks. The changes in her body were miraculous. The people of Troy might have declared her a goddess. After all, Lindsey's plan involved becoming one of the world's most beautiful women. Her new body required special care since, in her dossier, she described how much she loved all kinds of fatty foods and chocolates of any kind. One of the doctors who planned the changes to her DNA knew her eating habits could be an issue for "fashion model Lindsey." So, he made an unrequested change to Lindsey's new DNA makeup. She received a high metabolism. She could eat whatever she wanted and gain no weight, yet the change wouldn't require her to eat constantly. When she ate little, her body shifted into a "normal" metabolism.

Eleven months in the tank meant she endured only liquid foods and no companionship for an awfully long time. Of course, after her mind-waking state, she was able to communicate with the other Tankers. Lindsey had always been a talker. Two months after leaving her tank and eating only hospital food containing the required caloric and nutritional content, Lindsey wanted something good to eat.

Finally in her hotel room at the Hyatt, she craved a big American meal topped off with a chocolate ice cream sundae with extra hot fudge.

She dressed in a stylish dress that made a nod toward Ralph Lauren designs. The rustic outfit fit her new tall slender body perfectly. When Lindsey had moved into the hotel before going into the tank, she had eaten at many of the restaurants in the area. But she couldn't wait to get back to Uncle Bear's Barbeque Hut, two blocks away. She felt like a little girl heading out for a picnic.

Unfortunately, it was lunch time on a weekday and the place was packed.

Lindsey approached the hostess. "Table for two, but no one will be joining me. I'm hungry and need the space."

The hostess laughed and found her a corner booth that just happened to become available after Lindsey flourished the Twelve-Gen black credit card and requested the young woman immediately charge a one hundred new dollar tip for herself.

Lindsey knew what she wanted: the All-American BBQ Feast for a Pig, a meal for five or six people. Lindsey planned to eat it all by herself.

When the waiter came, Lindsey ordered a large chocolate malt milkshake along with the feast. She informed the waiter she planned to eat it all herself and asked him to bring the milkshake as soon as possible and keep more coming when it ran out.

The milkshake arrived in a tall glass and the texture appeared smooth. She could see waves of dark chocolate inside, accented on top by whipped cream and a bright red cherry. After only one sip of the delicious shake, the meal came. It had taken only about ten minutes for the feast to arrive. Her jaw dropped a bit as she surveyed the restaurant crowd and the server setting up stands for the two metal trash-can-lid "trays" holding her food.

That was incredibly fast!

The food circled the trays, mimicking a color wheel. Red ribs with a touch of barbecue, slices of dark-brown brisket with just enough fat, half of a baked chicken, thick brown well-cooked fat Texas fries, followed by the glistening yellow perfect cobs of corn.

Along with a bowl of baked beans, a bowl heaped high with coleslaw and a grouping of cornbread muffins, it made for a glorious down-home feeling.

Where do I even start? It all looks so delicious. I haven't had a great meal since leaving the tank. The brisket is probably both the best tasting, but the worst, health-wise, for a normal person. I wonder if I'm crazy for trying to eat all of this delicious food by myself. I don't care. I'm digging in!

As she lifted her fork, her eye caught a young man around twenty staring at her as he approached the table.

"Are you really going to eat all of that by yourself?"

He is quite the cutie! Lindsey laughed. "I think you're right. You know the old saying, sometimes your eyes are bigger than your stomach? Would you like to join me?"

He clearly admired her. "Yes, I'm alone today. I would love to join you. I think I can help you make a dent in your big meal."

His soft Russian accent crooned pure beauty. Something about it made Lindsey's skin warm.

"My name is Andrey Petrov, and I believe you are Lindsey Banks?" *I recognized your thought pattern.*

Lindsey blushed. His response meant he had heard her thoughts about his looks. She gathered herself quickly and leaned toward him to reply in a quiet tone, "Andrey, will you humor me? I want to talk out loud. I spent eleven months not hearing human voices, except distorted sounds through that liquid. Will you actually talk with me?" *Please!*

Andrey grinned. "Sure. We can talk in between bites of the feast."

Lindsey and Andrey started in on the greasy, messy, and ever-so-delicious fare and their verbal conversation. She talked about her home in Southwest Ohio outside a small town called Peebles. Growing up in the 1950s and 1960s in rural Ohio meant she was a farm girl. She grew up with a stocky figure and lots of strength. Her new body appeared completely different, tall and lean, though somehow, they had maintained her strength in her new body.

Andrey talked about his home in Stavropol, a small city in southwestern Russia. He described its location as 200 miles east of Sochi. Everyone knew Sochi had hosted the most expensive and over-budget Winter Olympics ever. In college, he learned to love history and took every course offered at the University of Stavropol.

He had written a historical dissertation about a group called TAMO. The intricate details he discovered about the secret organization made him famous. He found it all so amazing, he had joined the group and moved up through its ranks. Every so many years, they would initiate him into another level. At the time he became a Tanker, he was a Fifth Level TAMO member.

His dissertation leveraged his acceptance into the famous M.V. Lomonosov Moscow State University to teach history, one of the best universities in Russia. Some of his history studies took him around the world to help with the discovery of ancient artifacts. He figured it was the reason why the imperial grand master picked him to be a Tanker.

After two hours of eating and talking, their plates were empty, and all their drinks had been finished. Andrey paid for the meal.

Lindsey thanked him for being such a gentleman. "Dessert is my treat. Let's grab a cab and go to my favorite spot."

She made a call to the cab company. The auto-driver cab arrived after a few minutes and the two climbed in. The small two-passenger electric cab was a close fit, but they both liked the closeness. Andrey held Lindsey's hand, and she wriggled a little closer.

Lindsey leaned forward. "First and Main, Scottsdale," she relayed into the speaker.

When she turned her head, Andrey's face was inches from hers, his gaze on her lips. She completed the action. Their passion consumed the twenty-minute ride.

"First and Main. Thirty new dollars, please." The machine's voice broke the spell and they both laughed.

As Lindsey paid for the trip with her Twelve-Gen card, Andrey stepped out on his side of the car and ran around in time to open Lindsey's door.

She blushed. Farm girls weren't used to "city" gentlemen.

They stood in front of a store called the Sugar Shack famous for its Pig Sundae. It contained one quart each of chocolate, vanilla, and strawberry ice creams; and one cup each of hot fudge, caramel, and strawberry toppings. To crown the delectable treat, the store added a mound of fresh authentic homemade whipped cream with three cherries.

They went in and Lindsey modified the dessert by requesting three different kinds of chocolate ice cream instead of vanilla and strawberry. She exchanged the caramel and strawberry toppings with chocolate syrup and white-chocolate fudge sauce.

"This is obviously a chocolate lovers dream," Andrey said when the sundae arrived at their table.

The two chocoholics dug in with enthusiasm. As they ate, they shared thoughts of a passionate and sensual nature. Hard to believe, but they finished the sundae in record time.

While waiting for another auto-driver cab, Andrey remarked the food had created a little bulge in Lindsey's stomach area. He lightly rubbed it and smiled.

Lindsey turned a light pink. *We are going back to my place, and I won't take no for an answer.* She also included an image of what she had looked like in the morning wearing lingerie.

"Let's go!" Andrey gazed steadily into her eyes.

Her heart thumped, thinking about how this day would end.

By the time they arrived at Lindsey's suite, her little bulge had disappeared. The doctors had worked their magic. She could eat what she wanted without concern for her model body.

She experienced, firsthand, how perfectly the doctors had created Andrey's body, all six foot two of him. Their connection went beyond looks. They felt a completeness as they intertwined their bodies, thoughts, and passions.

They slowed down their lovemaking at around nine o'clock in the evening to share dinner delivered to the room. After their brief meal, the passion continued into the early morning hours. Both gained a clear understanding of how well they matched each other.

At five in the morning, Lindsey's suite door unlocked.

"Rise and shine, it's time to become an international top model," the sweet voice of her modeling coach called.

Lindsey bounded out of bed. "Give us a minute to get decent."

"Us? I thought you wanted to be a model and not just a pretty play toy." Her voice no longer sounded sweet. "Call me when you are ready to take this seriously!"

Lindsey ran out of the bedroom naked. "No! I'm ready to work."

The other woman scanned her from toe to head and shrugged. "Okay, take a quick shower, I don't want these magnificent designer clothes to be sullied. And get rid of that man in your room."

"Yes, ma'am!"

She ran back into the bedroom, mentally purring to Andrey to dress and leave by the back door. He left as she showered. She wanted to be a top model, and the help from this woman would make it possible.

She sent a quick last endearing thought to Andrey. *Ah, now I have two loves, Andrey and modeling, in that order.*

Andrey replied, *I love my history studies and you, and* not *in that order*. An emotional silent flow of energy between them followed. It contained only the soft energy of tenderness he had expressed to her all the previous night.

In the following days, after Lindsey's modeling classes, she and Andrey met. Their love vibrated with energy and all the Tankers could feel the flow of love around the two of them.

Within a couple of weeks, notice came. Lindsey and Andrey had been picked to be part of the second Dragon's Tooth expedition.

They barely made it downstairs that morning in time to meet the team for the trip to Peru.

The Spaceman

The tooth at the hand of the spaceman was one of the few clues for the Dragon's Teeth that made sense. In the Nazca Desert, a geoglyph of a man in a space suit holding his hand up as if waving is widely known. It appears on the side of a mountain and can only be viewed fully from a thousand feet in the air.

The Dragon Prophecy said retrieving the key would require "a priest and four combined gifted ones." After centuries of discussions, the great TAMO masters had come to the conclusion that the word "combined" was the sum of the series associated with the number four: 1+2+3+4=10. So, in addition to an initiated Thirteenth Level TAMO member, it would require ten gifted Tankers.

The total team of eleven Tankers included Rob Worthy as a Thirteenth Level TAMO member he was considered a priest, Father Jonathan Ashton, Ryan Bentley, Daniel Wright, Briana Goldsmith, Martha Felder, Albert Sanders, Donna Andrews, Lindsey Banks, Nadia Belova, and Andrey Petrov. Cecilia Begay stayed behind in Phoenix. Steve and Sandy, the other two Tankers, also waited in Phoenix, while in recovery from their library trip.

Even though the Nazca Desert was well known, transportation there could be difficult. It would take a big helicopter to carry the team from the airport to the mountaintop.

☆ ☆ ☆

Nan Cromwell joined the team at the airport in Toronto, as the representative of the TAMO staff. She chose to say almost nothing to Rob during the trip, no matter how sexy he looked in his red and gold priestly attire. Air Canada was one of the few airlines flying into Lima, their first stop in Peru after an eight-hour trip.

They traveled the next 275 miles aboard a large vintage Bell 412 helicopter. Dan and Ryan served as pilot and co-pilot to fly them to Nazca and the hand of the spaceman.

In the late afternoon, the helicopter took them eastbound from the coast to the mountainside where the spaceman had been etched into the western side of the mountain.

About five miles out, Nan yelled out, "Dan, put the copter into silent mode and hover it for a bit!" She'd been watching their approach through high-powered binoculars.

He immediately changed the helicopter settings to hover as quietly as possible. The plane stopped its forward motion.

Nan pointed and gave Rob the binoculars. "Rob, look at the mountain and the hand. Zoom in and let us see what you are looking at." She touched his hand so she would view in her mind the same images.

He opened up the doors in his mind to all the Tankers, even the ones not in the aircraft.

I'm looking at the side of the mountain at the right arm, our destination. I see a circle of five strangers A priest with his Catholic robes and collar, plus four others. Each holds hands with the person beside them. The two beside the priest are touching his shoulders. The priest pulled in his hands to a position of praying over the center of the spaceman's hand. It looks like they are following our ritual but with only five people, not the needed eleven.

A light is shining out of the middle of the spaceman's hand. It looks like a laser going up the arms of the priest. It is circling around and around all five people. The priest pulled his hands away from the center, but the light did not stop. It continues to go round and round the circle, and it's growing so bright, I can't see what's going on.

He paused, then blew out a quick breath.

The light went out. And no one is left standing there. They are gone, like the light.

The images burned into Nan's mind. *Gone. All five people gone.* She pressed her hands to her thighs to control their trembling.

"We've seen what happens when the wrong ritual is performed for the key. We *will* succeed! We know the key is there. We have Rob, a true TAMO Thirteenth Level priest. We have the additional ten gifted ones. We have the required eleven."

She paused and gazed directly into the eyes of each team member seated in the back of the helicopter. "Again, we will succeed! We *will* succeed! Everyone, say it out loud like you mean it."

They did. The exercise clearly calmed the group, and Nan sensed from their thoughts that everyone believed, deep down, they would obtain the Dragon's Tooth.

Once the helicopter got underway again, it took only a few minutes to land at the base of the mountain of the spaceman. They easily hiked up the hundred-foot mountain, not even breathing heavily as they reached the spaceman's right hand.

A bit of black soot covered the ground around the hand. That made it obvious what had happened to the previous team.

Nan did not climb all the way up. She stayed low enough on the mountain to see, but lower than the edge of the hand engraved into the mountain. The dragon must not think of her as a twelfth member. No way was her team going to end up like the last one.

The eleven took their places. Rob—dressed in his golden hooded robe, red sash, and golden boots—stood at the eastern-most section of the hand. Everyone else wore short-sleeved shirts. They circled the geoglyph hand-in-hand. Nan had asked Andrey and Lindsey to stand on either side of Rob. The couple's love energy would surely help in the ritual.

✰✰✰

At Nan's mental signal, Rob began. "Oh, great dragon, we are here to recover one of your glorious teeth. Soon we will have the full number of your teeth, and we will make you whole!" He clasped his hands and raised them in prayer over the center of the geoglyph's hand.

Light poured out of the ground again. This time, the light energy did not move into his hands. Instead, it wandered around the outside of his golden hooded robe and up the outside of the arms to his shoulders. The tingle-inducing light reached Andrey and Lindsey at the exact same millisecond. The love of those two flooded Rob, and he felt its warmth touch the other Tankers as the light split to circle in both directions. It moved from hand to hand and flooded all the remaining Tankers.

When the two sections of light joined at the last clasped hands, the energy broke like a wave and returned, brighter and more quickly, back around to Rob's arms and into the ground.

Below him, though blurry like a heat mirage, the TAMO symbol appeared with its signature ruby encompassing the light energy they had all been experiencing.

The beam of light burst forth from the ruby again, brighter but cooler in feeling. This back and forth motion continued until the light encircled the team eleven times. It then faded back into the ground, leaving only the thinnest filament of light between the ground and his right hand index finger.

A bit of intuition took hold of Rob's mind, and he abruptly yelled, "Think of love and close your eyes tight!"

Through their bond, he sensed the Tankers' initial shock at his vehemence, then a turn to calming Love. For the twelfth time, Rob watched the energy pour out again. The powerful tingle running up the right arm of his robe, and the unnerving feeling of both Lindsey and Andrey rising up slightly into the air on either side of him. As the energy passed to each person, he felt love and surprise. They all were lifting off the ground in turn.

The light flashed bright one last time and the ring of energy broke. Everyone dropped to the ground, exhausted.

Rob lifted his head up first. On the ground within the circle where they'd fallen, a golden object shaped like the TAMO symbol lay on the ground. In its center, a large diamond was set where the ruby had been. He stood to retrieve it. When he picked up the key, it felt cool to the touch.

☆☆☆

Nan ran up the last few steps to Rob. He touched her hand and broadcast to all, *We have succeeded!* He also sent an image of the key.

A helicopter roared up from the back of the small mountain. Its door gaped open, and a 50-caliber gun pointed out.

"If you want to live, put the key into the basket!" The woman's voice blared through a bullhorn.

The gun fired off several hundred rounds around the Tankers, to emphasize her point. A basket lowered from the helicopter. Nan took the key from Rob, scowled, and placed it in the basket.

She and the team watched the key go up into the sky, and the craft disappear into the east.

Rob had placed two fingers on her arm and was projecting the scene to all the Tankers everywhere. Their great success... ruined with the key stolen. Like the key at the library, somehow, some evil faction knew where the Tankers would be and arrived at precisely the right moment to steal the keys from them. Through Rob's touch, she experienced the frustration and sadness racking the team. These emotions of the team were similar to the emotions Rob had made her feel when he shut her out. She immediately withdrew from him and started down the mountain.

The members of the team all cried as they returned to the helicopter in the twilight of the day. She watched the sad bunch settle themselves back in the copter. Nan needed to somehow boost their morale.

"Look at all of you! Each sporting a wonderful 'tan.' It makes you glow in the night. You have each shared the energy of the key!"

That earned a few halfhearted smiles, but the team remained silent all the way back to Toronto where Nan said her farewells and disembarked.

They had all done their best, but now TAMO needed a plan to find out who was leaking information to their nemeses.

Paris

During the week after the Peru incident, Lindsey continued her training with her mentor, the former Victoria's Secret model. Despite her serious perspective on dedication to the craft, the woman was wonderful to work with. The woman said and thought encouraging words to her protégé.

Even though Lindsey's body had healed all the scars from the tubes that kept her alive in the tank, the changes to her body and face had taken her a while to adjust mentally. As she looked into the full-length mirror at her perfect nude body, and new face with its perfect nose and high cheek bones, she still found it difficult to internalize the image as the new Lindsey Banks. Her gleaming ocean-blue eyes complemented her perfectly cropped brown hair which would eventually grow below her shoulders. She pulled on her silk dress and looked in the mirror again. It fit her size 0 body like it had been tailored for her. She thought of the Victoria's Secret models around when she was fifty. No doubt, she looked like one.

Her first photo shoot loomed later in the day.

Am I ready? She glanced again at her new form. *Heck yes, I am ready!*

She headed for the airport with one suitcase and devised a plan to build a new wardrobe to match the new her. Soon she would arrive at her photo shoot *in Paris*! She could not imagine anything more amazing.

The round-trip first-class ticket hid in her cute Prada handbag. She remembered her accidental meeting with Miuccia Prada, the daughter of the original company owners, when they both had been shopping in New York. Now the company was a giant conglomerate making money under the family name.

An auto-driver limo picked up Lindsey outside of her Phoenix hotel and drove her the fifteen minutes to the airport. With the help of the project director, she had a brand new passport and international driver's license. She didn't think she would need the license but wanted to come prepared. The modeling agency had everything set up for her in Paris.

Even so, she brought her Twelve-Gen card. She had collected money for eleven months while in the tank, the two months of solitary learning about her new self, and the additional three months of model training. Her card had more than 380,000 new dollars on it. There was very little for her to even spend the money on. She did not need to work. She wanted to work as a model and attain her dream. After the two-hour nonstop flight from the Phoenix airport to the Charles De Gaulle airport outside of Paris, her agent met her at the gate. Even with all the modern security, her agent had wrangled a way to arrive there as she got off the plane. The agent directed her to the area to pick up her bag, where a porter waited for them. The three went past the normal customs screening to a special gate.

The customs agent stared at her in a very admiring way. "You look beautiful today, Miss Banks! Your agent showed me some of your photos and they are marvelous. Enjoy your stay in France."

Lindsey picked up on the custom agent's thought. *She is so lucky to be born naturally beautiful like that.*

The comment made her chuckle to herself. She knew intimately how her old duck body had been transformed into this swan.

It took only minutes from disembarking the plane to identify the limo waiting outside on the street. As they opened the outside doors, photographers everywhere started taking pictures, yelling at her to smile and look this way or that. Lindsey already had her own paparazzi, thanks to her enterprising and efficient agent.

Using her mental skills, Lindsey posed for a few seconds but closed the mental door keeping her from hearing the "normals." She didn't want some jealous person's bad thoughts to spoil her first time in Paris.

Paris, as she inhaled her first breath of the city, smelled amazing. All these people together had created the special scent: a mix of sweating bodies combined with many different colognes and perfumes. Her new form and enhanced mind could take it all in or discriminate down to the owner of a particular scent. She loved her new body. The excitement of new discoveries never seemed to end.

Her agent gestured for her to step into the limo. It whisked them away toward her very first professional photo shoot. As unusual as it sounds, the car was driven by a human being. The car was unlike any vehicle she had ridden in during the last ten years: a Mercedes stretched to fit six people in back in a luxurious manner. A bottle of authentic French champagne sat open, and her agent poured her a glass.

The limo traveled from the airport down many side streets. The driver wanted to show her the beauty of the real Paris. As they started down the Avenue des Champs-Elysées she could see the famous Arc de Triomphe at the top of the small hill. The driver only went halfway around the monument, as the metal barriers had been opened for him on one side. He pulled behind the Arc into a waiting spot.

On that side, Lindsey and her agent found dressing rooms tucked away for all the girls. It made it easy for the models to change into various outfits quickly and conveniently. With eleven other models, Lindsey expected a long day for the photo shoot.

She didn't get to spend much time in the dressing room. A quick change into new lingerie and dress in "street" clothes. The photographers wanted to take some casual photos.

As she removed her clothes, she was photographed. As each piece of clothing came off, they took pictures. As she undressed, she moved in a sexy but not trampy way. When down to her lingerie, the model assistants touched up her hair and makeup and adjusted her clothing. When she was perfect, she joined the first two models in front of the Arc for photos.

Lindsey was amazed at the speed of the cars as they rushed around the Arc. The automatic electronic drivers had made that possible, and not one accident had happened there in a long time.

Lindsey found her first full day as a model fun and tiring. At the end of the day, all the models hopped into stretch limos that quickly whisked them back to the Ambassador Hotel. The hotel supplied the luxury most models desired. Built in the 1920s art deco style during the middle of the last century, the hotel recently had finished a complete renovation. They touted a particular five-star feature: no robot helpers worked in the hotel. This hotel's supreme luxury happened only via human labor. Unlike in the previous century, the staff was well paid.

The models were the first occupants on the remodeled fourth floor. The original single room accommodations on the floor had all been converted into two-room suites. The bellman escorted the girls up to their rooms. When the bellman opened the twin doors to Lindsey's suite, a feeling of exhilaration flowed down her spine. A sitting room opened up in front of her, decorated in the art deco style with an added French flair. All the furniture appeared handmade. From where she stood, she caught a view of the Eiffel Tower through her bedroom window.

She thanked the bellman, but he stood and stared at her. It had been a *long* time since she had been in a hotel with a living breathing bellman, but it only took a second for her to catch his thoughts.

Is this girl going to be cheap like the rest or am I finally going to get a decent tip? That company is paying almost 6,000 francs a night. Aren't these girls being paid anything?

She opened her purse and pulled out three 1,000 new franc notes and gave it to the man. With an exchange rate of 5.85 it was a great tip of more than 500 new dollars.

His initial thought lightly touched her mind. *I'm so glad we went back to the franc and dropped the silly Euro money.* Lindsey was always amazed at what she learned from people when she listened to their thoughts. Needless to say, he smiled, bowed and closed the double doors behind him. *She is a beautiful woman who understands money. I'm glad she is different from the rest.*

She should have been exhausted after all she had been through. Instead—now a professional model... in *Paris*! —she was totally energized. She didn't want to rest at all. She was ready to go. The hotel was located only a short walking distance from the Galeries Lafayette where she planned to do some Paris fashion shopping to fit her new body. Not only did she have a loaded Twelve-Gen card, but the company that hired the models had given each of them thirty thousand francs or about 5,000 new dollars. The company told the models to spend it on clothes and other items for themselves. Added to the fantastic amount of money her agent had secured for her modeling, she was well set.

As Lindsey turned around to leave, something white caught her eye sitting on the edge of the dark-green comforter on the bed in the other room. She walked with the grace of a model to the bedroom. A white gown lay on the bed there. Next to it lay an amazing white set of soft ladies' wear, similar to what she'd modeled all afternoon.

A real white mink stole nestled next to those with a lady's hat sporting real feathers. Mink was almost never used in clothing anymore. The animal lovers had pretty much ended its availability in the United States, and the rest of the world had followed the example.

At the side of the bed sat a pair of white high heels accented along the edges with sparkly gems. As she sat on the bed to examine the shoes, a purse fell to the floor beside them. Matching the shoes, the purse was covered with an accent of what looked like diamonds. An envelope peeked out of the purse.

She picked up the purse and the envelope. Inside she found a ticket to *Phantom of the Opera*. An attached note read, "Dress for dinner and the show. Be in the lobby at eight tonight. I will meet you." The note was signed, "A."

A twinge of excitement ran from her head to her toes and back halfway between. Somehow, Andrey Petrov, her "close friend" made his way to Paris.

She picked up the hat and a small, elongated box tucked inside it fell to the bed. She opened it to find a beautiful necklace, a long, elegant oval of diamonds connected to a two-inch TAMO symbol pendant in gold. The arms of the cross connected to the diamond strands. The center of the star and cross featured a detailed flower in full bloom centered with a large ruby.

As if that was not enough, she discovered a diamond bracelet also connected by a smaller version of the TAMO symbol.

She loved everything Andrey had given her and could not wait to see her love again.

She reached out to Andrey's mind. *Thank you, my love. It is all so beautiful. I will see you at eight. I love you.*

I love you, too! Even more than I love spoiling you.

Lindsey closed her mind to all but her own thoughts again. It was time for a short nap, a bath, makeup, and dressing. She was pressed for time.

☆☆☆

Lindsey looked stunning in her gown and all her accessories as she walked off the elevator. Her height, slim figure, and ample bust, noiselessly broadcast her as a main attraction for someone. Men of all ages stared at her, and Andrey knew from their thoughts how much they all wanted her. Could she sense he wanted to be at the head of the line? She abruptly turned toward the bar and met his gaze. She immediately scanned his white tuxedo and focused on his gold necklace dangling heavily with a larger version of the TAMO symbol. The ruby at the center glowed with energy so he'd seen no need for diamonds in his more masculine version of the necklace.

You are fabulous! He hoped she caught the emotion behind the thought as she came to him.

The phone in his pocket buzzed as she approached him. He pulled it out to look at the number, shook his head, and frowned. He knew instantly what it meant. He could see her disappointed look, so she must have also known what it meant. He answered the phone and talked for the briefest of moments, hung up, and put the phone back in his vest pocket.

He lit up with the most brilliant smile he could muster and pulled her close to him.

"I'm sure you guessed that was Nate. They have a lead on the location of the next key. We are to meet them, to become part of the twelve, tomorrow outside of the small Siberian town of Vanavara. Nate has scheduled the flights and papers we need. We are to leave at five tomorrow morning and should arrive by evening at their small airport."

He noted her pout and returned it. "We can still enjoy the show and dinner. Afterward, when we come back to the hotel, we can stay up all night."

She answered by kissing him. That derailed their plans nicely. They skipped dinner and the show and went directly back to Lindsey's hotel apartment. Room service promptly delivered a nice light dinner of escargot, Caesar salad, and a local French fish cooked in a white wine sauce and lightly covered in pearl onions and capers. The white wine, a Cabernet Sauvignon Blanc, came from the Chateau Montelena Winery in California. Andrey thought it would be fun to share a California wine in the middle of France. The wine steward obtained the wine without a word, but the 900 new dollar charge for a 150 new dollar bottle of wine said it all.

With a light alcohol buzz from the wine after the meal, Andrey picked up Lindsey in his arms and carried her to the bedroom. They finally slept around three in the morning.

Siberia

The international flight from Paris to Moscow only took half an hour. A smaller plane took them from Moscow to the Siberian Vanavara Airport outside of the town of Vanavara. This leg of the trip was more than three times the distance and used a plane which was much slower.

They finally arrived a few minutes before six. The night started, as usual, dark and cold. Nate and Daniel met them and handed Lindsey and Andrey each a heavy jacket, hat, and scarf. The couple had traveled with only the clothes on their backs. They quickly put them on and ran inside the building. Russian efficiency dictated the airport needed no heat because it was so seldom used. At least the building protected them from the wind. They could bundle up properly for the ride to the "hotel."

The "hotel" facility comprised a block of twenty bedrooms, all only big enough for a small single bed, a dresser, and a sink. Bathrooms and showers were communal.

Lindsey and Andrey met the others for dinner in the restaurant on the first floor—more of a pub than a restaurant.

Their rough-hewn table might have been in the building during the Russian Revolution more than a hundred years ago. They sat on benches since there were no chairs. The food tasted hearty, but no one dared ask what it was. Drink options consisted of only vodka and a single brand of Russian red wine with a brackish taste, though the wait staff assured the team the wine was a famous Russian brand.

After dinner, they all went up to Nate's suite. It was big enough to hold a standard-sized bed, a couch, a table, and four chairs. Most everyone stood around or sat on the bed.

Nate clapped his hands once, then rubbed his palms together, as everyone's attention focused on him. "Based on evidence of the photographs associated with the two keys we lost, we believe the keys are not inert metal. They are also mechanisms capable of protecting themselves and of knowing if the procedures used by the key hunters follow the exact details for key extraction given in the prophecy.

"We believe the June 30, 1908, Tunguska event, which scholars say was a meteor explosion in the atmosphere, was instead one of the keys protecting itself from the meteor. There was no impact crater, so the meteor never made it to Earth intact.

"The meteor was thought to be on the order of two hundred to six hundred feet in diameter and it burst in an explosion three to six miles up in the air. Only tiny pieces of it ever made it to Earth. Right below the center of the blast on Earth, in a circular area, no trees have ever grown back."

His team members shook their heads and rolled their eyes, clearly incredulous at the story. They knew how dangerous the keys could be.

"We will travel to what our sources believe is the eye of the blast site. Our guides, Evenki hunters, will meet us here at the hotel at four tomorrow morning and take us only partway, about ten miles south of the site. The trip will be difficult and take most of the morning. When our guides decide they will go no farther, they will make camp while we take the vehicles forward. The Evenki hunters fear what they call the Valleymen but provided no more explanation than that.

"Our vehicles and the aerial maps will get us the rest of the way. We hope to drive in, do what we must do, and be back at the camp before dark tomorrow night. All of you have been given rugged warm clothes for the trip. Now get some sleep and no monkey business."

Nate pointedly looked at Lindsey and Andrey, Sandy and Steve, and Martha and Albert. If anyone had any comments or thoughts, no one shared them. All mental walls stayed up.

☆☆☆

In the morning, even before the sun rose, a group of Evenki hunters met the team. One Evenki climbed into each of the four vehicles. The rugged vehicles did not have auto-drivers, nor did they have power steering or automatic transmission. Luckily, the average age of the team members being ninety meant many of them knew how to drive a standard stick shift.

Steve drove the vehicle holding Sandy, Nate, and the chief of the hunters. They took the lead toward Tunguska. The chief sat next to Steve and said nothing but gave him mental directions. The chief knew Steve had the gift, though he did not know how the chief knew.

When Steve had opened his mind to the thoughts of the chief, his mental words were almost nonexistent. Instead, he watched the lights at the front of the vehicle out as far as they would go. When they needed to change direction even a little bit, the chief would project an image of what Steve needed to do. The image contained information not visible to Steve's eyes or senses. When he received an image, he repeated it to the other three Tanker drivers, Ryan, Daniel, and Briana.

The roughness of the road caused Steve a great deal of stress. He did his best to ignore it, since that small discomfiture amounted to only the tip of the pending iceberg. Late in the morning, he received an image of a great wall from the chief. The Evenki hunters would go no farther. The team stopped their vehicles as quickly as possible and unloaded the gear as the sun came up in the east. The hunters would prepare camp for the team's return.

As Steve started down the road with Nate as his guide, he felt the fear of the hunters watching the team leave. He knew the hunters would do as they promised and make camp, but he also knew they would not be there when the TAMO team returned.

The aerial maps were easy to use to navigate to the center of the blast sight. The driving was not fast, and Steve had to depend on Nate. After a few missed turns, Nate reached up and touched the back of Steve's bare neck. Immediately they had mind-to-mind communication. The driving went much faster after that, and the team knocked those few miles out in no time.

After an hour, about a mile from the final location, Steve started seeing things. They looked like people. The figures jumped in front of the vehicles, but when "hit", the beings disappeared. It took a while for Nate to understand what was happening, and he sensed the heightened confusion and anxiety from his team members, who obviously saw the ephemeral beings as well. Via a thought to Steve, Nate urged all of the team members to manage their fear.

Build your walls, people. What you are seeing is the result of the key. This key is more powerful than the other two we've encountered. We are close.

The last mile was the quietest any of the team members had encountered since leaving the tanks. They all felt it at once. No shared thoughts. Complete mental silence between the team members.

✰✰✰

All the vehicles stopped. The place they needed to be had been found. It just felt right to Nate. He got out first but waited for the rest of the team to climb out of their vehicles before saying anything.

"Everyone, we don't have much time. Gather together in a circle holding the hand of the person next to you and make the biggest circle you can make. I may not participate in this. Only those with the gift may do so. I will guide you with my voice. At a particular point, I will tell you to open your minds to one another. Be sure you only open your minds to one another and to no one else.

This will be a tricky maneuver. I am hopeful the results will be worth it."

The circle they formed was more than seventy feet in circumference. Nate witnessed the last two team members as they grasped each other's hands to close the human ring.

"Close your eyes. Take three calming breaths. Breathe in through your nose. Hold it while I count. One, two, three, four, five, six, seven, eight, nine, ten. Breathe out through your mouth. A second time, breathe in through your nose. Hold it for my count of ten."

He counted again.

"Breathe out through your mouth. For the third time, breathe in through your nose and I'll count."

He did.

"Breathe out through your mouth. Now, think of the Earth with all of its natural energy. Absorb into your minds the good Earth energy. Keep your walls up and doors closed. Continue to absorb more energy from the Earth."

He gave them all a minute to envision it.

"In your mind, form this mental energy as a ball. Wait. Condense it and make it more powerful. Now open your minds to your team members only and send the energy you have in a counterclockwise direction from one mind to the next. Faster and faster. When I give the signal, all of you, at once, put up your walls and close your doors and push the energy back into the Earth. Ready? I'll count to three. One, two, three, *now!*"

Even Nate felt the Earth shake. They had obtained the result he wanted. A three-dimensional image of a key hovered a few feet above the ground about five feet from the inside edge of the Tanker circle.

"Everyone keep the energy flowing to the Earth for another minute."

Nate walked the distance to the hovering key. He literally walked inside it and put a marker where the base of the cross touched the soil.

"Everyone break your concentration, open your eyes, grab a shovel, and come here. Our time is limited. We must work quickly."

As the team members opened their eyes, each focused on the shimmering 3D key image with Nate standing in the center of it. When they disconnected hands, the image of the key disappeared. They quickly grabbed their shovels from the vehicles and ran to Nate.

He had drawn a rectangle on the ground around him. He explained, "We want to dig a rectangular hole about three feet by four feet. I do not know how deep the key will be. It will be in a protective box. So, dig as fast as you can. It will be tough getting through this frozen ground, but slow down when you hit something sounding like metal."

Four at a time, team members dug small divots of Earth from the indicated area. The ground would not let them dig any faster. When the first four grew tired, the next four took over. In two hours, at three feet of depth, they heard the first clang as their shovels hit something hard.

Nate's hole had been drawn perfectly. Six inches showed around the outside of the box. Another hour passed as they figured out a way to lift the box out.

As soon as they secured the box in the lead vehicle, Nate climbed into the backseat with the box beside him. "Pack up, and let's get out of here as quickly as we can!"

Everyone ran to the vehicles.

"Go, go, go!" Nate yelled.

Steve took off but kept his mind completely closed. They had driven for about forty-five minutes, about five miles from where they started, when Nate put his hand out the window and gestured for the vehicles to stop. Nate opened the door, stood in the opening, and pointed in the direction from where they had come.

A small mushroom cloud had formed in the near distance. After a few seconds, they heard the almost deafening sound of the explosion.

Nate waited for it to pass by. "That, my friends, is our evil enemy, AKUA—the Ancient Universal Knowledge Association—

trying to prevent us from retrieving this key. Had they dropped a bomb on the area while the key was still there, we all would have died as the key protected itself."

Nate climbed back into the vehicle and motioned for the team to move out and do it quickly.

On the ride back to camp, no one said or shared anything. All the Tankers kept themselves closed off from the others. This was serious. It was no longer an adventure. People had been hurt and could potentially die.

The imperial grand councilor tried to remember the trail for the ride back to the camp. In the dark, he missed a few turns which required the team to backtrack. It ended up taking four hours to reach the camp. Not a single light welcomed them.

The team members quietly left their vehicles while the two military men, Daniel and Ryan, went to investigate, handguns at the ready. Ten minutes later, they all received a thought from Daniel, *All appears clear. No sign of the hunters. All their gear is gone. It's okay to come on in.*

Steve orally relayed the message to Nate.

Since retrieving the box, no one on the team had gotten any of the flashes of mysterious people. Whatever had been protecting the area was now gone.

The Box

All the members found their tents. The six smaller tents were big enough to sleep four but, without the hunters, they could sleep two in each tent. Everyone paired up with their favorite Tanker.

Sandy and Steve were settling in when the imperial grand councilor called from outside, "Steve, we need you in my big central tent in five minutes with your TAMO robes. Tell Rob."

Steve sent the thought to Rob who was bunking with his friend Cecilia.

Steve and Rob arrived together. The two carried their priestly garb with them. The tent door gaped, and Nate looked uneasy at the two as they came through it.

"Close the tent opening, gents. We are going to need some privacy. Put on your sacred costumes."

After they had changed, they approached the pinkish red container liberated from Tunguska. It sat on a table in the center of the tent and looked like a solid box with no seams. As the three walked closer to it, the red ruby in their TAMO symbols started to glow. The closer they came, the brighter the rubies shone. When they stood next to the chest, the glow from the rubies revealed buttons on the top of the box. Each button was numbered with Roman numerals ranging from one to twenty.

Steve crinkled his face as he watched the box change. "Now what?"

Nate waved his hand over the box without touching it. "The papers from the Vatican indicated it would take three to light the way for the twelve to be seen. The admonition of the papers warned that pressing the wrong numbers would be fatal. But I know what I must do."

Before Steve or Rob could respond, Nate reached out and pressed the number one, the number two, and then stepped back. It continued to glow from the red rubies, but the color of the box itself started to change. It went from the pinkish red color to the deepest of magentas. Abruptly, the three rubies stopped glowing, and the box became a dark sapphire blue. A small lip appeared all the way around the container several inches from its top.

The three worked together to lift the lid. Inside, a plastic-like blanket covered the contents. Nate lifted the blanket to reveal a large version of the Hermetic Cross, Star of David, and the flower. The ruby at the center of the flower started to pulse in red light. Each time the light went out, the rubies at the center of each person's necklace pulsed back a light of equal strength. This went on for five minutes until the ruby in the box's symbol turned clear.

A burst of energy pulsed through Steve's body.

Nate clapped a single clap. "We have successfully received the blessing of one of the Dragon's Teeth. I assume you both felt the added energy?"

Steve glanced at Rob, who nodded. Steve grinned at the amazing feeling of the soft energy that vibrated through him.

"We are finished here for the night then. I will lock things down. You two can go back to your tents and I will see you in the morning."

Steve and Rob changed back into their traveling clothes and left the tent. Steve didn't know what to think, and Rob agreed. They had each expected more. The Peruvian key had given them a much better light show.

Sandy had fallen asleep and left a lantern burning for him. He undressed and climbed into the double sleeping bag. He felt warm and cuddled close to Sandy. She opened her eyes and grinned.

You are glowing a faint red color. Do I have to play fire chief and put out the flames?

Steve didn't say a word. There would not be much sleeping going on in their tent tonight.

Early, the clank of pots and cups woke Steve out of a groggy sleep. *Must be Albert.* The former math teacher had drawn the short straw to make the coffee, tea, and set out the pastries left for the expedition by the hunters.

Steve tried to go back to sleep, knowing it was going to be a long day. They did not have a guide to lead them back to the little town. It was going to be a struggle finding the way back.

As Tankers woke up, they slowly gathered around the fire. The sun had not yet risen even though it was nine o'clock. The fire served as their only warmth and light.

Eventually the last of them—Nate, Rob, Steve, and Sandy—joined the campfire crew. When they showed up, the others stared at the newcomers with confused and mocking expressions.

"What's wrong?" Nate patted his arms and chest as if looking for something amiss.

"Do you think we've all gone crazy or something?" Steve quipped in a sarcastic tone.

Briana's whole face showed a smile. "The three of you have a very dark tan you did not have yesterday. Even Sandy has a light tan."

Nate looked at his hands and at the other three. "I guess this is the mark of those who have been in the presence of the master key." He inclined his head to the side and glanced at Sandy. "Or someone who has been quite intimate with a person who has seen the master key."

They all laughed. It was something to remember.

Upon finishing the light breakfast, the team struck the camp and loaded the tents and supplies back in the vehicles. Everyone climbed into their respective vehicles and the trip back to the town began. Nate spearheaded the effort. He used his maps to try to figure their way back. Many times, they had to stop while Nate examined the area, looking for tire tracks. During the slow process, they ate whatever light food and water was available. Instead of a four-hour trip, they didn't arrive in the town until around ten that night.

Rooms were ready and waiting. After a change of clothing, they met again in the dining area for some mystery food. When Nate and Steve did not come down, Sandy explained they wanted to remain with the key but would appreciate it if someone would bring dinner up to Nate's room. They ate and drank their fill and, as each finished, they took some food with them to Nate's room.

By the time everyone gathered in Nate's room, Nate and Steve had been given a great feast from all the samples brought up from the dining area. Everyone was quiet. They stared at the box sitting on the table. The box appeared like a dirty old container which had been dug out of the ground. None of them had seen it in its glory state like Nate, Rob, and Steve.

They waited patiently for Nate to finish eating, wanting to know what would happen next.

With a gregarious belch and a sigh, Nate pushed his plate away.

"We are in a difficult country that is neither ally nor friend. Getting in here was relatively straightforward for all of us. Tomorrow, all of you will fly back to Moscow. From there, I recommend you take two weeks off while Father Jonathan and I move this key to someplace safe."

They all heard his next thought. *The Center of Silence will be the place for it.*

"You all deserve your vacations. You have become skilled with your talents and your help is welcomed by TAMO. Each of you have been given lifetime memberships, and you will all be given ways to contact me or the imperial grand master for personal consultation about your TAMO studies. Even though money will play little in your futures, your Twelve-Gen cards have been updated with an additional 100,000 new dollars. It is a pittance in comparison to the work you have done. Go spend it. Travel where you please. Be sure to make your way to places to help you recover your minds and bodies. Take the full two weeks before you return to Phoenix. We will need to reconvene as a team once we have put together our exact plan to retrieve the next key."

Home from Siberia

The next morning, everyone arose before the sun and waited at the Vanavara airport just outside the little town where they had flown in two days before. Father Jonathan was carrying the master key wrapped tightly and placed in a backpack on his back. Nate carried a satchel of ten kilos of gold.

The team wanted to be sure Father Jonathan, and the imperial grand councilor left without trouble before the rest flew out later. The two travelers were expecting a jet to fly in and pick them up at seven in the morning. Only Steve and the imperial grand councilor knew who was coming. At seven o'clock exactly, a black corporate jet landed at the little airport. The jet's door and steps lowered from inside the plane. Two people disembarked. The first, a man in very plain clothes carrying a Russian-made Avtomat Kalashnikova rifle over his shoulder.

No doubt the woman behind him was his superior. She wore a sable knee-length jacket with high black leather boots. A sable Ushanka, Russian hat with flaps, covered her head. As she took each step, her coat slipped open to show black stockings under her short skirt. All the men gawked at her.

Steve stepped forward. *Team, this is Katia Poklonskaya and Alex Buzhinzky. I met them in Phoenix. Katia's father is a New*

Russian. We would call him Mafia in the U.S. They are here to help get the imperial grand councilor and Jonathan out of Russia safely with the key.

He didn't turn his head to look at Sandy, but he closed the doors in his mind to everyone but her. *Sandy my love, I met Katia during my first months out of the tank, before you and I met. We were lovers and her thoughts cannot be read unless you touch her skin. She is a character, and you can expect her to do almost anything. I just want you to know you are my woman and my forever love, always.*

Katia walked right up to Steve and gave him the standard Russian friends greeting, three kisses on his cheeks, left, then right, and left again. With each touch, Steve was able to read all her emotions and thoughts. She wanted him to fly off with her. Steve had left his mind open to Sandy, hiding nothing from her.

Sandy narrowed her eyes in obvious displeasure and sent a response. *Steve, I know you are my true love. I do not fault you. My anger is at her arrogance.*

Katia said, "Thank you, Steven, for these lovely clothes. I was able to get them with the travel money you sent for this trip. Which of your two friends need my help?"

Steve took Katia by the arm and walked her over to introduce her.

"Katia, this is Father Jonathan, and TAMO Imperial Grand Councilor Nate Conway."

They both reached out and shook hands with her. Nate gave Katia the satchel. Katia looked at them with knowing eyes, turned around, and marched back up the airplane steps. Jonathan and Nate followed her. Alex followed them. In less than ten minutes, by seven fifteen, the plane swiftly departed.

The other Tankers' flight arrived late, at eleven thirty that morning. In the Moscow airport, the eleven Tankers were separated from one another by Russia's FSB, an intense equivalent to the American FBI. All of them stayed in touch mentally and sent images to Father Jonathan who communicated with the imperial grand councilor.

The story was the same. An FSB agent asked each Tanker a series of questions and they were answered exactly the same.

"Where have you been?" asked the FSB officer.

"I went to the area of the Tunguska blast."

"What were you doing there?"

"I wanted to see the incredible destruction of the meteor from more than a century ago."

"Did you take anything from that area?"

"No, I have only what I came with. All that I have is in my bags."

"Where are the other two members of your team?"

"I don't know, they left by a different route. I came directly here to Moscow."

The FSB did not like the answers, but they could do nothing. To be sure the team had nothing extra, the FSB tore apart all their suitcases. They literally ripped the suitcases to shreds. The clothing was picked through, and the FSB officers kept what they wanted. The team members each received a large plastic garbage bag that contained the remainder of their clothes. The team was told to leave Russia within twenty-four hours, or they would be jailed as spies.

After the interrogation, the team boarded various flights to travel to different spots around the world. They split up and went their individual ways. Each had their own idea of where to go on vacation. Only Cecilia wanted to go home to Phoenix. Steve and Sandy went to the French Riviera to live it up in the most expensive hotel they could find. They wanted a classy hotel with a view of the beach. Martha and Albert flew to Monte Carlo to try their hand at cards. Rob, Ryan, Briana, and Daniel headed for the relaxation of the sun, beaches, snorkeling, and good food of Cancun, Mexico's best five star hotel.

Andrey and Lindsey returned to Paris. Her photoshoot had been put on hold during her week's absence. It should have cost the magazine a lot of money to delay all those professionals in Paris. TAMO picked up all the costs for the model's downtime and extra expenses of the magazine. The other models had no problem being on a short well-paid vacation. No one said a negative word when

Lindsey returned. In fact, all the models were happy and ready to get back to work.

Nate and Father Jonathan did not vacation. The first leg of their journey, they shared a flight with Katia and Alex from Siberia to a city in southern Russia, Rostov-on-Don. The city was both modern and old at the same time. There, Nate and Father Jonathan were to meet up with Katia's father, Konstantin Poklonsky. He headed the New Russians in the southwestern part of Russia.

The Russians were not unfriendly when they met the two TAMO members due to the presence of Alex and Katia. Father Jonathan's job was to watch everyone's thoughts for signs of danger.

The discussion started in the back room of a seedy bar. Their hosts insisted that they share vodka and food. Every few minutes, their hosts joined their guests for another shot of vodka. Father Jonathan's Tanker metabolism prevented the alcohol from having much of any effect. When Nate said he could not drink any more, Father Jonathan stepped in. He caught a mental image of the Russian's feeling insulted.

Jonathan got Nate off the hook. The twenty-something looking Father Jonathan told the Russians, through Katia's interpreting, that old American men can't hold their liquor. Jonathan assured the Russians that Nate would drink one shot for every four shots the others drank. That mollified the Russians, who waited to see what would happen to Father Jonathan. Of course, they could not keep up with him, though they tried.

After everyone had quite a lot to drink, the Russians appeared to totally sober up and started haggling. Initially, they asked for six kilos of gold to make the special travel arrangements, especially turning their blind eye to the cargo that Father Jonathan carried in his backpack. After some haggling, Nate was able to whittle them down to two kilos of gold.

Katia, holding all the team's gold, gave the two kilos to her father which cleared the way for Nate and Father Jonathan to make their way to Toronto under Poklonsky's special arrangements.

After a long, roundabout, and mostly uncomfortable trip for the two travelers, they finally arrived at the Toronto airport. Several members of the Center of Silence met them, and Father Jonathan turned over the precious backpack. With profound thanks, the Center's representatives handed him the first-class plane tickets for the trip back to Phoenix.

The first key had made it safely to Canada.

Rob and Nan

Rob contacted the imperial grand councilor by phone. He really wanted to get in touch with Nan. He had spent several weeks' time to resolve his issue with the blackmailer. He was sad that many weeks had passed since their time on the plane. Things associated with the search for the keys had progressed so quickly. During that time, Rob had been unable to reach Nan on her phone number. He thought maybe she had changed her number. He even went hunting for it on the net but found no new number. Her phone was completely unlisted.

The imperial grand councilor made the call to the Center of Silence, talked with Nan, and later that day, returned Rob's call.

"Nan has spent the last weeks since your flight together worrying about you. Your connection was so strong with her. You never contacted her after your little fight. At this point, she says she doesn't want to speak with you ever again. You hurt her. I have spoken with the imperial grand master, her grandmother, and explained we have been out of touch hunting for the keys.

"The imperial grand master apparently had a talk with her because Nan just contacted me by text. Let me read you exactly what she wrote: *'Tell Rob to meet me in Toronto tonight at the*

Rebellious Bistro at ten.' That is all I have, make of it what you wish. the next step is now up to you."

Rob thanked the imperial grand councilor, but the timing was not perfect. Though already noon in Phoenix, he decided he had to try. Thanks to his monthly stipend with Twelve-Gen, he arrived at the Phoenix airport in time to make a flight. Unfortunately, last-minute tickets were expensive and the only one left was in first class. The 6,500 new dollar cost was exorbitant, but he paid it. The plane would get him there by five in the evening Toronto time. He would have plenty of time to find the bistro.

During the one-hour flight, he went into deep meditation about what had happened to him with Nan.

"Ladies and gentlemen..." The captain's voice interrupted his meditation. "I'm sorry to report there is an issue going on at the Toronto airport. We have been diverted to the Quebec main airport to refuel. When things are resolved, we will fly you back to Toronto. Again, ladies and gentlemen, I am sorry for the delay this will cause."

Rob still wasn't too worried as the plane landed in Quebec at five-fifteen that evening. Passengers were given the option to stay in Quebec and take a flight to Toronto at their leisure or to stay in the boarding area and return when the Toronto airport gave the "all clear" signal. Rob decided to stay at the gate.

While waiting, Rob scanned all the news outlets on his phone. He read several articles. From the reports about the Toronto airport, apparently several men armed with long swords had attempted to avoid security. The airport went into immediate lockdown. The Royal Canadian Mounted Police had been called in. They expected to give the "all clear" by midnight.

Rob was devastated. No way could he travel back to Toronto in time to meet Nan. He started to wander aimlessly from the gate. A long time later, at nine-forty-five, he happened to look up and noticed the name of the bar he was passing. It was the Rebellious Bistro. He thought to himself, *What a horrible coincidence.* He went in and sat down, totally despondent because he could do nothing to make it back to Toronto and find the other Rebellious Bistro.

For a late night, the place was swamped. Apparently, many people were rerouted here and waited for planes to fly them back to Toronto. Rob ordered a Lover's Rebellion, one of the bar's most famous sandwiches, according to the menu. His choice amounted to a Reuben on rye with a fancy name and big price tag.

While waiting for his food, someone came up behind him and put a hand on his neck. One finger touched his skin.

"Buy a girl a drink?"

Rob did not have to look up at the quiet voice. The accompanying thoughts streaming from the other person came tinged with both anger and joy. He knew who it was and opened his mind to her so she would know what had happened in the weeks since their fight.

I wanted to tell you more about this evil man thinking he could blackmail me. He doesn't know of my resources to end the false issue. I did know you being near me could put you in danger too.

He stood and turned around. "I cannot tell you how sad this whole situation has made me." He held out a palm to her, inviting her to take his hand.

Instead, Nan jumped into his arms.

"I forgive you, you big fraud."

Rob cupped his hands on either side of her face, took in her big smile, and stared into her eyes. He melted.

Her lips twitched downward slightly. "I wanted you to feel lost like I have been for the last several weeks."

Rob relayed his subsequent questions through their gaze.

She raised her eyebrows. "The Center of Silence received a message to not go to Toronto today. We have supporters everywhere who hinted there would be a TAMO-related shutdown at the airport. The imperial grand master issued a required five-day holiday for all the staff, so the center is empty of all personnel. She even took the Tunguska key with her. I knew, if you cared, you would try to make it to Toronto for our meeting. I also knew this restaurant here is the only Rebellious Bistro in Canada. This being the closest major Canadian airport, I also knew you would be diverted here. I meditated with all the energy I could muster to encourage you to find your way here by ten tonight. I have a luxury room set up for us at one of the nicest hotels here in Quebec, The Fairmont Le Chateau Frontenac inside the city walls of Old Quebec. It recently finished a multimillion-dollar renovation. The Churchill Suite comes with a bed and breakfast package. A steal at only forty-four hundred Canadian dollars per night. Grandma is paying for it as part of the Center of Silence getaway."

Rob's heart slammed a beat against his ribs. She had forgiven him.

They finished their dinner together and leisurely walked hand in hand to the hotel. No one, not even the Tankers who could read minds, heard anything for two full days. On the third day, while eating lunch in bed and watching a silly TV program from the last century called *Sex in the City,* their show was interrupted.

A news flash identified a gas leak causing an explosion at an old resort in Nova Scotia. Rob held Nan's hands and cast his thoughts out to all the other Tankers. He wanted news and details immediately.

The Gas Leak

Early in the morning, Sam received another mental call from the anonymous Tanker. He or she had learned to change their pattern of thought. Each mental contact she received from the Tanker seemed to have a different mental signature. This time the thought woke her up in the middle of the night.

Sam, TAMO has the primary key, the Siberian Key. I think it is being kept at the TAMO Center of Silence. Those evil people must be stopped!

She immediately called Mario and repeated what she had heard. She remembered their night together after she brought him the book from the Vatican. He had been very thankful. In fact, he had been thankful multiple times that night, and even stayed for breakfast. This time his voice held a worried tone. He said "thanks" and hung up the phone. Not a very satisfying conversation.

The mid-morning news erupted with details about the giant gas leak explosion in Nova Scotia. The explosion had apparently destroyed a large, remodeled resort owned by TAMO but caused no deaths or injuries. The photos taken by local drones showed buildings totally flattened. It looked like a tornado had gone through the complex individually hitting each building.

Sam worried it had happened because of the information she gave Mario.

Around dinner time that day, Sam experienced a scream of death within her mind. It was awful, like nothing else she had ever experienced. She recognized the patterns as the painful communication shifted from one pattern to another—the final thoughts of the Tanker who had been in contact with her. When she tried to make contact, she found nothing. The Tanker and his or her mind were gone.

When Sam finally saw the nightly late news, they reported another explosion in downtown Phoenix. The news confirmed her suspicions. It appeared the newly renovated floor of suites at the Hyatt had also suffered a gas leak explosion. The news said two to four lives had been lost. Police were sifting through the wreckage and taking DNA samples from body parts.

☆☆☆

Nate's information from an AUKA informant had saved the personnel of the Center of Silence. The Center of Silence was only a place. It could be rebuilt. His informant did not know about what was to happen in Phoenix.

The deaths in Phoenix troubled him the most. Three Tankers had occupied their suites in the hotel when the bombs went off. Father Jonathan Ashton would be remembered for all the help he had given TAMO over the years. Cecilia Begay had brought her knowledge of tribal Arizona to the team, and Donna Andrew's pleasant thoughts had always been welcomed. All three would be sorely missed. At least they didn't suffer. They died almost instantly, with no time to say goodbye or even mentally contact their comrades.

The loss impacted the team, as it was no longer comprised of fourteen Tankers. Only eleven Tankers remained. Twelve had been needed for the ritual in Death Valley. Twelve had been needed in Russia. Nate remembered how, throughout the prophecy, it talked about the number twelve. Could they find the remaining keys with only eleven people? That question would only be answered by the hunt for the keys.

The Issue with Samantha

Samantha didn't like what happened the last time she talked to Mario. She did not want to be responsible for more death and destruction. Of the two keys she helped procure, the Vatican Key had been the smallest and easiest for her to handle. She decided she would focus on stealing the Vatican Key from Mario's boss, return it to the TAMO group, and work with them instead of AUKA. If she had time and opportunity, she would obtain the other key too. For her plan to work, though, she needed to find out where the keys were being kept.

Samantha contacted Mario and asked if they could meet at her house, using her finest sexual innuendo, and Mario quickly agreed. Retaining the memory and experience of an eighty-five-year-old but offering the allure of a twenty-year-old body, she embodied the perfect enticement to ply information from Mario.

When Mario came to her door, she met him dressed in a shimmering nightgown. It made her intentions immediately clear to Mario. She shared some pleasantries and mentioned the Vatican as she took him up to her bedroom.

Mario could not help but think about the clandestine storage location of the Vatican book and key. They had not even put the book in a secure location. It sat on a bookshelf in a library in a home in the Encanto area of Phoenix, a single story bungalow owned by a cranky old man. Mario's mental image of the man showed him to be very wealthy, but the man had his habits.

When Samantha made similar hints about the key from the spaceman's hand, she got nothing from Mario. Apparently, someone else in AUKA knew the whereabouts of that key. She figured she could settle for one key.

Samantha continued to make slight comments to cause Mario to think more about the old man. She soon knew the man left the house at eleven-thirty every morning. He went for lunch at a particular restaurant where other members of AUKA talked about how they must preserve mankind and keep the bad people of TAMO from ever getting the twelve keys.

She had enough information. She gave Mario the pleasure of his life. She knew it would be the last time she would see him. Mario left happy and without any knowledge of what he had revealed to her.

☆ ☆ ☆

The next day, Sam watched the old man leave at precisely eleven-thirty. She walked to the back of the house to check the door. Locked. With a little struggle to use her credit card to shimmy the mechanism, she was able to open the back door.

She walked in, went looking for the bookcase, and discovered it in the living room. With a little hunting she found the book containing the Vatican key. She could not believe her luck. The book had been wrapped in brown paper, the only one wrapped on the bookshelf. The old man had no sense of security. Before leaving, she wrapped another book of the same size in the brown paper. If her luck held, the old man would not notice the loss for a long time.

Samantha didn't know the exact location of the Spaceman key, but entertained the thought that it, too, might be here in the house. While she thought of this idea, the front door opened. With the old man's early return, she would not have time to search for the other key. She quickly snuck out the back door. She had come in and out of the house in less than ten minutes.

Her successful retrieval of the Vatican Key and book made it necessary for Samantha Sampson to disappear and no longer exist. With a little effort and some old contacts from a former time in her life, she obtained the papers and other items for a new identity. At home, she packed her bags with all the things Mario had given her, and left the house unlocked with the keys sitting on the kitchen counter. With the help of an auto-driver cab, she visited the bank and moved her earnings of two million dollars onto a new card under her fresh name and identity. As far as Mario would know she had vanished. Samantha planned to never talk to that horrible man ever again.

Samantha reached out to try to mentally link with any one of the other Tankers. She was unable to reach the person who had previously communicated with her. She didn't know who it was or why they wanted to help her. She came to the conclusion that one of the people who died in the hotel explosion had been her Tanker contact. For what she had planned, that was good. She was done with the traitorous Tanker and severed her contact with Mario.

The Tanker she finally contacted mentally was Daniel. She asked him if he would set up a meeting with the imperial grand councilor at the New Moroccan restaurant. He agreed. The three of them would convene in the neutral restaurant in downtown Scottsdale, Arizona. Despite its name, the restaurant embraced old Morocco, so they would sit on the floor and eat their meal from communal dishes. Shared food meant less chance of introducing poison into anything she ate.

Sam arrived early and requested a table in a small private alcove.

When Daniel walked in, Samantha noticed his eyes widen when he recognized her. She smirked a bit, recognizing his instant attraction to her. He had only seen her in her eighty-five-year-old body way back during the Tanker briefing session, but clearly was intrigued with her new look. She gestured for him to take a seat on a floor cushion next to her at the round low table.

Shortly afterward the IGC arrived and seated himself to her left with the threesome making a triangle around the table. His vibe radiated curiosity and a slight wariness.

They shared some meaningless small talk and ordered a typical Moroccan meal. After the food arrived, Daniel—in a show of good faith—reached into the first bowl to retrieve some meat. With his other hand, he retrieved rice from another bowl and placed both foods in his mouth. He rolled his eyes to show how good it tasted. After swallowing it, he reached for his cup of Moroccan beer, chugged it all down, and grinned at Sam. Too nervous to smile back, she simply delved a trembling hand into the food too.

Their serious discussion began with the obvious. Samantha pleaded her case simply.

"I don't like what happened to your people or what the AUKA stands for. To prove I am done with them, I will open my thoughts fully to you, Daniel. You will be able to tell if I am keeping anything from you. Then, you can relay anything you feel is pertinent to the Imperial Grad Councilor."

Both men nodded in agreement, and Samantha closed her eyes and pressed her lips together. She totally opened her mind to Daniel, even allowing him to see her many rendezvous with Mario. She relayed to him her truth as a simple woman without deceit. She sent him her intention to work with AUKA purely for monetary gain, with no malice against the TAMO organization. Before the rejuvenation, she had been old with no money. She chose to restart her life.

She kept back one small, but important, thought. She wondered if he would ask her about the hidden information before she revealed it.

Daniel verbally shared with the IGC what he had learned. Samantha knew that all he said was what she had told Daniel mentally, with no embellishments.

Upon absorbing the information, Nate extended his hand to Samantha.

"You have our belief that you do, indeed, want out of your current situation. We will work with you to help you integrate with our group and secure your new identity. I understand you have made a name change. We will make the change legally permanent in the most discrete manner so no one else will know."

She shook hands with the IGC, who smiled at her.

Samantha didn't return the friendly gesture. Instead, she reached into her purse and pulled out the book secured in a tight brown shopping bag. She carefully handed the covered treasure to the IGC.

He looked inside the bag and gasped for a moment, then pressed his lips together in a knowing smile.

"This makes your joining us even more poignant. We now can continue our quest for the next keys without worrying about this one. Thank you."

The IGC inclined his head toward her in obvious appreciation.

She bowed her head in apology.

"I am sorry I couldn't find out where they hid the Peruvian Key. I never was fully linked into their organization. I only dealt with Mario. He assigned me only to pick up the keys from your team. Once we retrieved the Peruvian key, the pilot dropped me off at an airport to find my own way home, and he took the key someplace after that. I really am sorry."

She knew that handsome Daniel already knew this from her thoughts, she revealed it when she handed over the hidden book. For whatever reason, he hadn't relayed her sadness about the incident to the IGC. Still, it was good they both now understood her remorse for her actions.

Daniel grinned at her. *I really like this lady.*

Samantha picked up the thought that escaped from his mind.

She finally smiled back.

Africa, Victoria Falls

Nate told Steve he had made a plan to challenge Samantha. She would fly to Africa with Ryan, Dan, and Steve. The Dragon Prophecy writings stated with clarity that a combination of two gifted ones, one of whom needed to be a priest, would be necessary to recover the African Key. That translated to the serial value of one plus two which meant three gifted ones.

On the trip, Dan would participate in the ritual. Ryan would serve as pilot, guide, and observer since TAMO wanted someone to report back if things went horribly wrong. Prior experience had mandated that at least one person on the team should be a priest. Steve, being at the Thirteenth Level, met this need.

The number of people needed to retrieve a key was based on the correct understanding of the Dragon Prophecy. The whole team remembered watching another group attempt to obtain the key at the hand of the spaceman in Peru using an incorrect interpretation. The Tankers knew too well about the admonition associated with each of the Dragon's Teeth. The searcher must do the ritual correctly *"or surely ye shall die."*

The team headed to one of the Seven Natural Wonders of the world. They believed the key was sequestered inside the Victoria Falls.

The Prophecy said, "I will be there for you in the dry season hidden by my curtain."

With the rainy season at its end and as the water flowed over the falls to a maximum degree, they expected it would probably take a while to find the section of the falls indicated by the prophecy. They had to locate this special section where the key would be found during the dry season.

Back in the olden days, around 2020, the trip would have required three stops, from Phoenix to New York, to Johannesburg, and to Victoria Falls, and thirty hours of flight time. After terrorists destroyed the whole of Manhattan and the surrounding areas, the team was left with a multi-stop trip. Instead of a four-hour direct flight from New York to Johannesburg, the flight would require multiple stops in several African countries and take more than a day. They would fly in slow antique airplanes. A day to travel anywhere was such a crazy length of time given the current technology.

Daniel seemed to be growing close to Samantha. Steve could sense them both blocking him out of their thoughts. He remembered how he and Sandy blocked everyone during their first several weeks together. As Samantha opened up to him more and more, he appeared to see her in an ever increasing positive light. When Daniel spoke her name out loud, any Tanker nearby sensed the positive emotions pouring from him.

The first flight left from Phoenix for a one-hour hop to the next stop. Samantha and Daniel disappeared during the short flight. Steve watched them leave their seats at about the same time.

Ryan raised his eyebrows and met Steve's bemused gaze. The veteran must have noticed too. "I wonder if..."

Fifteen minutes later, the "missing" team members returned with that special glow about them. Things had definitely changed between Daniel and Sam. Steve grinned at Ryan, who chuckled quietly.

The trip was uneventful after that little diversion. On arrival in Barcelona the team showed the customs officials their passports and special TAMO cards, and customs waved them through. No one even checked their luggage.

Finding a flight to Johannesburg was relatively easy, but all the airlines used the old slower planes which meant another fourteen hours of flying. TAMO always purchased first-class seating. Sam and Daniel kept disappearing into the back of the plane and when they returned happiness fueled their smiles. By the fourth time, Steve knew the two had fully bonded.

The customs agents in Johannesburg differed greatly from those in Barcelona. In fact, they pulled the team aside and tore apart all their luggage. Perhaps they objected to seeing a black man holding hands with a white woman. Historically, the Afrikaners no longer remained friendly after the genocide of almost all the white farmers in the 2000s. The customs officers pretended to look for something. When they found the golden hooded robe and boots, they asked Steve to fully explain the purpose of the garb.

He explained the clothes bore religious meaning. He produced a paper from the imperial grand master, explaining in laymen's terms the importance of the clothing items. The customs official only glanced at the paper and told the team to leave as soon as they could.

Their next plane took off thirty minutes later for another three hours on the leg to Victoria Falls. The weather caused the team to endure a rough flight. Dan and Sam stayed seated, held hands, and smiled at each other often. Steve was sure the couple was enjoying a great mind-to-mind discussion.

"Bumpy" barely described the landing at Victoria Falls International airport in Zimbabwe. Once inside the airport, the team collected suitcases and went to customs. Like Barcelona, they showed their passport and special TAMO cards and moved easily through the customs process.

The last leg of the journey would bring them to the falls themselves. The TAMO office had arranged for an old Bell 407 helicopter decked out with an open door and a crane. The crane was a simple device, a long wire on a spool at the end of a beam. At the end of the wire were four loops for two people to hold onto the wire with one hand and one foot. In this way two people could be lowered or lifted at once.

The fueled-up copter stood ready to take them the twenty miles to the falls. Ryan and Daniel ran through the preflight checks. Steve and Sam locked down the luggage in the back. When finished, they all hopped in, put on headphones, completed the checkout and Ryan took off.

They landed first on the helipad at the guest information center. The team left the craft to talk with one of the guides to ask what the falls looked like during the dry season. For some reason, none of the guides would talk with them.

Ryan picked up on the thought of one of the men they had yet to approach.

Those superstitious natives of ours! Afraid if they talk about the dry season, it will come quickly and be worse than normal. If these yanks have money, I will tell them all they need to know.

Ryan whispered this to Dan and the team approached the guide. After a clandestine exchange of some hard gold currency, the man whispered to the team that, during the dry season, most of the falls became but a trickle of water. On the western edge, the falls always continued. The team recognized their destination goal. They thanked the guide and left.

The ride was quick, what with the mile-long series of falls almost in front of them. Even their goal of the western edge lay only a little more than a mile away. The helicopter flew along the thundering falls. The wet season made it a magnificent sight. Nearing the falls at the west end mimicked a flight in the middle of a rainstorm except the sun shone brightly overhead. As they came to the base of the falls, the sun's rays showed a glimmer of what was probably an old goat's path that led up into the falls, east of their goal.

Though they saw no place to land the helicopter near the top of the falls, a small plot of dry land offered a spot where three members of the team could be lowered. Ryan put the helicopter in hover for Daniel to lower Sam and Steve down to the base of the falls. Once the two were down, Daniel hooked himself up and, using the detachable controls, lowered himself as Ryan kept the helicopter steady.

The team of three donned their rain gear and backpacks. Climbing upward, they followed the goat trail. One hundred feet below the top of this section of the falls the trail led them behind the falls and continued on an inclined slope.

They tramped under and behind the falls where the trail continued but grew smaller and smaller. They climbed to approximately the center of the falls where they found an indented carving with ancient lettering above a defaced image of something below.

None of the three could decide what to do. They sensed the key was close by but could not see it. They looked and hunted for more than an hour but had no luck in their little quest. Hoping to find another path, they traveled back towards the pickup point on the original goat path.

Steve prayed for a new path to take them to their goal but to no avail.

This trip was a bust. As a team, they decided to wait until the dry season to hunt again. Sam was the first to go up back into the helicopter, followed by Daniel. Steve grew impatient when Daniel did not respond to his mental requests to be lifted up to the copter. When the winch finally started and cranked him up, he discovered Daniel and Sam in a deep passionate kiss.

Nate had confided in Steve that he hoped the trip would show what Sam was made of. Steve still held some negative feelings about Sam. She had been the one at the library. He would continue to watch her, though it was hard to stay angry at her. He could feel the positive energy flowing from Daniel towards Sam.

Even though the team did not find the key, Sam integrated well and worked with her team on the search. Except for Sam and Daniel falling in love, this trip failed to meet success expectations.

The four traveled back to Phoenix, this time bypassing South Africa. The plane trip exceeded the thirty hours to Victoria Falls because they traveled eastward via Dubai and straight back to Phoenix.

Stonehenge

Four weeks after the retrieval of the Tunguska Key and the failure to retrieve the African key, Lindsey's first photoshoot completed successfully. Pick up any of the top model magazines and her photo appeared in it. Her advertisement videos found their way onto all the broadcast and online outlets in dozens of languages. She was becoming a very wealthy woman.

A quick phone call to Lindsey in Paris made gathering the team easy. Nate knew any one of the Tankers could contact the rest anywhere around the world. Lindsey relayed Nate's oral request to the rest of the team to meet in London in three days. They needed to meet before the winter solstice, less than a week away.

Nan knew TAMO was putting all its resources into figuring out where in Stonehenge the key would be found. They could not dig up that large of an area to find a small box, they had to follow the clues. Apparently, "something" would happen at sunset on the day of the winter solstice, but they did not know what.

Lindsey and Andrey took an auto-driver limo from Paris to London via the Chunnel. The car and train expressway under the channel between France and England still functioned fully. As always, the team stayed in the best hotels.

Nan flew in the TAMO private jet with Rob from Toronto to London Stansted Airport. The jet, slower than commercial flights, took four hours. Especially after their time together in Toronto, she needed the flight time to discuss their relationship. Of course, their talk convinced her she had totally forgiven him. She just knew they would be together forever.

Something about that touch of his and their direct mind-to-mind communication made their closeness even more intimate. Still, she remained a little cool and aloof. It was fun to tease him. Besides, making up would be so wonderful. That gave her something to look forward to.

☆☆☆

The remaining Tankers flew into either Heathrow or Gatwick, depending on where they had been vacationing. Sam's presence with them made the imperial grand councilor feel a little better. With her, the team included twelve members plus Nan and himself. The Dragon Prophecy had many requirements for finding the twelve treasures. By separating the team members, the likelihood lessened of some freak accident happening.

He, Nadia, Nan, and Rob had been invited to stay with the current Queen Consort of England, Catherine. She used to be known as Kate Middleton or the Duchess of Cambridge. At a little more than fifty-five years of age, she remained in the British Royal Family. She told the IGC over lunch that she and her husband hoped to reign longer than Queen Elizabeth II.

Lindsey, Andrey, Steve, and Sandy were sequestered at the Dorchester Hotel, originally built in the last century, in 1931. The hotel suites they picked were side by side with an adjoining door and overlooked Hyde Park. Even with their fat bank accounts, the room cost 4,079 new dollars per night, not including meals, so the team members acted delighted to have TAMO pick up the charge for the suites. They certainly all knew the old adage, "To stay rich, use other people's money."

Down the street, Albert, Martha, Daniel, Sam, Ryan, and Briana stayed at 45 Park Lane, a very modern hotel. They could walk down the sidewalk and meet with the others or stay in their rooms and communicate with the rest of the team via their mental gifts.

Nate had two days to plan. On December 21, 2040, at six-thirty-three in the afternoon, the winter solstice sunset marked when they would hold the Stonehenge Key ceremony. The imperial grand councilor spent a lot of time trying to figure out exactly what was needed to find that Key.

Of course, the Tunguska Key had reacted positively to the presence of three TAMO Thirteenth Level priests. This time they had four, the Guardian Nate, the Sacred Speaker Nan, and the two new Thirteenth Level priests Rob and Steve. Soon after the treasure ritual had revealed the true Phobos sphere, Nate used TAMO's extreme financial strength to convince the British government to reserve the sunset ritual at Stonehenge for the TAMO team.

The government had asked for and received billions of new dollars to guarantee no other people would be near Stonehenge around the predetermined time. To assure their privacy and secrecy, a curtain ten feet taller than the tallest monolith encircled the ancient monument. They left open the entrance area for the team and for the area where the final rays of the solstice sunset would appear.

In the past forty-eight hours, a blast of northern artic cold air had dropped the daytime temperatures to an unheard-of minus twenty degrees Celsius. With the wind blowing, the wind-chill caused the temperature to plummet to minus forty degrees Celsius. The expected temperature high on the day of the winter solstice was expected to be minus twenty-five degrees. A north wind was bringing the coldest winter storm in English recorded history. Nate believed the weather had something to do with the Stonehenge Key and the presence of the gifted ones.

The team met via mental thought discussion. Nate donned his official role as the ICG and mentally discussed with the team what needed to be done. He held hands with Nadia, and she sent the thoughts to the other Tankers in their various locations.

Nan also held Rob's hand to be a part of the discussion too. The IGC told the team members to remain separated until it was time to leave. He didn't want to experience any other setbacks like the mugging in the Vatican Library, the loss of the key at the hand of the spaceman, the terrorism at The Center of Silence, nor the bombing in Phoenix.

First and foremost, it looks like we will be facing the coldest day on record for this area, he explained mentally. *I know that all of you were prepared for Siberia, but this will be twice as cold as the wind whips through Stonehenge. The four initiates of the Thirteenth Level TAMO degree will dress in their special robes. These will keep us warm. The rest of you should shop today. Go buy the warmest clothes you can find. Be sure the clothes have minimum metal in them. When you dress for the trip, wear no jewelry except the TAMO symbol. As always, to make you stronger, get a good night's rest. We will leave for Stonehenge at two p.m. for the two and a half hour drive. Be sure to eat a hearty lunch. We should arrive in plenty of time to dress and orient ourselves.*

The day of the solstice started out colder than predicted. By the time the team assembled in front of their lodgings at two that afternoon, the temperature had dropped another ten degrees.

The limos were all driven by human TAMO members. Nate was taking no chances with electronic auto-drivers. The limos came, one to each location, picked up the team members, and drove them to Stonehenge. They had to park in the tourist parking area, a distance of about 500 feet from the monument. The government had done as requested. No one wandered in the area.

The team dressed in their heavy clothes and went out to the center of the monument. Nate used a serious tone to announce, "The four of us dressed in gold will stay at the center of the henge around the altar stone. We will form the flower while the center stone will represent the ruby. The rest of you will form the remainder of the TAMO Symbol. We have drawn our symbol on the ground using the mystical combination of earth, water, and fire—sand, salt, and sulfur. Each of you shall take up a position at one of the ten points, the four points of the cross, plus the six points of the star. We have twenty minutes before sunset. It will be cold waiting but get into position now."

The team spread out and took positions. Each person had a view of the center altar stone.

As Imperial Grand Councilor Nate, the Sacred Speaker and Thirteenth Level Priests Steve and Rob approached the center altar stone, their amulets started to glow ever so slightly. Even though the altar stone was partially covered, Rob and Steve made up the final two inner positions of the flowery rose's west side and the eastern center. Nan and Nate took up north and south positions near them. As soon as they positioned themselves, their necklaces glowed a little brighter. The imperial grand councilor felt they had set things up correctly. They simply needed to wait a few minutes for the sunset.

The wind had stopped, yet the cold had increased even more. The four stayed warm even though they only wore their thin garments. The imperial grand councilor regretted the others had only regular clothes to keep them warm.

From their positions in the inner circle, Steve faced Rob and Nate faced Nan. By looking over Rob's shoulder, Steve would be able to see the location where the setting sun shone through the massive stones. The shadow from the stones slowly crept longer and approached the altar stone. The closer the shadow came, the brighter the rubies in the initiate's necklaces glowed. When the last rays of sun touched the altar stone, the rubies on the initiates became fire red.

According to Nate's expectation, each ruby would send a mental thought out to its wearer. Given the expressions on the other team members' faces, that appeared to happen to them, too. From the four rubies of the initiates a circle of light formed. The light expanded and reflected off each of the four and radiated out to the other team members until the lights outlined the full TAMO symbol.

Where the center lines crossed from the gilded four, another light started to form. The altar stone appeared to lose its solid state and to rise up out of the ground. On its flat surface a series of roman numerals printed out with precision from one to twenty.

The imperial grand councilor stepped forward. The light from his ruby continued to mark the spot on the stone. Moments before he touched the number twelve, he remembered what one of the young neophytes had asked with such innocence when learning of the legend of the Dragon's Teeth.

"Isn't twelve really the numbers one and two?"

He prayed she was right. He pressed the number one followed by the number two and stepped back into position. When the ground began to shake, the imperial grand councilor thought he might have made a mistake.

The temperature started to rise. Within a few minutes, the snow on the ground in the area marked by the symbol had completely melted and then evaporated. From the center of the altar stone rose a rectangular box about half the size of the one found at Tunguska. As the last beam of light left the altar stone, its stone solidified again. When it became whole, a box sat on top of it

When the rubies in everyone's amulets faded from red to clear, like diamonds, the imperial grand councilor walked back into the center and picked up the box. The center of the altar stone looked no different than it had twenty minutes before.

By the time they walked back to the limos, the temperature had normalized to three degrees Celsius with no breeze. The coldest day on record for England had ended.

Nate, Nadia, Rob, Nan, Steve, and Sandy drove back to London and immediately to the airport. In one hour, the group lounged in a private high-speed plane that would take them from England back to Toronto. The flight was uneventful, except for the amorous adventures of Steve and Sandy, not to mention Rob and Nan.

About halfway through the flight, the four stood up together, walked to the back of the plane, and closed the galley curtains. If you didn't know about their love, you would have thought the noises resulted from meal preparation.

Once the team arrived in Toronto, Nate stored the Stonehenge Key in a secret vault in the Toronto Lodge, relieved to finally secure the third key.

The Number of 12

Imperial Grand Master Julie Bernard was worried. AUKA was going after the Dragon's Teeth at the same time as TAMO. Somehow, the two groups hunted for the same keys in the same order. This situation had to be discussed but only the Thirteenth Level initiates could participate in the conclave. Julie instructed the imperial grand councilor and the sacred speaker to bring the Thirteenth Level initiates to the Toronto Grand Lodge.

More than five-hundred Thirteenth Level TAMO initiates lived in locations scattered all over the Earth within many lodges and other sacred locations. Each initiate played a part in learning about the Dragon's Prophecy and the written works associated with it.

Some initiates completed their Thirteenth Level initiation and become reclusive. They spent the rest of their lives examining a single portion of the prophecy and wrote volumes about it. Over the years, their writings became part of the Dragon Prophecy—in turn, studied and written about.

The prophecy and knowledge of the Dragon's Teeth had been discussed at length for almost one hundred centuries. The only people who knew what a Dragon's Tooth looked like included the original high priests, more than three-hundred centuries ago, and their designated successors throughout the centuries.

Obtaining and keeping the Siberian Key allowed the select members of TAMO to understand what a key looked like and the power of a key. After seeing and examining it closer, the highest level TAMO members began to review the research and throw out all the wrong guesses and philosophizing from centuries of discussions. With a real key in hand, they could also tell much of what was true in the additional works related to the prophecy.

The Dragon Prophecy documents were old and fragile. Even though they were written on hides, the material did slowly disintegrate. Each century, to preserve decaying content, the original prophecy would be copied by hand, retaining all the markings and words of the original document handed down at the beginning of the TAMO organization.

Constant references in the original prophecy related that all rituals must be done perfectly "or surely ye shall die." Always, the dragon says, "Bring me the number of twelve of my teeth. Do not only bring me the first tooth. Do not bring me the last tooth with a few others. Bring me the number of twelve of my teeth and make me whole again, or surely ye shall die."

Many verses made no sense. A paragraph called "The Great Discovery" read, "*Ye must listen to the newest of the ancients who is so young and so new to the life of the dragon.*" Many had written about this, but no one really knew its meaning.

With the keys accessible, the time came for a consensus of all the dragon's followers to decide what it all meant and what needed to be done.

Steve received his invitation to attend the meeting of the Thirteenth Level TAMO members. He and Sandy took the first flight they could catch from Phoenix to Toronto. During the whole flight and the travel to their hotel, Sandy tried to explain in many different ways why she felt in her gut she needed to be there too. He continued to explain why she could not come to the lodge, that only Thirteenth Level initiates could participate.

She finally opened her big, beautiful eyes, stared into his, and reminded him she was like Ruth in the old bible. "Don't urge me to leave you or to turn back from you. Where you go, I will go, and where you stay, I will stay. Your people will be my people and your God my God."

With that combination, Steve was unable to tell her no. He said he would try to include her, though he internally hoped someone at the lodge would prevent her entry. Besides, she did not know the password of the Thirteenth Level of TAMO or their very sacred secret sign.

☆ ☆ ☆

Sandy admired Steve, dressed in his Thirteenth Level priest's clothing. Quietly, he had built a mental wall to block her out, stating he felt he must focus on the problem of the Dragon Prophecy without distraction. Sandy had dressed in a fresh spring outfit that mimicked the priestly garb.

An auto-driver cab delivered them to the lodge where everyone also wore the same priestly garb. Everyone but Sandy. She did not care. Her intuition told her she needed to be included in the meeting.

She lowered all her mental walls to take in the thoughts of all the wise men and women in the room outside of the main temple. She caught some familiar thoughts from Nan and Rob. She quickly left Steve's side and went to see them.

When they saw Sandy, they hurried up to her and each gave her a big hug. Physically touching Nan allowed her to read her friends' thoughts at the same time. Each wondered what she was doing there at a gathering for only Thirteenth Level TAMO members.

She answered easily, *I have been on the quest for the keys. I have seen and been in the presence of three of them. I have the knowledge of the Dragon Prophecy in my mind from touching those around us. At the age of seventy-four, I am one of the oldest people here. I'm downright ancient! I guess I am the youngest of the 'gifted ones.'*

In their minds, Nan and Rob recognized something about what she had relayed to them, but they appeared slightly confused. Her friends locked eyes, nodded to one another in some form of agreement, and turned their gazes back to her.

Nan took Sandy by the hand. *I can't exactly put my finger on the importance of what you just shared, but we both believe you must be in this meeting. Everything is going to work out. We will talk to the IGM.*

They approached the guardian at the entry door and asked to see the IGM on a pressing matter. Though she was in the middle of preparing for the conclave, Julie came out to speak to her granddaughter, the sacred speaker.

Nan, who carried a lot of weight in the TAMO organization, explained her feelings about the need to have Sandy present for the talks.

After a series of questions for Sandy, the IGM agreed she could enter, but that the rules required her to know the password and the Thirteenth Level sign to enter. Julie reminded Rob and Nan they may not explain the prompts to Sandy. They agreed.

The IGM went to the guardian of the outer door and explained Sandy would be attempting to come into the conclave but must first give the password and make the sign. If she did not, he was to expel her from the temple.

Sandy did not look worried at all. She smiled and opened her mind to all of those entering the lodge temple door. It only took a second to know the secret password for the Thirteenth Level. Anyone approaching the door would think about what to say to the guardian, *The tooth is the key.* That was easy.

The physical pass sign proved slightly more difficult. She concentrated and found many of the entrants had to focus on doing the sign correctly. The guardian would pull the person close and let them whisper the passwords to him. Then he would hold his hand out to the petitioner as if to shake hands. Instead of shaking the guardian's hand, the petitioner would claw the back of it. Thus, the petitioner showed their right to enter and to help the dragon find her teeth.

Sandy stood in line with the others. When it came to her time to petition the guardian for entry, she gave the password and sign as though she had been doing it for years. The guardian let her pass.

She waited inside for Rob and Nan, followed them, and sat down next to them.

A knocking came at one of her mental doors. She opened it and Steve flashed in, *I love you. You are my one and only. I can see your beauty from the other side of the room.*

She looked up and smiled at Steve on the other side of the Temple. She could feel his longing from across the room.

When everyone had entered the temple, the IGM, wearing the dragon's head, went to the center of the temple to light incense and candles as part of the opening ritual. Once completed, she went back to the dragon's chair at the east of the Temple. Before sitting she removed the dragon's head and glanced from side to side at the members in the audience.

"We have three keys. A fourth key has been stolen from us and a fifth key appears to be missing. We, all together, must decide how we shall obtain the twelve keys to return them to the dragon on Phobos. All of you talk among yourselves for half an hour, let's see if we can find a solution."

Sandy, not being a true Thirteenth Level member, sat and listened to all of what the people thought and said. Most focused on how to get back the missing key or how to quickly find the other keys. She had been working with Steve for about a month, learning about TAMO. They had started from the first Neophyte levels of the TAMO lessons. She had finished the Sixth Level and was only at the beginning of the Seventh Level, which involved the learning of numerology, and the power of numbers stored in letters and words. All the talk in the room made her focus on her lessons. She abruptly understood why the same thing was said many times in the words of the Dragon Prophecy. She stood, placed her hand over her heart, and stared at the IGM. At first, conversations continued all over the Temple but, one by one, the people in the Temple saw her standing in her nonconforming gown.

Sandy stood for almost fifteen minutes until the Temple went silent and the IGM looked up from her mediations. "Lovely little dragonet, speak thy words to those around you," the IGM said.

Sandy inclined her head in acknowledgment of her permission to speak.

"Dragon masters here in the present and those in the past, hear me. I ask you to consider the words of this small lowly dragonet. I have come here to the council of the Thirteenth Level with the knowledge of almost three quarters of a century and the body of a twenty-four year old. I have gone through my studies and am in the Seventh Level."

Communal gasps emanated throughout the room. No one under the Thirteenth Level was supposed to be present at this gathering. That did not stop Sandy.

"All of the documents talk about the number of the twelve keys. I'm new with TAMO, but my question to all of you is simple. Isn't the parity of twelve really three? Twelve is made up of the numbers one and two which, added together, make three. Doesn't that mean we only need three keys? We have three keys. Are we not done?"

Sandy sat down and opened her mind to all in the temple. She was sure Steve and Rob did the same.

Every single person was evaluating her words against their knowledge of the prophecy. Each and every one came to the same phrase in the old document that they had memorized. They all thought it almost simultaneously, *Ye must listen to the newest of the ancients who is so young and so new to the life of the dragon.*

The IGM stood. "Ye must listen to the newest of the ancients who is so young and so new to the life of the dragon."

All in the Temple nodded their heads in agreement.

The IGM held out one hand toward Sandy. "This dragonet looks only twenty-four. She is indeed one of the ancients who has gone through rejuvenation. She has become young again. With the help of her friend, she has become a member of our order. She is quickly learning our knowledge and our ways. I don't normally open suggestions to a vote, but this is a special time. All those in favor of putting the full power and funds of the Traditional Ancient Mystical Order toward our endeavor based on the words of the prophecy apparent today, say 'So mote it be.'"

The answer sounded out loud and unanimous.

"So mote it be."

The IGM donned the dragon's head and rose to leave the temple. Everyone in the room also stood in deference to their leader, upon her departure, the members left the Temple one row at a time.

Next Stop Mars

The new urgency of the need for a Phobos mission, to return the three keys to the dragon, would require changes in a Mars-bound spacecraft owned by The Space Company. Its ship was originally designed for forty people to start the Mars colony along with a crew of five and a massive quantity of supplies. Now though, TSC's silent partner, TAMO, needed the ship for its mission. Before that could happen, TSC must be convinced to give up the ship and colonization plan.

On the positive side, the trip would require less technology because there would be no need for a heavy gravity lander. The big issue centered around the travel to Mars taking almost six months. The timing depended on the positions of Earth and Mars in their respective orbits. The original planned mission was when Mars would be in opposition to Earth on March 11th, 2044.

The requirement for an earlier launch meant the systems engineers would have less time to test the ship. But, with the change in destination, time to launch, and number of passengers, they needed only to complete facilities on the craft for the crew of two, plus eight passengers. The schedule allowed no time for live training. However, some of the TAMO members would be able to go through simulator training to serve as the crew.

✩✩✩

Ryan Bentley and Daniel Wright had flown to The Spaceship Company's headquarters in Florida as soon as the "go" decision had been made at the Thirteenth Level conclave. On the speedy and comfortable private TAMO jet, they arrived near the end of the workday.

The grand lodge had been a big investor in The Spaceship Company's ventures for many years. Ryan and Daniel took a letter from the imperial grand master to give to Sir Richard Branson, the president of TSC. Branson was not even in the US when they arrived. They would have to talk to the General Manager and CEO, John Shaffer, who was in the office. Mr. Shaffer would not take a meeting. Through the secretarial area camera, he had seen the men arriving. Daniel picked up his thought.

They look like they're only nineteen or twenty years old. Way too young to be of any use to the company.

He told his secretary to explain he was too busy to see them.

The Tankers gave the letter to the secretary, who took it into the CEO's office. Even the letter of introduction from the imperial grand master made no difference. The mental image from Mr. Shaffer was quite clear.

Whoever this imperial grand master is, I don't care. Those children will never get an appointment.

The office day was ending. Ryan and Daniel were told that they would have to leave for the day also. Before security arrived to escort them out, the two explained to the secretary they would be back the next day to wait for an opening in the CEO's schedule.

The secretary gave a weak smile and said good night. Daniel heard her thoughts. *I wish I could help them, but the boss is the boss, and he said, "No meeting, ever." I feel sorry for them.*

The next morning, Ryan and Daniel showed up at the corporate headquarters when it opened at nine o'clock. The secretary told them there would be no meeting. Ryan and Daniel remained polite. They simply sat quietly and patiently and exchanged friendly conversation with the secretary. Outwardly, they appeared quiet. Inwardly, they had both opened their minds to listen to what was going on.

The twenty-something secretary had looked at them many times, especially Daniel, who she clearly considered most attractive. They probably appeared to her to be three or four years younger than her. She obviously wanted to help them.

Daniel hoped to use that information and her attraction to him to his advantage. He talked with her pleasantly most of the day. After lunch, he considered asking her out for dinner. He decided not to when her thoughts shifted into prurient desires and thoughts of what she wanted to do to him when she got him home. Daniel knew it would be fun, but their business with the CEO was more important. Besides, he was deeply in love with Sam.

Finally, late in the afternoon, Daniel and Ryan decided to call in the "big guns."

Daniel tried contacting the imperial grand councilor through Nadia while Ryan mentally listened in. He found it exceedingly difficult to get through even to Nadia. She had built up a thoroughly strong mental wall. Daniel kept the pressure up on Nadia's mind.

After an hour, her mind finally relaxed and let down her mental walls just a little. He reached her in that mental twilight between waking and sleeping. Daniel's sent a simple message.

I must speak to Nate! He repeated it multiple times.

She groggily answered, *Oh, Daniel, I thought I was having a dream. Nate is right here, let me reach over and touch his hand.*

He immediately connected through her, and Daniel was able to relay the information. The response was quick and simple, *It shall be done!*

Daniel had no idea what would happen. He only knew they would have their meeting soon.

Nate rolled out of bed and called the secretary of The Space Company's owner on a special private line.

"Jane, it's Nate, I need to talk to Richard. It's urgent."

"He is in China today working on a special deal," she responded quickly and efficiently. "But I am transferring you now."

The phone clicked several times, and an elderly voice said, "This is Branson."

"This is Nate. The dragon has his twelve teeth."

Even as only a Sixth Level TAMO member, Richard understood the urgency. This statement had not been used in many thousands of years.

"What do you need?"

"First, I don't appreciate your people keeping my two TAMO members waiting for more than a day to meet with the CEO."

Nate went on and explained about the need for the TAMO team to commandeer TSC's new spacecraft currently in orbit because it was needed to go to Phobos instead of Mars.

Branson responded. "I'll call the company CEO, John Shaffer, and explain he is to give your people anything and everything they ask for regardless of cost." His tone sounded terse. "Your people will be given carte blanche, no matter what they ask for."

The phone clicked and Branson was gone.

Nate held Nadia's hand again and was able to mentally get through to Daniel. *It is done!*

☆☆☆

Only ten minutes later, the CEO came out of his office with his hand outstretched to shake both Tankers' hands.

"Good afternoon, I'm John Shaffer, the managing director and CEO of The Spaceship Company. I apologize for the wait. Please come into my office and tell me what you need."

Daniel explained about the mission to Mars and the training he and Ryan would need. Daniel kept his mind open to interpret the mental words and attitude that came from Mr. Shaffer. His mind was full of fear of his boss and a desire to obtain whatever they needed. He wanted the young men out of his office as soon as possible.

While they sat in his office, Shaffer made several calls to set everything up. Afterward, he explained how they would go to Colorado the next day to train for piloting the new spacecraft.

After several hours, the news finally reached the imperial grand master. She was pleased with the results of the imperial grand councilor. *Things are coming together.*

Farewells and Sandy

Steve knew he would be one of the members on the Mars trip. Before that new risk and considering all the other dangerous situations they had been in together, he wanted to make Sandy an honest woman. But he did not want to marry without his family present.

After making their happy decision, Sandy and Steve took off on the next available flight to Washington DC. None of Steve's family knew the two were coming. They arrived at eleven that night at Steve's daughter's home in time to watch the four girls drive off in their auto-driver car for a Friday night of bar hopping. Tiffany sat in the command position. Steve could see the house was dark so he decided they would follow the girls. He told his auto-driver to follow the car in front of them. Life was so much easier with the new technologies.

He opened his mind to his family to see if he could find out where the girls were going. He had let Sandy hear what was going on too. Most of it was young lady talk which Steve ignored. But one string of thought he recognized.

How come they think I can't find the "New Ultrabar?" It's on F Street, and I even can use my free pass to get us in. I guess I'll have to explain again that the designated driver picks the place. Even if the auto-driver does all the driving.

Steve was sure that was Tiffany. Second-born tended to need to continually stick up for themselves.

Steve suggested a fun idea to Sandy.

Let's play a trick on Isabella, Tiffany, Caroline, and Evelyn. We will get to the bar, and I will see if I can pick one of them up.

Sandy quickly replied, *I know you look like a young man, but sometimes you act like a lecherous old goat.* After a full giggle and approval of Steve's idea, Sandy spoke out loud to him.

"Why don't you walk up to them and talk to them like they are your granddaughters. I think that will be 'trick' enough. Listen to their thoughts, you will see."

Steve grunted in agreement.

Their auto-driver followed the girls' car and when his granddaughters arrived at the bar and went inside, he and Sandy tried to do the same. They became separated from the girls because the young women went right in. Fifteen minutes, and two fifty new dollar tickets later, they gained entry. The bar had four levels, so he and Sandy split up to try and find the girls. She started on the bottom floor, and he went to the top floor.

Level four featured "old" albums from 2010–2020. Steve liked the music. A lot of it included remakes of 1970–1980 music.

Sandy, I'm bad. The music here is like what I grew up with. I'm going to get a drink and look for the girls after that. Sandy's response included a simple image of her in one of her very skimpy lingerie outfits. It was her way of saying, *Okay but remember who you came with.*

Steve walked over to the bar to order his drink. Since the music played at a pretty loud decibel, Steve had to raise his voice to get the attention of the bartender.

"Barkeep, give me a Drambuie on the rocks with a water back!"

Steve yelled the words right as the music stopped. Everyone on that level knew what he had ordered. He picked out a thought that came to him, *That's the drink Pop-Pop drinks. I wonder who that guy is.*

A glance around along with interpreting several thoughts between the girls helped him pinpoint the girls' locale. He imaged a thought to Sandy.

Fourth level to the right as you come through the door.

Steve paid for his drink and walked over to the girls. He reached the table and took in their appearance. The young ladies were all definitely "dressed to the nines." They also engaged in an intelligent conversation about school and work, beyond their interest in dancing with some of the handsome men in the place. A guy would be lucky to meet any one of them. The girls already sipped on drinks. At the age of nineteen, Isabella and Caroline were both only allowed to drink beers. Tiffany and Evelyn had some foo-foo girly drinks in front of them. He was sure Tiffany's drink was nonalcoholic. She always followed the driving laws.

Steve sauntered up to their table.

"Can I buy you ladies another round?"

He opened his mind to hear their thoughts. Isabella and Caroline thought essentially the same thing, *A cute guy my age wants to buy me a drink. He is welcome to, but he better not want anything for it. He looks so familiar.*

Tiffany and Evelyn, being the older twins, thought similar thoughts too. *I'll take the drink, but this guy is too young for me.*

The oral answer Steve received from the girls came simultaneously, "Yes, that would be nice!"

He waved down the waitress and discreetly gave her his Twelve-Gen card. He leaned in toward her ear and whispered his request.

"Put the four girls' tab on this card and bring them a round. Please also bring me another Drambuie on the rocks with a water back, and a Merlot for my girlfriend who will be here in a minute. Also, add a 200 new dollar tip for yourself."

The conversation came through a bit awkwardly for Steve as he wasn't sure what to say.

He tried, "How are your school years going, ladies?"

Evelyn's mind said, *That's a pretty personal first question but I don't want to blow him off until the drinks come.*

Each answered verbally and concisely described as much as they could without saying anything too personal. The efficient waitress went away and came back within only a few minutes. As she was serving everything up, Sandy showed up and picked up her drink. You did not have to be a mind reader to see the confusion in the girls' faces.

Steve continued with his agreed-upon tactic, though he found it hard to stay serious. Somehow, he managed to talk with just a small smirk.

"Isabella, Caroline, Tiffany, and Evelyn, this is my fiancé, Sandy Haspure."

The girls' expressions became even more confused. Evelyn, the oldest by five minutes, took charge as she normally did.

"Who the hell are you and how do you know our names? Are you some sort of creepy kinky stalker trying to be with four girls and your fiancé?"

The girls' minds were all in agreement.

Steve couldn't stop himself. The trick on the girls was going so well.

"Well, Evy, I thought you would like to meet her." He pointed to Sandy.

The only person who ever called Evelyn "Evy" was her Pop-Pop. Reality hit these smart young women all at once.

They responded in unison, "Pop-Pop! Is that you?"

The "gig" was up.

"Didn't I tell you girls last year that some young guy might come up and talk to you?"

They all laughed as the younger twins brought up two more chairs to the table.

The six of them talked for several hours. When they all finally left the New Ultrabar together, they squeezed into the family car and headed back to their Georgetown home.

On the way, his granddaughters revealed that both their mom and dad were expected home sometime in the early hours of Saturday morning. They encouraged Steve and Sandy to take the guest bedroom when they returned home.

Steve left a note for Alisa and Mark and put it where they'd see it when they arrived. Sandy told Steve she felt very much at home and welcomed in this house. They fell asleep in each other's arms, their minds calm and open.

Knock, knock! A loud rapping sounded on their door. Steve woke right up. He could hear the positive thoughts coming from the other side of the door, as could Sandy, from both Alisa and Mark.

Sandy covered her naked body with a sheet but before Steve could cover much, the door opened, and Alisa came flying in.

"Dad, what are you doing here? Why didn't you call ahead? We would have wanted to be here when you arrived! Who is this lovely creature next to you? Is she my soon-to-be new mom? It's about time you remarried. You dirty old man!" She pulled up short as she focused on him. "Wow, look at you, Dad! You look like you are twenty years old—" One hand flew over her mouth, her eyes widened, and her lawyer persona overtook her excitement. "Oh, how rude of me. Get dressed and come downstairs and have some coffee. Mark will wake the girls."

Mark still stood in the doorway. He grinned and waved hello, then turned toward their daughters' rooms.

At almost noon on Saturday, when they had shared hours of talking and reminiscing around the kitchen table, Steve finally got down to the reason for their visit.

He explained as much as he could about the trip to Mars and how no one knew how the trip would end. The trip was designed to travel only one way, so he felt the importance of introducing Sandy to his family. He and Sandy wanted to marry right away with family and friends present, so it needed to happen Sunday, the next day.

The whole family was happy that Steve had found his second true love and that they would get to see them marry. Steve recognized Alisa's forced smile. He knew she was happy to see her dad remarry but, at the same time, expressed sadness that the newlyweds would soon be gone, possibly forever. The two sets of twins looked at the couple with tears flowing down their cheeks, not knowing what would happen, but knowing the two lovers would at least be together.

Arrangements were made for several of their Tanker friends and TAMO members to come and stay that night, or to arrive the next morning for the sunset wedding. Nate and Nadia flew down from Canada later that day. Andrey and Lindsey flew in from Paris. The four arrived barely in time for the Saturday night rehearsal dinner. With Alisa and Mark's family of six, plus Steve and Sandy's friends, it made for a nice even number of twelve participants for the rehearsal dinner.

Steve pulled some strings and laid out a considerable amount of money to secure a last-minute dinner location for that night. The dinner was at one of the "new" best restaurants in Georgetown where the chef flew in fresh "authentic" ingredients every day.

The menus listed no prices. Steve heard the girls worrying about how their share of the dinner would be paid. The other Tankers apparently heard the young woman's thoughts too.

Nadia stood up and scanned the group with a pleased expression. She held her glass of water aloft as if she planned to give a toast.

"I have been so well taken care of by my love, Nate, that I have been unable to spend but a little of the stipend I receive each month. It is my pleasure to pay for all and anything you want tonight. Consider it my gift to Sandy and Steve, from Nate and me. So, enjoy!"

Everyone placed their orders: everything from a vegetarian shepherd's pie to a twelve-ounce authentic filet mignon. Nadia even ordered several bottles of champagne.

"Since I'm buying, I'll make the first toast as soon as we all have a glass of bubbly in our hands."

Three waiters arrived almost immediately with three bottles of authentic champagne from France. Everyone knew even the cheapest bottle cost in the hundreds of new dollars, and these bottles topped the vintage. The waiters opened the champagne and poured the liquid treasure. Everyone at the table stood and raised their glasses.

Nadia raised hers and inclined her head toward the betrothed couple. "We have known Sandy and Steve for a little over a year and have come to think of them as family."

An image went out to all the Tankers of a spring day in the Ukraine with rabbits and baby deer snuggling up to Sandy and Steve as they fed the animals little morsels of food.

"Nate and I love them both and wish them many years of happiness and love for each other and the many children they will have. May they have a safe trip. May they both return to us quickly and safely!" She finished with the standard TAMO ending. "So mote it be!"

The rest of the group responded in unison, "So mote it be!"

Everyone saluted, took a sip, and sat again. Each person at the table took a turn making a short toast. Steve, next to last, raised his glass and gazed at Sandy with big childlike eyes.

"If you can believe it, I met and picked up Sandy at a bar. Well actually, she tricked me into meeting her. We have become so close and several times I thought I was going to lose her. On one occasion she actually was in mortal danger, and I was tied up. Unable to help her. We survived that with the help of our Tanker friends."

Steve pointed his glass at the Tankers around the table.

"Each of you have become close friends. The bond we share cannot be measured in normal ways. You all can feel my love for you and how much I love my partner, Sandy! I am looking forward to our next adventure as husband and wife!"

At this point Steve was in tears. He raised his glass higher.

"I love you, Sandy!"

Barely able to choke out the words, he took a sip of champagne and sat down quickly to wipe tears from his cheeks

Finally, Sandy stood. In a full happy cry, she said, "Love you *all!*" She raised her glass in toast to her friends and family, sipped her drink and sat again with tears sparkling in her eyes.

The meal became very quiet after that toast, mostly because of the arrival of the excellent meal. Its touted tastiness and succulence and no disappointment. As the servers delivered dessert, everyone started to chit-chat again.

When the party had been going on for several hours, Nate stood. "It is almost midnight. As best man, I must make sure Steve gets to our hotel and does not see the bride until she comes down the aisle tomorrow on the south lawn of the White House. The President knows what we have been doing for him and our country. He is looking forward to meeting these 'kids' who are really eighty plus years old."

He gestured toward Steve's daughter. "Working with Alisa here, we have convinced the chief justice of the Supreme Court to marry these two unworthy people. The President took only a little convincing to let us use his home for this affair on such short notice. I'm sure everyone in DC will wonder what special event happened there that never appeared on the official White House agenda."

Everyone at the table chuckled and commented to one another about the good news, Nate grabbed Steve by the hand and dragged him out to the waiting human-driven cab. Steve didn't even get to say good night to his family. He did send a message to all the Tankers including Sandy.

Love you all! See you tomorrow at sunset.

☆☆☆

Mark and Alisa hosted Sandy. Her beautiful white silk designer dress arrived in the morning, along with the designer and a seamstress. It required only minor adjustments.

The rest of the family had dressed in formal attire of burgundy and black. Mark had called his youngest sister to come as a guest who brought her two little daughters to be the flower girls. The two girls were dressed in matching frilly pink colored dresses. They were ready to walk down the aisle first with baskets filled with dark red rose petals. The whole wedding party had somehow color coordinated the reddish colors for the wedding.

Sandy had no living parents, so her Tanker friend Rob had agreed to walk her down the aisle.

Rob, where are you and Nan? I don't want to have to walk myself down the aisle!

Sandy, we only just landed at Baltimore Washington International. We will meet you at the White House in twenty minutes.

Sandy was her normal positive self. *You two better make it or you're dead!* She sent an image of a beautiful wedding with Rob escorting her down the aisle. She showed him the gorgeous long white dress that showed off her young figure in a see through lace but covered her essential parts with a satin opaque film. Her train flowed down her back touching the floor.

Her friends made it in plenty of time, though it took a bit to get through the guards at the front of the White House. Not to mention the large crowd trying to see what big wigs rated a wedding at the White House.

The bridal march started. After the bridal party and the darling flower girls in pink satin, Rob walked Sandy down the steps at the back of the White House into the rose garden, and down the satin white aisle to where Steve waited in his stunning white tuxedo with a long tailcoat. Rob turned to Sandy and lifted the veil away from her face.

The chief justice officiated with a typical wedding ceremony. As the sun cast its last pink and red rays onto the clouds forming a pink roof over the couple, he ended with, "I now pronounce you man and wife. You may kiss the bride."

All the Tankers caught the chief justice's thought. *You, son, don't deserve such a hot woman!*

The Tankers all sent images of joy to the couple as Steve leaned in and gave her a long passionate kiss. Steve's smile as he came up for air made the whole audience smile and applaud.

So, started the life of Mr. and Mrs. Steve Johnson.

The reception inside the White House entertained the small gathering of people for the rest of the evening. Around midnight Sandy and Steve said goodnight. As they left the White House and headed back to their daughter's Georgetown home, their friends and family threw rich colorful biodegradable confetti at Sandy and Steve.

Their arrival at Alisa's home culminated in a night of wedded bliss and debauchery consummated more than once during the short night.

Monday morning came too early for the newlyweds with an early but pleasant breakfast. Everyone needed to be somewhere before eight that morning, so Sandy and Steve said their goodbyes, hugging and kissing everyone including the pets. They hopped into an airport limo to take them to the airport for their flight to Colorado and the next stage of their adventure together.

Nadia, Nate, and the Moon

It was not the first time that Nate had complained about his aches and pains. After all, his body belonged to a man of sixty. His lover, Nadia, had the beauty and body of a twenty year old. Neither of them thought for a minute, despite their disparate looking ages, that they should be with anyone else.

The two of them entered the dragon's temple in the Phoenix TAMO lodge. Its beauty and details were obvious as Nadia looked at the intricate brass pieces and tall carved Egyptian style columns that held up the ceiling containing frescos of mystical figures from the past. In recent weeks, she had talked continuously about making arrangements to enhance the lodge with real gold elements instead of the brass. That day, she looked around and made comments about what improvements to recommend, but suddenly noticed Nate was no longer walking beside her.

She spun around to see him ten feet away kneeling on one knee and holding out a small box toward her.

Nadia hurried back and stopped before him, both hands covering her mouth.

He opened the box to reveal a gorgeous diamond ring set in a miniature cross and star with a beautiful deep vivid red ruby in the center of the flower.

"Nadia Belova, will you marry me?"

Her face lit up with joy and she let out a squeal.

"Yes!"

She held out her left hand to him.

Nate rose and carefully placed the engagement ring on her finger. A perfect fit. He reached into his pocket and brought out two tickets and handed them to her.

"These tickets will take us into near Earth orbit in two weeks. From there we will go out to the big U.S. moon base. There, I have arranged for us to be married in a private ceremony. The governor will do us the honor of performing the ritual."

She clasped her hands over her chest, eyes sparkling. "Oh, Nate—"

He leaned in and placed a gentle kiss on her lips. "There are several passages in the Dragon Prophecy that involve the moon. Since no one places much value on Moon real estate, I was able to secure an agreement from several governments and the moon governor that allows me to buy a large parcel of the surface. It stretches twelve miles by twelve miles on the dark side of the moon in the Mare Tranquillitatis. My idea is to live there, which will ease the pains of my old body."

Nadia cradled his cheek with one hand. "You mean we could live near the Sea of Tranquility, ease your discomfort, and I could become the Moon Goddess of our estate?"

He grinned and took her hand. "Well, TAMO can do what they want with the property. I will own the 144 square miles on the surface, but TAMO owns a wedge-shaped piece under it, down to the moon's core. I'm sure it will take quite a while before we can build anything there, but it is a start. Will you come to the moon with me and be my bride and the queen of our TAMO Moon kingdom?"

Nadia gave a little jump and pressed her hand against his neck. "Yes! Whither thou goest, I will go."

The ancient reference to Ruth in the Old Testament of the Bible brought his lips into a sweet smile until her lips thoroughly vanquished it.

☆ ☆ ☆

Nate spent the next two weeks putting his finances in order. He needed someone on Earth whom he could trust. After a discussion with Steve, who gave his consent, Nate contacted Alisa's law firm and asked them to take care of his finances. The firm would be paid .002 percent of the value of all of Nate's assets. It represented a big win for the firm, with an almost guaranteed twelve million new dollars of income each year. It meant work for the associates and profit for the firm.

The Moon Colony had been built into the side of a crater. Those few people with windows lived at the crater's edge. Even with the small 5,000-person population, shops provided limited goods from Earth. Many other shops had goods manufactured on the Moon. Food and moon-style clothing were easily purchased but expensive.

Nadia decided she would convert her Twelve-Gen card to moon dollars. The funds on her card held the only finances she owned in the world. Nevertheless, Nate's hints at financial investments had given her a lot of profit, even after paying the crazy fifty percent U.S. profit tax. She was set to be able to buy what they needed in their new moon home. The cost of shipping items to the moon was extremely expensive.

Though Nadia donated all her earthly clothes to charity, of course, she kept all the lingerie. It was lightweight, and none would be available in her new home. She even added to the collection by purchasing a white bridal set to make Nate's wedding night one he would never forget.

After packing and heading to the airport, the flight from Phoenix to the Colorado launch location took only fifteen minutes. They arrived in plenty of time for the pre-boarding as required by their tickets.

The launch craft held forty-five people and sat on top of a fat multistage rocket. The technicians gave the couple lightweight launch clothes and told them to pack everything else in their suitcases except their phones and tickets.

The preparation for launch took longer than the flight to the airport. A guide showed them into their own small first-class cabin where they sat somewhat comfortably in chairs with their backs to the ground. *Up* was the direction of space after all. They waited more than an hour and a half, periodically hearing the launch director's "L minus" countdown until launch.

Finally, the launch director's voice came through their comms, "Ten, nine, eight, seven, six, five, four, three, two, one, and liftoff!"

The three gravities of pressure during the liftoff were hard on Nate, but he smiled the whole time. Nadia screamed like a little girl with the joy of the ride. After about ten minutes, they entered into the same Earth orbit as the space hotel and the inside of their ship went weightless. They enjoyed the weightlessness by "playing" in their cabin together. It took ten hours for the craft to catch up to The Spaceship Company Orbital Hotel and dock.

The plan was to stay one night in the low gravity of the spinning hotel, and the next morning board another spaceship to take them to the Moon colony.

They left the craft walking in the light gravity, which allowed them to feel which way was up and to keep their feet on the floor. Their hotel room was small, about 180 square feet, about the size of a small inner cabin on an ocean cruise ship. In space, that was considered a large suite. Because they would not see their bags until they arrived at their new Moon home, an off-the-rack set of clothes hung in the small closet for them, with complete instructions on what to wear for meals and for sleeping. In the tiny bathroom they found all the toiletries they would need.

The next morning, after a light breakfast and cleaning up, Nate and Nadia put on lightweight space suits in preparation for the next leg of their trip. The Interplanetary-One vehicle was designed to travel from the hotel to the Moon, land at the colony, allow people to disembark, pick up return passengers, load freight, refuel the rocket tanks, and return to Earth. It was a twenty hour trip each way.

Nate and Nadia boarded with no issues. Except for their phones, everything else was issued by TSC. On this leg of the trip, cold food was made available in their cabin. The room was about half the size of the hotel room from the prior night, though only a full-size bed made the room seem larger. A view of everything around the ship appeared on the monitor screen in the cabin. At one point they pointed to the great dock where the Mars ship sat ready for its launch.

Their short hop to the Moon proved uneventful. The landing of the spaceship next to the colony was the most exciting part of the trip as they could see from the monitor screen everything the pilots saw.

Going through customs only required the presentation of their phones. All their baggage had been scanned and manually examined multiple times since the beginning of their trip. Even so, the Moon's customs team had to take one more look. Before customs finished, the governor arrived. He greeted them as VIP guests and personally took them to their penthouse suite. He talked the whole way to the suite. Nadia let Nate listen to the words. She listened to the governor's thoughts, which matched his blabbering. The governor was excited about officiating at their upcoming wedding.

The moon suite they had rented had been sitting on the market for almost a year since its completion. It had never been occupied. The original price had been 200 million new dollars per year. They had rented and paid for two years in the penthouse suite which featured three floors and a Moon surface/Earth view. To entice them to lease, the final price had been cut in half, so they'd only paid 100 million new dollars per year. That amount barely made a dent in Nate's finances. He had done well as TAMO's imperial grand councilor. What the organization invested in, so did he. The fact that TAMO needed him on the moon meant that they paid for the suite.

The price of the penthouse came with a butler, maid, and cook. Nate and Nadia would be well taken care of. They would choose each of the staff positions from a catalog of people wanting to work on the moon. They found eight butlers, five cooks, and four maids to interview. Nate and Nadia interviewed them all online from Earth via video communications links. The two-second delay between the questions and the answers challenged everyone but, after the online interview, the couple picked four butlers, two cooks, and two maids to physically come to the Moon. It would be expensive to do the final in-person interviews, but Nate and Nadia wanted to hear the applicants' thoughts before accepting them.

Within a week, the candidates arrived. As Nadia was introduced to them, she listened carefully to each of the candidates' thoughts. This first butler and the next two butler candidates were not acceptable because of their many unpleasant thoughts. One even planned to rob them of goods and money. The fourth butler candidate, John, was the same age as Nate. His family had a great history of serving the aristocratic families of England on Earth. John also had attained the Ninth Level membership in TAMO. The first maid and cook met with Nadia's approval right away. The rest of the candidates for those positions were released and either sent home to Earth or to other interviews on the Moon.

Both the maid and the cook wanted to be there and to do good work. The positive attitudes might have been because of their TAMO memberships. The maid was Eighth Level, and the cook was Eleventh Level.

The wedding was set for one month after their arrival. The governor invited many of his friends to "show off" the two new VIPs. He allocated half of his people to the bride's side and half to the groom's. The actual wedding was to take place in the large colony meeting room, big enough to handle a quarter of the 5,000 people in the colony.

Nate was expected to pay for the wedding and the reception, and he agreed. He felt it would be a good gesture to the colony.

The butler would walk Nadia down the aisle and the maid and cook had agreed to be the maids of honor. The lieutenant governor stood in as the best man. For the Moon, this would be a very fancy wedding.

The marriage ceremony and the following reception were a big success. All the Tankers attended in absentia, as Nadia broadcasted the whole ceremony to them. She loved images more than talking, and projected images of all the people around her at the wedding and what each person thought. She had learned to not even consider what people were thinking, but instead serve as a conduit. She passed onto the other Tankers all that she saw and heard. The information would be interpreted later by other TAMO members.

For the Tankers, the most interesting part came when Nate kissed the bride and both his and her thoughts were broadcast to the listeners.

Nate knew in his gut that being on the Moon was the right thing. His gorgeous young-looking wife would help him and explore with him. What a great benefit to Nate and to TAMO. He knew, somehow, he would build the first off-planet TAMO temple for the dragon on their plot of land on the dark side.

During the wedding ceremony and reception, Nate picked up something not quite right with the moon colony that he asked Nadia to broadcast. It troubled the Tankers.

The Preparation

Upon arrival in Colorado, the whole team started training on the new spacecraft designed to take them from Earth orbit to Mars and to the moon of Phobos. The pilot training and simulation was given to Daniel and Ryan. The general training for the others involved only the company VR simulator. This was the first spacecraft of its kind, and the VR was the best training available to the team.

The new team did not have the luxury of waiting and preparing several years for the spaceship to be ready. The very next window of time that Mars would be closest to Earth would be February 6th, 2042. The travel time would be about six months using the Hohmann transfer orbit calculations. That meant the team must be ready to launch around August 3, 2041. There would be no time for a maiden run of the new craft. Its first trip anywhere would be its trip to Phobos. The spacecraft needed to only have the minimal supplies necessary for the trip to Phobos and for two years in suspended animation in the tanks. The team knew it might be a one way trip. The quick loading of the craft meant they loaded only enough fuel, food, water, and oxygen for the two pilots. Six months of these supplies would allow for the survival of the two pilots, who could remain awake for the whole trip if necessary. Minimal supplies would sustain the others who would put themselves in a comatose state by entering tanks similar to those used previously for their rejuvenation. With no immediate return trip to Earth planned, they would pack enough extra provisions for two months with the whole team awake.

After the Phobos mission was completed, most of the team would return to the tanks to sleep. They would remain sleeping until the resupply ship came. Earth would send the needed fuel and food for the return trip by rocket after the team succeeded with the keys.

Two Tankers, Albert and Martha, planned to stay on Earth to serve as eyes and ears for TAMO. Nate and Nadia were to remain on the Moon as TAMO's representatives to the Moon government. The remaining Tankers—Andrey, Briana, Lindsey, Rob, Sandy, Steve, and Sam—would make the trip as passengers. One TAMO member, Nan, decided to make the trip to remain with Rob. Ryan and Daniel would go as the crew of the vessel named *TSC Enterprise* by the Tankers after a craft in a twentieth century TV series. TSC, of course, stood for The Spaceship Company, a subsidiary of the Virgin group that owned the spacecraft.

The team had only been in Colorado for a month when news came that fifteen weapon-laden rockets had been launched by various countries towards Phobos: three military rockets launched by China, five by Russia, two by Japan, one by India, and four by America. The rockets, all on a one-way trip, would accelerate to the highest speed possible for travel to Mars, leaving enough fuel to maneuver when they reached Mars' orbit. All the rockets launched with the same mission: "destroy Phobos." Each carried a single weapon varying from an energy weapon to nuclear explosives.

That did not worry the imperial grand master or the imperial grand councilor. They had seen what had happened in Tunguska when a meteor approached only one of the major keys. The Russians should have known about the minimal odds for success. Back in the previous century, their space probe disappeared when it attempted to land on Phobos. TAMO's only worry came down to whether the TSC spaceship would take off on time. The rockets headed to destroy Phobos would not even reach it before the new *TSC Enterprise* spaceship launched.

The rockets were still a month out from Phobos when the Tanker's team assembled and was flown from Earth to orbit in three different ships. Each ship carried three or four team members and one of the three keys. The imperial grand master and the imperial grand councilor wanted to take no chances with the possibility of losing all the people and keys in one "accident." Luck stayed with them, and all personnel and keys arrived at *TSC Enterprise* docking bay without incident.

The separation from the ship building rigging caused a monumental event. Camera crews traveled into orbit and lingered on all sides of the ship to transmit the details of the launch back to Earth and out to the moon.

It remained quiet on the bridge as the pilots, Captain Daniel Wright and First Officer Ryan Bentley, worked as a team to maneuver the craft out of its dock. The voyage of *TSC Enterprise* was underway.

It took only a week for the ship to reach maximum acceleration which created a one gravity, 1G, force on all the occupants and simulated Earth's gravity.

No one wanted to go into the tanks until the military rockets made it to Phobos. If the rockets succeeded in destroying the metallic craft, the team would work with the people in Colorado to plot a new trajectory to return the ship home.

The day the rockets reached Phobos' orbital space finally arrived. One hour remained before the first rocket would reach the sphere and the team gathered on the bridge to watch the screens of the extended radar on the *TSC Enterprise.* They could manufacture an image simulating all of the rockets' positions. The military rockets had been programmed to match speeds so they would deliver their energy pulse and nuclear payloads on Phobos in a pattern of continuous explosions.

The American rocket first approached Phobos with an energy pulse weapon. A flash on the simulation screen registered as the energy pulse left the rocket. Seconds later the rocket itself struck

Phobos. The simulation could not show any details or results of the explosion. The whole team watched the monitor anyway. During the next hours, each subsequent country's rockets exploded on Phobos. Everyone would have to wait to determine any results.

Finally, all the rockets had exploded on Phobos, and the simulator was recalibrated to assemble a new image of Phobos' space. The unexpected result revealed not a scratch on the Phobos sphere. The observatories on Earth confirmed the results. No damage to Phobos along with visual proof that the rockets had disappeared off the radar in a puff of light only hundreds of feet from the target.

The time had arrived for TSC *Enterprise* to make its voyage.

The team members finally consented to go into the tanks, expecting six months of discussion and speculation as their bodies slept and their minds communicated.

Nan, who had not gone through rejuvenation, did not have the tank experience of the Tankers. She expected a simple six month rest and discussions with Rob. The couple's constant mental contact while touching had started to open Nan's ability to both transmit and receive thoughts to those near to her, but the lovers didn't want to take any chances during their trip to Mars. They had asked for and received a double tank in which they would lie touching. In that way they could continue mind talking with each other and the rest of the Tankers while in their coma state.

The ship could fly itself to Mars without human intervention. The crew would only be awakened early if the on-board computer had an issue with some unexpected occurrence. Everyone hoped for an uneventful trip.

Travel to Mars

The plan involved waking the team after the ship flipped 180 degrees to point its engines toward Phobos instead of Earth and fired to start decelerating. Slowing would bring the ship close to zero acceleration when they arrived at Mars' orbit.

Unfortunately, the unexpected did happen. Four months into their "sleep," the Tankers received an urgent mental message from Albert on Earth.

"A missile launched by an unknown party is headed for your ship. Estimates say it will reach you in the last week of your travel. Be aware and take the necessary action. Martha and I are trying to locate the source, to act from Earth. Nate and Nadia are working on the problem from the Moon as well. One of us will surely determine the source of the launch."

The "sleeping" Tankers discussed the situation for several days. Captain Daniel finally relayed the result. They would still have enough time to take action even if they waited to be brought out of the tanks on schedule.

That happened. When the time came, the captain and first officer revived first on their own. Briana Goldsmith, the onboard nurse, awakened third. If anything, critical happened, she would apply her nursing skills, and subsequently consult the computer. If

she and the computer could not find a solution, they would call
to Earth.

☆☆☆

Steve exited his tank fourth and welcomed the noxious-tasting
blue electrolyte drinks from Briana. Like all of the others, he exited
the tank naked and went to the showers to clean up and dress. As
each person finished, they would help the next person out of their
tank. Within four hours, everyone was out, showered, dressed, had
eaten, and gathered on the bridge.

Steve wanted to know what was being done about the
incoming rocket. He surely wasn't the only one. Only three weeks
remained before they would synchronize orbits with Phobos. In
only two weeks, there could be contact of some kind with the
incoming rocket. Captain Daniel stayed in constant mental
connection with Albert and Martha on Earth, and with Nadia on
the Moon. As usual, Steve marveled at how mental thought traveled
instantly between locations, like the group was sitting and talking in
the same room.

So far, the people at home had only one clue about the rocket.
It had been financed by the group called the Ancient Universal
Knowledge Association. According to Sam, those were the awful
and dangerous people she had the misfortune to work with. She
blamed them for the destruction of the Center of Silence and the
deaths of the people in Phoenix. The IGC had, months ago,
indicated it was also probably AUKA who should be held
responsible for the tactical nuclear bomb that barely missed the
team at Tunguska.

Both the imperial grand councilor working from the Moon
and the imperial grand master working from Earth were pulling in
all the favors owed to them to search for the launch location and the
control center for the rocket. They felt that information to be close
at hand.

The IGC's contact at the Lunar South Pole colony came
through with some detailed information about the location of the
launch and control sites. They said they'd discovered them in the

Sahara Desert in the southwestern corner of Egypt. With nothing around for many miles, the suspected compound showed up as only a few deserted shacks on the satellite images.

Even though the United State had tried to destroy Phobos with American rockets, the current situation differed. The *TSC Enterprise* contained Americans. The IGM was able to talk to and convince the President to send an elite SEAL team into Egypt. They hoped to sneak in and destroy the missile from within the control center by using the missile's own self-destruct code.

The IGM sat with the President in the Situation Room with several other officials, and Tankers Martha and Albert. The IGM held hands with Martha and the President held hands with Albert. In this way, the four of them could all see instantly what the Tankers saw onboard their spaceship.

The White House Situation Room was set up so all could see on the split screen what happened in the desert. Martha transmitted this image to all the Tankers. The second side of the split screen allowed the remainder of the officials to see a simulation of Phobos, Mars, the spaceship with the Tankers, and the approaching rocket.

A five minute delayed image came from the *TSC Enterprise* showing what was being recorded from the ship's onboard cameras. The live mental feed directly from *TSC Enterprise* astonished the President with its clarity and timeliness, far exceeding the various simulations and delayed images.

As the SEALs approached the area of the shacks, it was obvious the buildings themselves served as camouflage for the underground complex. The special force approached the central shack which prior reconnaissance suggested was the control center.

As they approached, gunfire broke out and a firefight began. A half squad of the SEALs broke off from the main group.

The second team headed around toward the back of the building and approached a series of large well-hidden vents. The team broke in through the vents and started the search for the rocket control console.

In the control room, they overpowered the engineers, found the console, turned the self-destruct key, and pressed the button to send the destruct signal to the rocket.

The timing was going to be close. Everyone waited impatiently for the signal's five-minute travel time from the Earth to the deadly rocket.

The President and the IGM, along with those in the Situation Room, waited. The simulation showed the rocket unchanged. The image from the Tankers on the *TSC Enterprise* appeared in real-time in the minds of the President and the IGM.

No one on Earth knew if the self-destruct signal had been hit in time. They focused on the screen as the rocket continued its intercept course with the spaceship.

The five minutes passed. The signal should have arrived. They should have seen an explosion. The self-destruct had failed. In only six minutes, the rocket would destroy the *TSC Enterprise*.

On the ship, the team prepared for the worst. At the IGM's suggestion, they grouped together on the bridge, joined hands, and meditated.

With four minutes left, as a group, they transmitted out the thought of Love in all directions. Even the Tankers on Earth and the Moon locked their minds together in final thoughts of Love for mankind and all entities everywhere. It was the only thing they could do. The best thing they could do. If the team on the spaceship was going to die, it would be with their comrades and loved ones.

With only three minutes left, Steve left the meditation to be the outward observer while the rest continued and concentrated on sending Love. The radar on the *TSC Enterprise* registered a small craft about the size of a small car leaving Phobos at extraordinary speed. Surprise and hope filled all of the Tankers' thoughts as they saw the screen through Steve's eyes.

The Tankers continued to send Love.

Even though the *TSC Enterprise* was still one week from Phobos, the little craft had already covered half the distance between Phobos and the spaceship in under a minute.

With less than a minute left, the small craft flew within a few hundred feet of the rocket, between it and the *TSC Enterprise*. The radar registered an explosion. The small craft destroyed the rocket. It missed the spaceship by less than a thousand feet.

The Tankers and those connected to them jumped up and bellowed joyous whoops and hollers. The why and the how remained unknown but the team and the *TSC Enterprise* were safe and could continue their voyage.

In the Situation Room, everyone cheered. The trip to Phobos had been saved!

Martha and Albert thanked the President for his help. They and the IGM left in hopes that all would be well when the *TSC Enterprise* arrived near Phobos.

☆☆☆

The *TSC Enterprise* team would reach Phobos in fewer than seven days. During that time, the ship continued to slow down. All of the members prepared for their individual tasks for when they reached Phobos. Much needed doing prior to arrival. Preparing the lander for the final flight from the ship to Phobos involved everyone. Each team member worked on a task.

Ryan and Daniel split time between the bridge of the *TSC Enterprise* and the lander. They made the final pilots' landing preparations and tested out the operations of the lander as best they could. Sam stayed with Daniel and helped where she could.

The Thirteenth Level TAMO members—Steve, Rob, and Nan—were responsible for unpacking the keys from their large safety crates and securing them in the lander for more accessible usage. The Tunguska and Stonehenge keys were left in their original boxes. The smaller Vatican key remained in the security box created by TAMO. The keys would be removed from their boxes later upon landing on Phobos.

Briana, with Sandy's help, brought the medical supplies into the lander. They checked them and doublechecked them.

Lindsey and Andrey took responsibility for the spacesuits. They made sure all were examined and ready for the landing party to wear.

The arrival day finally came. The Tankers felt confident everything had been prepared for success. Captain Daniel steered the *TSC Enterprise* into orbit along with Phobos. He positioned the ship right above the obelisk at about ten miles out. The lander had more than enough space for the eight people. Designed to fly in the atmosphere of Mars, it could also fly in close to zero gravity. Even with this light amount of gravity, leaving Phobos would require some extra thrust. The lander had more than adequate power for that maneuver.

Final preparation began. Nan, Rob, and Steve donned their priestly gear. The three removed each key, one box at a time, and laid them carefully on individual golden cloths made of the same material as their priestly robes. That would make it possible for the keys to be carried by the three teams.

As a key was removed, one of the three TAMO priests spoke the words indicated in the ancient Dragon Prophecy texts.

"Oh, Sacred Dragon, we come in peace. We have come to return your teeth. We bring the number of twelve of your teeth."

Once removed from their boxes with the prayers spoken by the three Thirteenth Level members, the keys could be handled by anyone.

As Steve touched the Tunguska Key, it made him giddy. His bare hands warmed as an energy flowed through him filled with great joy, love, and lightheartedness. He wanted to keep holding it but, instead, placed the key in its special golden shroud. The energy flow and giddiness passed, leaving him feeling empty.

The team had been split up into teams of loving couples. Sam and Daniel would stay with the ship. Briana, and Ryan—as first officer—would oversee the lander and the landing party. Steve and Sandy would exit the lander with the Vatican Key to make first physical contact on Phobos. Nan and Rob were to follow holding the Stonehenge Key. Lindsey and Andrey, as the final team, would bring the largest and most magnificent item, the Tunguska Key.

The teams, all dressed in spacesuits, carried eight hours of oxygen. Plenty for a trip expected to take two hours. The people on Earth had figured the surface of Phobos was comprised of magnetic metal. They based the assumption on a previous examination of the keys on Earth. The keys were made of some sort of metal not known to humankind. Current Earth scientists had no idea how to find or create such a metal. However, the scientists were able to find magnets that stuck to the keys.

If Phobos embodied a metal as found in the keys, the team's magnetic boots would keep them securely attached to its structure. If the surface was not of the same metal, they would try to rely on its comparatively lesser gravity. The Earth scientists determined the gravity was about .0057 m/s2 on Phobos, barely any gravity at all. Still, that small amount of gravity should be enough to keep the team members from floating off Phobos.

As pilot, First Officer Ryan and his assistant, Briana, were first to enter the lander. Briana had been taught enough to maneuver the lander back to the ship in an emergency should Ryan become unable to handle the controls or die. Both Ryan and Briana armed themselves with laser weapons. Their jobs involved keeping the lander secure and protecting the other three teams as necessary. No one else carried weaponry as their focus needed to remain on delivering the keys to the base of the obelisk.

The three couples entered the lander and strapped themselves in. Each of the three keys was held close by one appointed member. The golden shroud covering each key prevented direct contact between the key and the team members' flight suits.

The Dragon's Teeth

Ryan's launch of the lander from the hanger bay was picture perfect, Sandy thought. The flight took barely ten minutes from the ship to the base of the obelisk. Each team member enjoyed communicating images of what they saw to Daniel and Sam on the ship, Nadia and Nate on the Moon, and Martha with the IGM and Albert on Earth. All the team members could watch and listen in as they desired. The nearer the lander moved toward Phobos, the clearer the image became of the base of the obelisk.

The landing shook the ship as it hit hard on the surface of Phobos. Its impact also took focus away from the base of the obelisk for a few seconds.

Sandy first focused on the obelisk by leaning into one of the lander's windows. She transmitted what she saw to those not in the lander.

This is amazing! All around the obelisk, some 500 feet from its base, I see lander-type spacecrafts. The noses of every one of the vehicles are dug into the surface. They all are in bad shape even though they are about the size of a two-story house and twice as long. Three smaller crafts sitting near the obelisk look brand new as if built yesterday.

Steve craned to see better out of the window so Sandy moved back slightly and nodded to indicate he should share his viewpoint too. *Even more amazing are the small three dimensional models of places on Earth surrounding the obelisk. Each model is about twelve by twelve feet and three feet tall. I recognize a miniature of Vatican City. On the sub-ground level of the city, where the secret library is located, I see a light green glow.*

Yeah, Steve, and next to it is the area around Tunguska. Sandy recognized Briana's mental voice. *It looks like it would appear if you viewed it from the air before the nuclear explosion. In the center, where we found the key, there's another green light glowing.*

Hey, I see a red light in that section next to it, Ryan added, looking out the same window as Briana. Sandy grinned at his excited tone. *That's the Rock of Gibraltar, the northern pillar of Hercules. Do you see, almost at the top, the red shining? Just next to Gibraltar, you can see the southern pillar of Hercules too. The details are incredible.*

Sandy sent a mental emoji image of a mind exploding, and relayed, *These models obviously represent the locations of the dragon's keys. See, there's Stonehenge with a green light.*

Yes, Steve chimed in again. He pointed out the red light under the Wailing Wall in Israel, the Egyptian Sphynx, and the African Victoria Falls.

He mentally paused, studying the models. *Ah, beyond the falls, do you see the pattern of a large serpent created by a grassy mound? The design runs east and west with the head with jaws open about to eat an egg. The red light shines where the eye should be. Also, there's a plateau like one in the western United States. Halfway down the steep side of the plateau, see the soft red glow?*

Rob added his memories of the area. *It is in the plateau group my people consider the sacred plateaus. No one, except a priest, ever goes there.*

I recognize the Nazca Plains, chimed in Lindsey. Her eyes brightened at the memory of the ritual. *Several of the giant pictographs are there. There's the likeness of the man in a space suit up against the side of a mountain with a glowing green point in his right hand.*

Steve continued with a mental thought of the next red illumination he saw and the joy it brought him. From the Dragon Prophecy he repeated the verbiage to remind the others of what they were seeing. *In the mountains of Tibet, the Drepung Monastery nestles in a valley... the home of the Dalai Lama for centuries.*

With all twelve key locations spotted, Steve's attention returned to the obelisk. *Take a look at the door. Ryan landed us a hundred feet from the front of it. At its base you can see the large door that stands probably twenty feet square. It looks like the mouth of the dragon that is missing his teeth. A large tongue, frozen, flicks outward to the left. Look closely. Isn't that hole in the tongue shaped like the TAMO symbol? And those two humanoid statues half again taller than the door... their heads are definitely Egyptian. One is a bird and the other a jackal.*

Per the mental reactions of the Tankers on the ship, Moon, and Earth, Sandy knew each could not believe what their companions were experiencing.

Ryan had powered down the lander, so everyone took off their safety harnesses and headed to the back of the craft where they would put on their suits and exit. The six crew members prepared their equipment, tightened their helmets, conducted a self-examination of their gear, and went to stand beside their companion. One of each pair held a key wrapped in the golden shroud of sacred material. Steve held the Vatican Key, Nan the Stonehenge Key, and Andrey the Tunguska Key

Briana focused on each of the other team members. She made sure everyone had their equipment set up correctly.

We are making final preparations for leaving the lander. Everyone looks ready. In one minute, Ryan will remove the atmosphere inside of here to allow us an easier exit and reentry.

"Decompressing, now!" Came over Steve's headset.

The hissing of the air was audible even through their helmets. After only a few seconds, the ramp slowly opened to the outside and lowered toward the ground. When it touched, they faced the door in the obelisk. Steve and Sandy lined up on the ramp first.

He bowed to her. "Ladies first!"

Sandy continued to hold the rail as she walked cautiously down to the end of the ramp. She put a single boot out onto the surface and paused.

"One step for the future of mankind."

It was close to what the Apollo 11 astronaut had said many decades ago when Sandy was a girl. Her boot connected to the surface and made a magnetic click. She stepped carefully with her other foot. Her magnetic boots held.

Steve knew about low gravity and an exhilaration rose in him about touching part of an alien device. It made him feel like a little kid. He pushed off from the ramp with all his energy, flew up and over Sandy, and landed forty feet in front of her. His magnetic boots clicked into place and held his feet. Unfortunately, his mass took over and he fell forward. With the light gravity, he was able to use his one available hand and his boots to slow the downward progress, but he still landed face down. His boots unlocked from the surface, and he slid another ten feet before he gained control. He held onto his key like a football running back. No harm had come to it.

Sandy continued her steady walk towards him.

"Amateur!" she called out through her helmet mic.

To Steve only, she sent, *Honey, that was extremely dangerous, don't scare me like that. I don't want "until death do us part" to be today. I love you!*

Steve couldn't stop his face from turning bright red in embarrassment.

As it was, Briana's thought carried a worried feel. *Steve, are you alright? Your suit readings show irregularities in your blood pressure and heartbeat.*

That only added more embarrassment. Now everyone knew. *I'm okay. Thanks!*

In their minds and through their helmet radios, the Tankers heard, *"Geronimo! Russians will be first in this space race too!"*

In response, Lindsey screamed both verbally and mentally. "Andrey, *no!*"

Too late. Andrey had run down the ramp holding the rail for support and, just before reaching the surface, jumped. He did it with more energy than Steve. The Russian went flying in an arc over the heads of both Sandy and Steve at a height of about ninety feet.

Steve watched in horror as Andrey's speed increased in velocity with the descent of his flight. Unfortunately, at twenty feet in the air, he slammed into the top edge of the obelisk door and crashed down to the base. His boots locked his feet in place on the ground, but the force bent his knees, and the back of his head hit the ground hard. The Tunguska Key fell out of Andrey's hand unprotected by the shroud which was nowhere to be seen. He apparently had been holding the key, touching its surface with only his gloved hand.

Lindsey screamed again, "I can't hear his thoughts! Steve get to him quickly!"

Steve ran, carefully taking steps fifteen feet at a time. He reached Andrey and read the meters on his suit.

"He is alive! He must have knocked himself out. I'll take him back to the lander so Briana can take a look at him."

Steve opened his own golden shroud, laying it on the ground in front of the obelisk. He quickly placed the Tunguska Key in it beside the Vatican Key, careful to place it so the keys didn't touch. He lifted Andrey up. The man's mass required Steve to be even more careful as he started the trip back to the lander.

Everyone else had been told by Ryan to keep heading to the obelisk door. Steve managed to return Andrey to the lander though it took both Ryan and Briana to bring Steve to a standstill as he plunged into the airlock.

Ryan looked grimly at him. "Get back to the obelisk door. We need to close the ramp and put atmosphere back in here. We need to get Andrey out of his space suit."

I am Nowrai!

All of the Tankers stopped still. Those words had formed in their minds.

Have you brought me my teeth?

The voice in the minds of the Tankers was strange. It was nothing like anything they had heard before. The feeling was feminine yet mechanical and slightly rough.

Bring them to me. Ye all shall surely die if you do not bring me the number of my twelve teeth! Leave the injured one and come! Deliver to me my teeth. I have waited for thousands of years. Now bring them to me or I shall surely destroy all of you!

Nan, Rob, and Steve hurried to the front of the obelisk. Nan laid the third key down on the shroud beside the two Steve had placed. She lifted the Tunguska Key up from the shroud, protected by the priestly golden hooded robe under her space suit.

Steve knew she was remembering the adage from the ancient scrolls, *"Be quick of tongue."* The order of the placement of the keys was crucial. The bright woman placed the first key into a depression matching its shape in the tongue. As the key slipped into place, the depression filled and became like a solid tongue. When it solidified, the single door cracked down the middle, revealing its true form made of two large doors.

Again, in Steve's mind, and surely in the others' as well, the voice said, *You have given me my tongue to speak. Fill my mouth with the teeth in the order I have demanded! I must finally have the number of my twelve teeth. Continue correctly, or surely ye shall die!*

Nan stared at the remaining two keys. Steve's heart began to pound. He prayed that Sandy's solution was correct. The impression matching the Vatican Key was on the left side almost at the top of the door. The one matching the Stonehenge Key was on the lower right.

Nan picked up the Stonehenge Key and hesitated as she sent, *Next, we must fill his mouth as a clock may tick. That means clockwise. Should it be from Nowrai's point of view or ours?*

As if to answer the question Nowrai mentally sang out. *I am the center of the beginning of the human race on Earth. Now give me my teeth! You are about to die!*

Steve knew what they must do. He relayed to Nan, *Counterclockwise by our point of view will be clockwise by Nowrai's point of view.*

Nan picked up the Vatican Key, but she could not reach the indentation. Steve stood closest to her, so he picked her up to give her the height to fit the key into place. Like the first key, when it slipped into the opening, it blended into the side of the door as though it had always been there. A second later, the giant figure on the left turned to look down at them.

The voice boomed in Steve's mind again. *Give me all of my teeth! Without the number of twelve of my teeth, surely you all shall die!*

Sandy pointed to their third and last key. Steve picked it up and matched it in the position of the depression on the lower right of the door. The statue on the right turned to stare at them.

Both statues started to turn and move toward the team while two handles appeared in the door. Each of the two giants grabbed a handle and pulled. Simultaneously, a much quieter pleasant female voice filled Steve's mind.

Thank you for bringing the number of my teeth. Come! Please enter my humble home.

The Dragon's Lair

The newly mobile statues fully opened the doors and stared until Steve and Sandy attempted to pass through the dragon's mouth. Their movement through the open door felt strained like they needed to push through a barrier of some kind, but they made it through without harm.

What have we just passed into? Sandy asked.

You are free to take off your spacesuits and be my guests. The voice in their heads had become unbelievably soft and feminine. *Even with the doors open, no air escapes. The technology I use is highly advanced. Please come in and sit comfortably. But first, bring the injured man here to be healed.*

Steve relayed everything he had heard and seen to every Tanker.

Ryan and Briana relayed that they needed to put the unconscious Andrey back into his suit. When that was done, they carefully brought him to the obelisk, through the dragon's open mouth, and into the area where their friends waited.

Remove his suit and place him in the tank at your left. Do not fear. It will fill with liquid, and he will be healed.

Ryan and Briana did as the calm voice in everyone's minds told them to do. They carefully removed Andrey's suit and clothes and placed him naked at the bottom of the clear tank. The top of the tank sealed itself shut. They all watched as a blue liquid filled the tank and covered Andrey. He started to struggle, as if he could not breathe, then went limp. A light went on and the liquid became a bright blue. In a matter of several minutes, the liquid turned clear.

A smile came to Andrey's face as the liquid drained away and left him healed and dry. The lid receded and Andrey climbed out. He walked over to a rack on the wall and grabbed a robe made of the same material the priests wore and sat on one of the empty benches near the healing tank.

A shudder passed up Steve's spine as he watched the team approach the newly healed man. What they just witnessed involved a highly accelerated Tanker experience.

What a marvel, he sent to Sandy.

She beamed back at him and placed a hand on Andrey's shoulder.

Steve took a moment to examine their surroundings. The room was appointed in a spartan style with several long benches along the wall. This appeared to be an anteroom. He walked to the rack and motioned to the others to take off their space suits and put on the golden clothes.

With his priest's clothes already under his suit, he simply took off his space suit, planning to lay it on the floor. Instead, a series of small cabinets had appeared, just large enough for the team members to store their suits.

The beauty and simplicity of the room appealed to him, along with the sound of some light beautiful music. The clean air held the scent of pine, like walking through a forest.

He moved to the bench and sat next to Andrey. Though its surface looked hard it became soft and comfortable like a sofa when he sat.

"Let me tell you about your ancestors," Nowrai's beautiful, serene female voice said out loud. "Around 35,000 years ago, some of your ancestors came here from Orion to escape persecution. On their home planet, your ancestors were considered freaks, for they had only two hands and two legs. Those who considered themselves superior had six or eight arms, and some had four legs. Your people, a minority of the five billion people on Orion, were shunned. The two legged priests of that time decided to leave Orion and become a diaspora throughout the galaxy. Only 3,360,000 people came here as settlers in the thousand ships you see outside. You can see most of these large ships scattered across the surface of this moon craft. I have kept several of them in working order as I knew you would come. The first order of business for your ancestors was to leave our home planet."

Images of the beautiful planet and the harsh persecution their ancestors endured became a black and white movie on the opposite wall.

Nowrai, is that what you consider a good movie? Steve asked.

Oops, let me fix that. The movie changed to color.

Steve relayed what he saw and heard to the others not in the room. The images showed a great deal about the conditions on the harsh planet where their ancestors went within the Orion galaxy to temporarily escape persecution. The images also showed the building of this moon-like craft and its special gate. It launched with the craft, it traversed the universe via a wormhole created in front of itself and brought it here to the outer edges of their solar system. Slowly the craft parked in the orbit of Mars.

Nowrai, this movie would be better in 3D, Steve asked. *Why aren't showing us your best capabilities?*

Nowrai said nothing. Instead the wall became 3D.

The images continued with such depth and reality, showing large ships going through a gate at Orion, then a second gate that must have been a transition point to their final destination of Earth. The "movie" revealed the two towers that made up the gate on Phobos, and the ships as they came through the event horizon of the gate. The ships came in waves. The first two ships immediately went to Earth. These were filled with the scientists; biologists; and the technicians, who served as the priests of their religion.

Nowrai advanced the style of the movie again. Along with the 3D images and her continued oration there was now sound, smell of the salt air, and the feeling of the wind as things happened.

"In the beginning, the settlers occupied a small continent. In your mythology, it was called Atlantis." A large island with several mountains shown like a contour map with lifelike views on the wall. "In the center stood the tallest mountain." A bird's eye view from the top of the mountain appeared. "From its top, in the distance, you could see what they called the 'Pillars of Hercules.'" All of the western entrance of the Mediterranean could be seen in sharp focus. "The island contained no large animals but featured a vast variety of plants." The view swooped down from the mountain top in bird-like fashion showing how the island originally looked. "It took five years of work, even with the levitation tools and cutting tools they brought, for the two thousand to build a city for the remaining millions that would come later."

Steve watched in awe as the images continued. He could feel, as mountaintops disappeared, massive stones cut from the mountains were transported to needed locations, and the stone became welded into almost seamless walls. It was like a Lego set, building a city, piece by preplanned piece. It was so realistic that he could almost touch the details.

"The city island was well planned out." The bird flew high up over the island showing it all. "The city looked like the cross and star with the rose at its center, the symbol of their religion. At each point of the symbol in the city stood a tower, and in each of the towers they secured a key that coordinated with the other keys to maintain the city. The primary key lay at the center of the city at the top of the central mountain. The key of keys lit up the top of the mountain like a small sun. It obviously held great power."

The bird flew from tower to tower slowing just long enough to see the key that was associated with each tower, including the tower of the primary key.

Steve had become so involved with the story he had not looked at his teammates until that moment. Briana jumped up under the projection and her hand went right through the solid looking image.

I can smell the city and the ocean, she broadcast to Steve.

He relayed this to the others who were not present.

"With the completion of the city, the remaining ships came. Each ship would unload its passengers and supplies."

The view again shifted to watch people exiting the ships and going to various parts of the city.

"Then the crafts returned to the new moon of Mars. There, the ships buried themselves nose-deep into the side of the moon craft."

This time the bird view shifted to the bridge of one of the ships. Steve and the others were able to watch as the ships made one small jump after another until arriving back on the moon of Mars.

"Early in the migration planning, the priests had decided that, on their new world, they would not allow space travel for humans until they learned again about flight and obtained the gift. All of the settlers had limited advanced knowledge. Only the small group that built the city and the twelve priests kept the gift and the knowledge of their past."

Her oration stopped. The wall returned to its unassuming grey blankness.

"Oh, please excuse me. I have been a horrible hostess. Please come into our dining area and enjoy the foods of your ancestors."

A path lit up on the floor and a wall opened. Steve was first to walk the path to the table filled with delicacies from all around Earth which waited for the team's pleasures. The rest of the team members walked in behind Steve and sat at the long carved wooden table. One of the ornately carved chairs felt soft and conformed to his body. Sandy relayed to him that the banquet reminded her of those presented to kings in the past.

First tackled, the hors d'oeuvres. Each person consumed a different appetizer that appeared in front of them. Dan started breaking open the king crab legs with that familiar cracking sound as the shells broke. The Tanker laid bare the sweet meat and dipped it in the pure salted butter found in the small gold cup next to it.

I've never tasted crab as delicious as this.

The mental image of the exact taste accompanied the comment. Dan's favorite made Steve's mouth water. He himself devoured twelve of the escargot in front of him. They tasted like they had been cooked in white wine, butter, and garlic with a wonderful smell and delicious taste. He couldn't resist.

This escargot tastes like those served when I was in Paris forty years ago.

Steve sent the sensual taste experience so all could enjoy what he was eating.

Andrey sat in front of a pound of black Baluga caviar. The broadcast from him came with each tiny spoonful as it burst its salty taste onto the tongue. His every bite was followed with closed eyes and a lift of the corners of his mouth.

When the appetizers had all been tasted and removed by humanoid robots, golden goblets were filled with an orange liquid tasting of the finest Asian fruit.

The feast continued as Steve was served his favorite medium-rare steak, pierced with garlic. Though not authentic, it smelled and tasted just like the real thing straight from the grill. A side dish on the plate was a purple food that looked like a vegetable. Bringing a bite to his mouth, he tasted the wonderful, sweet flavor of fresh boiled beets. It brought back memories of long-ago people and loves.

After they finished the main meal, the robots brought desserts of all kinds to the table along with fresh coffee and tea.

Nowrai continued her presentation in a more urgent tone.

"It has been many centuries since I have had contact with humans on Earth. The ritual you did allowed me, an artificial intelligence, to link minds with you. I was designed to only work with people with love in their hearts. Without that ritual of love and energy, I can only talk to those I can see.

"Finally, I have someone who I can ask to help me. Something has happened on the other side of the gate in the Orion galaxy. It has been thousands of years since I have had any contact. I fear something horrible has happened to my AI friends and your ancestors who stayed on Orion. I implore you. Please, will four of you travel there to see what has happened?"

Steve discerned the desperation in her voice and relayed her urgency to all of the other Tankers. He knew they had to make this humanitarian trip for the sake of their ancestors.

"I have prepared three ships for you." Nowrai's voice had moved to one side of the antechamber near a 3D image on the wall. "These vehicles shown have the capability of close solar system travel by way of mini jumps. Enough power stores in the anti-matter containers to make the short hops, though they must be from one visible location to another. For instance, a trip from here to your Earth would take about ten hops in twelve hours. Most of that time allows the onboard AI to do the needed calculations. The hops themselves are instantaneous. In addition to this space travel, each craft is capable of atmospheric flight and landing."

A visual tour of the inside of one of the ships began via the projection.

"The first ship is a totally stripped-down version. This is to be a gift for Richard Branson and The Spaceship Company to replace the ship he lent to you. This ship will have no robot helpers, no weapons, and no cloaking device. It provides only sufficient outer protection of the hull to prevent damage while traveling within your solar system. Onboard is a medical facility at the same level as currently exists on Earth. A small piece of me, named Nowrai771, will be capable of running that ship.

"She has no knowledge of the construction of the ship, equipment, or any other aspects of knowledge that might compromise the other missions. She is only capable of flying the craft. Branson has been of great help, but his TAMO member level is only Sixth Level. The TSC CEO has limited knowledge about TAMO, and I cannot be sure he will not misuse the additional knowledge and capabilities contained in the other two ships."

Steve slowly inclined his head in agreement.

"Each of the other two ships will contain portions of me named Nowrai772, destined for the Moon, and Nowrai773, destined for the gate. These AIs know everything about the ships, and they contain the same knowledge as I do. Their limits are bounded only by the amount of energy they contain. The ships are capable of total cloaking. Neither your technology nor my ancestors can see them. Only I can see them."

This made Steve ponder what was to come. *Consider what we will experience in our lives together, my love,* he mentally relayed to Sandy.

She squeezed his thigh where her hand rested. *It's thrilling to think about,* she sent back.

"The ships have a full array of energy and missile weapons." Nowrai's tone became tinged with what Steve thought might be pride. "They contain probes to help with each of the two ships' missions. The outer protective skin of these ships can withstand attacks from all weapons known in this solar system and all weapons available in our original solar system at the time I lost contact. Each ship has fifty of the healing tanks sealed in the spacecraft's cargo area and one active, ready for use. The tanks can be used for healing a person, rejuvenating them, or for suspended animation. With the right raw materials, many other things can be produced by my AI daughters and their robot helpers. Even additional energy sources can be built."

Despite the AI's pleased tone, her continued hint of war concerned Steve.

"Human friends, we have a need for a hidden and powerful military base on the dark side of the moon. The mission to begin this process will be the job of four of your team members. The IGC has obtained the grants needed for the site on Earth's moon to begin building the base. We need the whole world to believe this is just a standard moon colony for the glory of TAMO. The world cannot know its true purpose. The last ship must go through the gate and find what has happened to your brethren and mine. You must pick the people who will travel on the three ships," Nowrai implored. "Speak amongst yourselves and let us all begin the next phase of our lives' journeys."

Epilogue

With mental discussions including all the Tankers, Nan, the IGC, and IGM, they worked on who needed to go in which ship. The AI computer Nowrai771 flew back to Earth with Sam and Daniel. Richard Branson was contacted as the ship entered Earth orbit and Sam explained some of the ship's capabilities to him. She agreed to meet Richard at his Colorado plant that night. Everyone wanted to limit who saw and knew about the special craft.

From their conversation, she expected Richard would know what to do with the ship and hoped he would take all the ships' technology to help the people of Earth. It might take years for The Spaceship Company to make new ships implementing the new technology, but Branson expressed how much he looked forward to the dispersion of the new technology to mankind, and to their meeting later that evening.

The nighttime landing posed no issues. The craft was able to hover and slide into a used rocket assembly building before the doors of the giant building closed. Nowrai771 lowered the ramp, and Sam and Daniel went out to greet Richard.

Sam's mouth dropped open at what she saw. Richard had come prepared with twenty scientists and engineers to examine the ship.

As soon as the three of them shook hands and shared introductions, Sam gestured for Richard to come see the ship and to meet Nowrai771. The AI was told orally to give Richard full access to the ship and all its capabilities.

Nowrai771 mentally sent to Sam and Daniel a single last word. *Goodbye.*

Later, as the auto-driver cab picked up the two Tankers and took them to the airport, Richard and his team initiated their discovery of the ship's capabilities.

Sam and Daniel would never see the results of Richard's efforts. The two were bound for the Moon to meet up with the IGC.

☆☆☆

Ryan started chatting with the AI Nowrai772, that was to take Briana, Ryan, Andrey, and Lindsey to Earth's moon. Their final landing place would be the center of the land purchased by the IGC. There, with the help of Nowrai772, the humans would begin the construction of the hidden military base.

Ryan instructed the AI to start their voyage by heading out to the asteroid belt. He knew the new base would require raw materials, and the AI was able to find and capture two large asteroids. One contained raw materials for fabrication of the new base. The second was a solid block of ice. From it, water, hydrogen, and oxygen could be produced.

The trip to Earth's moon was done while completely cloaked. From the outer asteroid belt to the Moon, the trip took a day and a half. A simple mental contact with Nadia gave Nowrai772 and the Tankers the exact landing coordinates for the location of the land on the moon owned by TAMO.

Even without the cloaking, nothing on the dark side of the moon would have seen them arrive. With an almost perfect mooring, the craft positioned the two asteroids on the surface below where the ship would land. The base would be built in the Armstrong crater, named after the Apollo 11 astronaut who landed just fifty kilometers away in Mare Tranquillitatis. The two and a half mile wide (4.21 km) crater lay in the center of the TAMO land, and its concave formation of almost half mile in depth (.7 km) would keep many prying eyes from taking too close of a look.

Nowrai772 landed next to the two meteorite boulders. For a split second, the asteroids were visible until the cloak expanded to cover the whole area where the base would be built. Those passing over would only see what the AI wanted them to see. For now, all would see only an empty crater.

☆ ☆ ☆

Steve had been told by Nowrai that Nowrai773 had been outfitted for travel through the gate. It was loaded with provisions to last several years. Rob, Nan, Sandy, and Steve were the final team members to take off from Phobos. When their AI had flown them about ten miles from Phobos, Steve and his immediate team watched the surface from the bridge. The large obelisk separated into two towers and the area between the towers started to glow. Soon a full pattern resembling water appeared. Nowrai773 told Steve that what the group observed was the event horizon of the gigantic wormhole gate. The gate looked like it was even larger than the other big ships crashed into the Phobos surface.

Nowrai773 warned its passengers to strap in and started the countdown, "Ten, nine, eight—" *Relax and we will leave. I can tell by your mental state that you are all prepared.* "Three, two, one. Enter vortex."

She launched toward the gate, accelerating at high speed.

When the ship hit the gate dead center, it was enveloped. Steve sensed no transition except a little nausea and discomfort for that second. The craft had been in the space around Phobos, suddenly was nowhere. From his sense of movement, it felt like traveling through a tunnel. The view from the bridge windows looked more like a blur.

The AI informed them with her calmest mental voice, *We will be traveling for several hours before reaching our destination.*

The novelty of the feeling and the unusual view kept Steve staring. He was not the only one.

Nowrai773 seemed comfortable communicating mind to mind when they were near to their arrival point. *Five minutes to reentry. Please be seated and strap in and relax.* It did not take long before the AI said, "Three, two, one. Exit vortex."

Just as he had been uncomfortable entering the gate, leaving the vortex left Steve with the same brief nauseous feeling.

The sight when they came out was incredible. The stars appeared different. No doubt, they had entered another part of the universe.

Steve relayed everything to the Tankers in the Sol system and to Nowrai on Phobos as the ship came to a stop.

In front of them hovered the symbol of TAMO, with the cross, star, and rose. The center bud of the rose must have been four times the size of Phobos. That center area flickered, apparently indicating another portal.

Steve studied the symbol in amazement for several minutes before he noticed the viewing panels around the bridge. In the screens focused behind the ship, he expected to see their exit point from the Phobos gate. Instead, he saw thousands of exit gates. Some were active. Some were dark. The series of gates made a half-sphere shape of the thousands of tunnel entrances. Looking back, it reminded him of the inside of a honeycomb.

His temptation was to investigate some of the other gates, but the AI headed forward to the rose. Steve knew they needed to find the beginning of man.

As the craft approached the rose gate, Steve heard a male voice in his head, *You are the first to return in more than 30,000 years. We who remain, need your help.*

Mankind's new beginning had started.

Request for Review

Thank you for reading Mankind's New Beginning: The Dragon's Prophecy and the Tankers' Quest for the Ancient Keys.

To leave a review:

1. Write your positive review.

2. Scan the QR code at the bottom of this page or enter the link below it.

3, Click on the website the code creates.

4. Follow the links provided to share your review on various platforms.

Your feedback is invaluable and greatly appreciated!

To write a review without using the QR code, please follow these steps:

1. Visit the Goneti Press website by copying and pasting the following URL into your browser: https://gonetipress.com.

2. Navigate through the menus to find the review submission page.

Acknowledgments

I would like to thank Book Shepherd Ann Videan, who advised me as my editor and helped polish the book. 

The book cover was designed by Carolyn Mirelez. She is part of the electronic ink graphic design team. 

Supporting Friends and Bata Readers

Thank you for your help and support Ann, Kristi, Natali, Nadia, Peter, Kelsey, Angel, Kitty, Roger, Wilhelmina, Steve, Harris, JC, and Alisa.

Typography Credits

This book uses the following fonts:

Aleo font, is licensed under the SIL Open Font License (OFL). The font was created by Alessio Laiso.

EB Garamond font, is licensed under the SIL Open Font License (OFL). You can find more information about this font at EB Garamond on Font Squirrel.

Libre Baskerville font, is licensed under the SIL Open Font License (OFL).

Open Sans font is licensed under the Apache License, Version 2.0. © 2011-2021, Google Inc.

Russo One font is licensed under the SIL Open Font License (OFL). The font was designed by Jovanny Lemonad.

About the Author

Charles Henry Sherbow

Determined author Charles Henry Sherbow fulfilled his lifelong dream by publishing his debut space-age science fiction novel in 2024. Extensive early travels with his family of seven children fueled the discoveries in his first book, and his love of family and friends is reflected in the story's characters.

Born in Baltimore, Maryland, in the 1950s, Charles grew up as a self-proclaimed geek and loner. He found solace in science fiction novels by Asimov and Heinlein. A passion for the genre led to a Masters of Science degree in Information Systems Engineering in 2014. Charles's subsequent career as a computer consultant took him across the United States, while his personal travels spanned Europe, the Middle East, and Eastern Europe.

As he embraced the philosophy, "Don't let your schooling get in the way of your education," Charles delved into metaphysical works with the Ancient Mystical Order Rosae Crucis (AMORC). Involvement with the fraternal order first ignited his passion for writing.

In his travels, he met a beautiful woman in Eastern Europe. In 1999, married the love of his life, adopted her daughter, and formed a true family.